CHRISTMAS STORIES
REDISCOVERED

CHRISTMAS STORIES REDISCOVERED

SHORT STORIES FROM *THE CENTURY MAGAZINE* 1891-1905

Edited by

BARBARA QUARTON

The Borgo Press
An Imprint of Wildside Press LLC

MMVIII

CONTENTS

INTRODUCTION

BY BARBARA QUARTON

A hush falls over a college library in early December. The fever pitch of finals week subsides. Professors post grades; one can almost hear the collective sigh of relief. As students and faculty leave campus for winter break, public places in the library become deserted. The stacks are blanketed in silence.

On one of those quiet December days, I sat alone in my office. After a hectic fall quarter, I was happy to have an opportunity to focus on new projects. I enjoyed a long, productive spell at the computer, and then decided to stretch my legs. Soon I found myself wandering contentedly through the library. Oh, the pleasure of browsing familiar stacks on a gray December day....

As I roamed the vacant stacks I allowed my attention to be drawn to the binding—the hard cover—of a very old magazine. The binding appealed to me because it was obviously original and it was beautiful in a way that few things are anymore. There were many volumes of this magazine, and the entire set took up several shelves. I spent a long time gingerly turning tanned pages and getting to know the layout of each issue. I examined the illustrations and photographs and, skimming the indexes, I marveled at the many now-famous fiction writers, poets, statesmen, and essayists whose works appeared in the magazine: Thoreau, Melville, Crane, Longfellow, Wharton, Twain, Chopin, and Muir, to name just a few. I fell in love with the short fiction and the essays. I had stumbled upon *The Century Illustrated Magazine*, and it was nearly one hundred twenty years old.

In December, Christmas is not far from my mind. So when I came across the holiday story, "Wulfy: A Waif," in the December 1891 issue, I read it...and was touched by it. Were other Christmas stories of the period as poignant? I returned to the stacks many times after that to hunt down and read all the holiday stories in *The Century*. Indeed, I discovered several literary gems.

Christmas Stories Rediscovered is a collection of fifteen Christmas stories first published in *The Century Illustrated Magazine* during America's Gilded Age, 1891-1905. Each story is introduced with a bit of historical or literary context. Respectfully, no changes were made to the stories; the reader will find original word spellings, punctuation, dialect, and nineteenth-century turns of phrase left intact. The stories reveal much about day-to-day life in a long-ago time. I hope you find great pleasure—and perhaps a new bond with your forebears—reading these charming old holiday stories.

WULFY: A WAIF

BY VIDA DUTTON SCUDDER (1861-1954)

The Christmas season magnifies the inequalities between the rich and poor in America. During the Gilded Age, many middle-class Americans tried to help those in need directly, either by doing individual charitable work or by getting involved in social reform movements. In the late nineteenth century, one such reform movement began operating "settlement houses," where workers lived among the urban poor and offered help. This story describes the experiences of a little waif and his effect on an idealistic young settlement worker.

My father's a good father; he don't hardly ever hit me," wheezed Wulfy.

"No, but he scolds him awful," interposed Jakey.

They were standing around Miss Margaret's chair—three little waifs of the street. Jakey, the Italian, with Murillo curves to mouth and eyebrows; Fritz Hutter, somewhat taller, his soft hat worn on the back of his curly head, his face sickly and sweet-eyed; Wulfy, the shortest of the three, his large and rickety head with its wide mouth, giving him something the effect of a Japanese doll. All the boys were dirty and ragged, but

9

Wulfy's rags carried off the palm. There was more hole than cloth. His face, overspread by a peculiar yellow grease, had a curious smile; at times it was a positive leer of worldly wisdom; again there crept into it something shy, appealing, and—could one venture to use the word—childlike. His eyes, when one could find them, were blue.

"He scolds him awful," said Jakey.

"Yes, but that's all right!" said Wulfy. "Yer see, he gives me two cents ter buy my breakfast, an' sometimes I'm hungry an' I asks him for fi' cents, and then he does scold; but that's 'cause he wants the fi' cents hisself, don't yer see?"

All this with an eagerly apologetic tone.

"How old are you, Wulfy?"

"I think I'm ten, but I might as well be twenty-five. I'll never be no bigger. I'm goin' to be a little man, yer know, like the little man at the dime museum. I went to the dime museum once, an' I saw a man swaller two swords!" This speech, somewhat mournful and meditative at the beginning, became gleeful toward the end.

"And you live alone with your father?"

"No. I ain't got no mother, yer know. There's a friend of my father's lives with us. I calls her aunty."

"And isn't she your aunty?"

No. She ain't no relation. She's jist a friend of my father's."

"O-oh," said Miss Margaret. Her knowledge of life was becoming enlarged. "And is this friend of your father's good to you?"

"She don't hurt me. An' my father's a good father now. When I was littler I couldn't dress myself 'cause my leg used to be so bad; he had to help me, an' course he didn't like that. Then it used to be hard. But I can dress myself now. He don't have to do nothin' for me. He's a good father."

The other boys, attracted by picture-books, had wandered away. Wulfy still stood beside Miss Margaret. There was some lop-sided deformity about the tiny, stunted fellow. His weak hands pecked at her dress, and an indescribable guilelessness shone paradoxically through his world-weary little person. He talked in a guttural, gasping fashion, hard to follow; yet there was no accent, except that indefinable accent of the streets which becomes one's mother-tongue as one descends into the region of the Bowery.

"I had a mother once. A mother's a good thing to have. When I was little, an' my leg was bad, an' I couldn't get dressed, I used to lie in bed and remember her; an' do yer know, sometimes I'd feel so bad, I'd feel as if I'd like to die!"

All this with no touch of sentiment, but with the same matter-of-fact tone in which a few moments before he had been telling of his ambition to own a nanny-goat and peddle newspapers.

Miss Margaret, however, who had seen less of life's hard realities than Wulfy, was still inclined to be sentimental.

"You wanted to die so that you could be with your dear mother again, didn't you, Wulfy?"

Wulfy looked sideways, with a scared expression.

"No, no! She died in the horspital."

Miss Margaret waited, puzzled.

"They said they put her in a box and buried her. 'Twas over on Long Island. I shouldn't be buried on Long Island."

"Oh, but Wulfy, don't you know? Your mother wasn't buried, the real part of her; she went to heaven, and you can go there too when you die."

Wulfy was blank. Evidently no impression entered his mind.

Miss Margaret looked at the forlorn little figure in silence an instant. Then all those lofty and etherealized conceptions of a future state which had been formed in the most advanced school of liberal theology slipped away from her, and she found herself saying:

"Wulfy, Jesus Christ, who is very good and who loves you dearly, died and went to a beautiful place called heaven on purpose that he might get ready a lovely house all for your mother and you. And when your mother died I think she went there, and I think she is waiting for you. Do you understand?"

Not at all. No more than if she had been talking Greek. With abrupt and disdainful transition, he announced:

"I won't die in the horspital."

The child quivered a little in speaking, like a frightened animal:

"They said they buried her, but they didn't, yer know."

"Why, what makes you think they didn't?"

The answer came reluctantly, in a hoarse whisper. Wulfy was evidently making a grand confidence.

"There was a sick man in a gutter. They took him to a horspital. They were *glad* to get him."

"Well?"

"He died. They didn't bury him."

"Wulfy, what do you mean?"

"They take the poor, sick people, and when they die they – make – castor-oil – out of them."

Miss Margaret gasped.

"Who told you that wicked story?" she demanded.

"The man on the corner."

"Now I want to tell you something." She took his two wee hands and spoke impressively. "That is a wicked lie. Do you understand?"

Wulfy gazed at her blankly, then repeated his statement with serene and sorrowful assurance.

"They make castor-oil of them. He said so, the man on the corner."

Nor could any amount of persuasion, then or later, shake in Wulfy's soul the mystic authority of "the man on the corner."

"But I wish she hadn't died," he went on drearily. "A mother's a good thing to have. Better nor a father. A mother can make yer clothes. A father, he can buy yer clothes, but shoh! what's the good of that? Costs him fifty cents to buy yer a coat. What's the good of spendin' all that money? A mother, she'll make yer coat; yes, and wash yer clothes too. I wish my mother hadn't died. Do yer know, my mother, she – used – ter – kiss me."

It was Miss Margaret's first experience of life in "the slums." Already she had begun to resent the opprobrium of the title; already felt that the frank and sturdy humanity of her neighbors deserved a more respectful handling. She found character more interesting here than on Fifth Avenue, because less sedulously concealed; at the same time, she recognized as the chief evil of this existence its crushing monotony. There was less room than she expected for the exercise of that somewhat high-strung compassion with which she had left her home. She was at first inclined to lavish a double measure of such compassion on Wulfy, for the sickly little fellow limped the streets all the bitter winter, foraging for himself like the sparrows, with the aid of an occasional two cents from his father. When asked at any hour to describe his last meal the answer came cheerful and invariable, "Coffee and Ca-ake"; these, picked up at the street-booths, formed the staple of the child's diet. His little shivering body showed here and there through his rags. He suffered much pain at times, and, though silent for the most part about his home-life, it transpired slowly that he did not dare seek the mean shelter of his father's tenement till after nine at night. And yet, for all this, Miss Margaret soon found that in a sense her compassion was wasted. Wulfy was as happy as the day is long. He would suffer hardship with the unconscious patience of a kitten, and the prevailing mood of his sunny nature was delight at the queer pleasures of street-life. Wulfy had been to school once, and liked it; but having been absent, he was turned out, and his place given to another. No one was to blame. What would you have when thirty applicants are sometimes refused at these public schools in one day for lack of accommodation! Wulfy, under these conditions, could hardly expect to be educated by his country. He had also, at one time, peddled papers, but a member of the S.P.C.C., seeing his shaky little legs, put an end to this occupation from mistaken kindness. So Wulfy became an attendant imp in the street-life of lower New York. He knew by heart all the theater-posters on the Bowery; he haunted the Hebrew booths on Henry Street in the evening, his small, ancient face watching like a child-Mephistopheles the evil that went on by the flare of the kerosene-torches. He joined in the rapture of barrel-bonfires, fleeing with all his small companions when the cry "Cheese it!" warned them that the "cops" were in sight. He was in the thick of every street-scandal, watching not only the row but the "flatteys"—a term which Margaret, highly amused, soon learned to know as the nickname bestowed on detectives by the hoodlums whose sharp eyes would pick out instantly, in spite of civilian garb, the flat-topped boot of the policeman.

There was nothing in the outer aspects of city-life among the poor which Wulfy did not know. There was nothing apart from the limits of that life of which he had ever heard. Full of strange superstitions that had no grace of fancy or of perverted faith; a thorough little materialist, with no vocabulary and no consciousness outside of the life of the body; conversant with evil of which the woman who talked to him hardly knew the name,— Wulfy was yet innocent in heart as the Christ-child. Scraps of child-wonder and desire were interwoven with his wizened knowledge. Every impulse was generous, and his whole nature set to sweetness. He radiated affection; to hear him talk, no little fellow had ever been so favored with friends. Now it was the kind "butcher-lady" who had given him a dinner; now he had gotten an "o'er-coat"—poor, flimsy little o'ercoat, looking as if it had been chewed—"off" of his father, and beamed with filial devotion.

Like all ardent natures, he had one great passion. It was for his sister. Poor waif! His little husky voice poured forth one day the whole pitiful story, while one hand rested confidingly on Miss Margaret's knee:

"Do you know my sister Milly? She don't live at home. She's a bad girl, my sister Milly. She's twelve years old, an' you can be a bad girl when you're twelve. Milly she come home late nights. Why, it was one, two, twelve o'clock an' she didn't come home! I'd sit up an' open the door; father he'd go to bed. But he found out as she come home late, an' he took her, and sent her off. The place where she lives, it's a place where bad girls live. My sister Milly's awful good to me."

"And do you ever see Milly now?" asked Miss Margaret, crying in her heart over the child's sorrowful knowledge.

Wulfy's whole face brightened with an inward radiance that at times changed him from a Japanese doll to a child-angel.

"I'm goin' to see Milly after Christmas. They've promised me I may. I ain't a-goin' to let 'em forget it."

"Are you glad Christmas is coming?"

"Yes," with the bright impulse that always came first. "Ye-es—" more dubiously, and with a clouded face. "Santa Claus don't come to my house, of course."

"Why not, Wulfy?"

"He only comes to houses where there are mothers. There ain't no mother at my house. He comes to Jakey's house. Last he brought Jakey a knife and a drum."

"Do yer s'pose," he went on eagerly, "as Santa Claus comes to the house where Milly is? There ain't no mother there, yer know."

A vision of the Reform School rose before Miss Margaret.

"I don't know, Wulfy," she said gently. "But tell me: if Santa Claus should come to you this year, what would you like to have him bring?"

Wulfy brightened. For once, he looked like a genuine, jolly little boy.

"I'd like a drum, and an orange, and a pony with real hair on wheels, and – and – and a nanny-goat. Only a nanny-goat couldn't get into the stocking."

"No," assented Miss Margaret gravely. "Now, Wulfy, Santa Claus visits this house, I am quite sure, and, if you like, you can come here Christmas eve and hang up your stocking. Would you like that?"

Wulfy's response was not made in words. Sticking out a spindly leg, he started with beaming face to strip off its grimy, wrinkled and antique casing.

"Not now! Not now!" interposed Miss Margaret hastily. "Christmas eve! and, Wulfy, mind you wash the stocking before you bring it."

Now Wulfy had aspirations after cleanliness. The first signal of his arrival was always a demand to "wash me hands"; and in a pan of hot water and a cake of soap he did delight. One day, when Miss Margaret had by vigorous scrubbing caused five pink fingertips to emerge from thick grime, she had said, on didacticism intent, "I think clean fingers are prettier than dirty."

"So do I," assented Wulfy; "but if you had a bad leg, and had to climb six pairs of stairs every time you washed yer hands, I guess yer fingers would go dirty." To which *argumentum ad hominem* Miss Margaret had instantly succumbed.

On Christmas eve arrived Wulfy, his face one wide smile. In his hand he bore a trophy:—"I washed it myself," he announced with unspeakable pride.

"I should think so!" gasped Miss Margaret.

It was a stocking. Rather it had been a stocking. Thick and slabby with dirt and grease it had evidently been dipped in water, squeezed out weakly by tiny fingers, and allowed to stiffen, rough-dry. Miss Margaret took it, handkerchief at face.

Wulfy viewed the stocking in her hand, and a shade of anxiety began to gather in his eyes. Toe and heel looked as if large bites had been taken out of them.

"Can yer tell Santa Claus something?" croaked Wulfy.

"Yes."

"Tell him, then,"—with a look of uncanny wisdom,— "to put the orange in the toe. It can't fall through, yer know, and it'll keep the other things in."

"I will," promised Miss Margaret. And with due solemnity the stocking was hung.

Christmas was not many hours old when Wulfy came to welcome it. His face was clean in spots, to do honor to the occasion. Miss Margaret took him to the fireplace, his small body tense with expectation.

Santa Claus had remembered! He had remembered everything. There was even the orange in the toe; only, as the stocking was after all a very wee one, it had to be a mandarin. But there were the drum and the pony with real hair, warm stockings too, and mittens, and a muffler; yes, and a knife, and candy and raisins, and a large gold watch which would tick vigorously for over an hour when wound up.

If Miss Margaret had expected a demonstration, she was disappointed. Wulfy received his stocking in silence. The unpacking was an affair of time, for the little hands trembled so that they could not lift the packages nor untie the string, yet no one else was allowed to lay finger on the sacred treasures. At last it was accomplished, and the objects were ranged in a semicircle, Wulfy, cross-legged, like a Hindu idol, in the midst.

Then he broke silence.

"I got a gold watch!" he said, with a shaky sigh.

Nor could another word be extorted from him. This he repeated over and over, gazing at the gilt object as if hypnotized. Not his coveted pony, nor his ball, nor his drum, could hold his attention long. His eyes strayed back to the glittering watch, which he dangled speechless before each new-comer.

It was time for Wulfy to go home; and the journey was a function of state. In vain did Miss Margaret offer to help to carry the packages; he shook his head with determination. "Yer may go with me, though," he announced graciously. "I'd ruther the boys." So Wulfy was laden like a small pack-horse, and started from the house, bundles under each arm and the full stocking slung over his shoulder. By Miss Margaret's side he hobbled joyful but exhausted. His feeble fingers dropped something every few steps, and not a raisin must be lost; his half-paralyzed side bent double under his burdens. As he jogged along, one boy after another of the street-urchins hailed him with surprise and glee, for Wulfy was known to them all.

"Hello, Wulfy!" "My eye, what a Christmas!" "Whatcher got?" met him on all sides. Wulfy's grotesque little figure staggered under its bulky bundles with the proud and serene air of an Eastern prince. Secure in the protection of Miss Margaret, he answered briefly but freely.

"I got a gold watch," was his response to every salutation. As they advanced, the walk became a triumphal procession. Boys sprang up from the paving-stones, poured from the alleys, dropped from the sky. In front marched Wulfy's special friends Jakey and Fritz, as a guard of honor; behind and around was a crowd of boys of all sizes, hooting, curious and envious, and in the midst trudged Wulfy, laconic in his triumph, his stocking bobbing on his shoulder. The bright gold of the orange showed through the jagged toe. He was growing pale and breathless when at last the cavalcade halted at the entrance to a dilapidated court. He surveyed his followers an instant in silence, then, croaking a little louder than usual, he announced:

"Yer can go back now."

And the boys went.

Miss Margaret waited. She hoped for an invitation to Wulfy's home. But she received none.

"Good-by," said Wulfy with dignity.

Thus dismissed, Miss Margaret murmured meekly, "Good-by," and turned away. But another thought had struck him.

"Wait!" he called. "Where are yer going?"

"To church."

Church was one of the ideas and probably one of the words which lay outside of Wulfy's sphere; but perhaps he associated it dimly with beneficent powers, for he sidled a little nearer and wheezed with a touching sweetness of manner:

"Yer might tell Santa Claus as I liked all this stuff."

For some time after Christmas Wulfy, to use his own phrase, did not "come over." There was nothing surprising in this. He was irresponsible as a squirrel, and often would vanish, no one knew whither, for a month at a time. But at last, on a bitterly cold day, he reappeared. His rags were a little more sparse than usual, his face looked pinched, but he wore his familiar smile.

"Wulfy," said Miss Margaret, "where are your new mittens?"

"I gave 'em to Jakey. Poor Jakey didn't have any," he said, looking at his blue fingers.

"And why don't you wear your nice stockings?" for the little legs were incased in the old rags.

"Them stockings weren't no good."

"Why not?"

"Sho! they fitted tight! Stockings ought ter wrinkle. Like these. Then they keep yer legs warm. See?"

Miss Margaret saw: Wulfy's wisdom was, as usual, convincing.

"I've seen Milly," he announced.

"I'm glad. Was Milly pleased to see you?"

"Yes. She kissed me," he said with shy pleasure. "They're good to her. She has puddens twice a week. I gave Milly my gold watch."

"Why, Wulfy! I thought you liked your gold watch."

"Like it! Guess I did. 'T ain't every feller as has a gold watch. Milly liked it too."

Every shred of his Christmas gifts had vanished. To trace them was impossible. The pony, it seemed, and the candy had also gone to Milly. The knife, the ball, and all the rest had doubtless been distributed among the members of the youthful procession which had followed Wulfy through the street in his hour of triumph. He had not kept a peanut for himself.

"Wulfy," said Miss Margaret soberly one day, willing to try him, "oh, Wulfy, where are your Christmas things? Aren't you sorry they are all gone?"

Wulfy looked sober too for a minute, and his worldly-wise little lip quivered childishly. Then a smile broke over his face, he gave a brief chuckle, as was his wont when pleased, and then croaked jubilantly: "I had 'em once."

Happy Wulfy! In this short sentence he had found a philosophy of life.

And Milly? Did Milly, who was a "bad girl" who had known a wild and secret life, did Milly care for a tin gold watch, for candy, and for a pony on wheels? Did she take them to please the little brother whose clinging loyalty may have been the one tie that held her to good? Or did the child perhaps still live in Milly,—poor Milly, who, although she was bad, was only twelve years old, after all,—and did she like the pony and watch for their own sake, with a little girl's affection? Who shall say!

Wulfy, at least, was happy. Santa Claus had given him the two greatest pleasures in life: the pleasure of possession and the pleasure of sacrifice.

Miss Margaret went home soon after this: it was a year before she returned to lower New York. The day after her arrival Wulfy "came over." He looked plumper, his face was clean, and his clothes were neatly patched. Altogether he was a far less uncanny object than of old.

"Good mornin'," said Wulfy, "I've got a new mother. She ain't a friend of my father's. She's a new mother—a real one. She cooks my meals. Look here,"—holding out a fine patch,—"she did that. Look at them pants. I got 'em off my father. She told him to 'em for me. Once I didn't go home, she thought I was lost, and, do yer know, she cried till she was black and blue. She was sorry."

With this wondrous climax he paused breathless and rapturous. So Wulfy was to know the joy of being missed, of being shielded! He was no longer to depend on the chance kindness of the butcher-lady or the grudged two cents of his father to feed his small body;

no longer would he laboriously scrape together stray pennies to buy for himself the shirts that barely covered his thin little chest. The waif of the streets was to be a waif no more. He was to know, though in a rough and poor fashion, something of the kindness of a home. Already the child-face, that of old showed only in rare moments, had become habitual to him; and the wicked and antique wisdom which had overspread it as a mask came back only in flashes now and then. The stunted body and sunny soul might know a little comfort at last. Life was sweet to Wulfy now.

Yet not all sweet. Still there was sorrow; still, disappointment, and desire unfulfilled. For Milly was not at home.

"I goes to see her," said Wulfy. "But I don't tell her about the new mother. I tell her its jist another friend of my father; for if she knew it was a new mother, Milly'd want ter come home. An' they say she can't come home—yet."

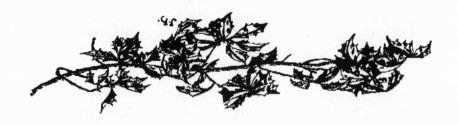

A CHRISTMAS DILEMMA

(A TRUE STORY)

ANONYMOUS

The dilemma in this story is probably familiar to most readers. During the Gilded Age, Christmas gift-giving expanded to include not just family—as had been the custom—but also friends, acquaintances, and business associates. For the first time in American history, people felt obliged to weigh the value of their relationships and give gifts accordingly. A Christmas Dilemma is a lighthearted look at a sometimes vexing social predicament.

"John," said Mrs. Spencer to her husband, "I don't know what to do about the Martins' Christmas presents."

Dr. Spencer looked up from the paper he was reading. "Do?" he said vacantly. "What do you mean?"

Mrs. Spencer laid her work in her lap and moved the student-lamp on the table between them, to get a better view of her husband's face.

"Come up to the surface, John," she said, "and listen, because I really need your advice."

The doctor rested his paper on his knees and "climbed over his glasses" at his wife.

"Go ahead," he said; "you have my attention."

Mrs. Spencer continued seriously:

"You know what a nuisance these Christmas presents have come to be between the Martins and ourselves, and how much I want to stop them; and yet—" She paused, and her husband's face assumed an amused expression.

"Well, my dear Ellen, my advice is, leave off sending them. It is the solution of the difficulty. It will immediately relieve the situation."

Mrs. Spencer nodded, and tapped the table with her thimble.

"It is what I wish to do," she said. "I am sure it is as great a worry to Mrs. Martin as it is to me; but the point is, how to leave them off. I cannot be the first to stop. Just suppose I should send nothing, and she should send the usual great basket with a present for every one of us—you, the children, the servants,—last Christmas she even sent a collar for Don,—I should die of mortification."

Dr. Spencer took off his glasses and looked gravely across the table at his wife.

"I have often thought," he said, "that there were too many women's societies in this town; but I see the need for one more—a Society for the Suppression of Christmas Presents. Send out circulars, beginning with Mrs. Martin. You ought to get a large and enthusiastic membership."

Mrs. Spencer sighed, and took up her work again.

"You don't advise me at all," she said; "you only joke, and I really think this is a serious matter."

"My dear Ellen, I am willing to advise you, but the whole difficulty seems to me a ridiculous one. There is only one thing to do. Stop short now. Suppose she does send you a basket? It will be the last time. It's the shortest and simplest way to end it."

"I might," said Mrs. Spencer, meditatively, "not

send anything at Christmas, and then, in case she does, I could return them presents at intervals throughout the year—on their birthdays, at Easter, and so forth."

"Good Lord, Ellen," hastily interrupted her husband, "don't do that! You'll have her returning the birthday and Easter presents. It would be worse than ever."

"Yes; I am afraid that would not do, after all," said Mrs. Spencer, looking more troubled than before.

Dr. Spencer reached out for the poker and tapped open a lump of soft coal on top of the fire. A blue flame shot up through it, and a little spiral of smoke licked out into the room.

"Ellen," he said, emphasizing his words with taps of the poker on the grate, "take my advice: cut it short, and just bear it if you do have to take presents from her this year. Carroll Martin is a man I shall never respect again after his course during the last election, and anything is better than carrying on this perfunctory friendship. We no longer see enough of any of them to justify our exchanging presents, and I am sure Mrs. Martin will thank you as much as I shall if you will take the bull by the horns now and be done with it."

He looked at his wife, but she did not answer. Her eyes were bent upon her sewing, and her expression was unconvinced.

Dr. Spencer set down the poker, took up his paper, and settled himself back in his chair again. He was not one of those who go on and split the board after they have driven home the nail.

"You have my opinion," he said, and went on reading.

The Spencers and Martins had been, some years before, next-door neighbors. The Martins were then newly married and strangers to the place, and the first

Christmas after their arrival, Mrs. Spencer, in the kindness of her heart, had sent over a bunch of flowers, with a friendly greeting, to her young neighbor. Her messenger had returned with Mrs. Martin's warm thanks, and a pretty sofa-pillow, hastily snatched up and sent to express the little bride's pleasure and gratitude.

Such a handsome gift, in place of the "thank you" expected, had decidedly taken Mrs. Spencer aback, and when the next Christmas came, she took care to provide a pretty pin-cushion for Mrs. Martin and a dainty cap for the baby who had by that time been added to the family. This occasion found Mrs. Martin also prepared, and she promptly responded with a centerpiece for Mrs. Spencer, an ash-tray for the doctor, and a doll for their little Margaret.

From this time on each year the burden grew. Several children had been added to both families; each one was separately remembered, and, in the old Southern Christmas fashion, presents for the family servants had been added to the list, one at a time, until not only nurse, coachman, and cook had been included, but, as Mrs. Spencer said, the previous Christmas had even brought her a collar for the dog.

During these years both families had moved. Both had built new homes, on the same street, it is true, but a block apart, so that they were no longer near neighbors, and lately the two men had been on opposite sides of a bitter political contest. "Warmth had induced coolness, words had produced silence," and the relations of the two families had become only formal.

The Christmas presents had been kept up only because neither woman knew how to stop, and as Mr. Martin had in the meantime made money, and become, according to Southern standards, a rich man, Mrs. Spencer felt more than ever determined "not to be beholden to them."

On the evening in question she said no more, but the night brought counsel, and next morning she informed her husband that she had decided what to do. She would buy the presents as usual, but she would wait, before sending them on Christmas morning, to see whether Mrs. Martin sent to her. "And if I do not need them, I can put them up for the children next Christmas," she concluded triumphantly.

Dr. Spencer did not approve of this ingenious plan, but his wife persisted. "Not for worlds" would she have a great lot of presents come over from the Martins' and have nothing to send in return.

Christmas morning came, and, while dressing, Mrs. Spencer told her husband that she should send little Jack out on the front sidewalk with his fire-crackers, so that he could keep a lookout down the street and report any basket coming from the Martins'.

Hers was packed and ready. Every bundle was neatly tied up in white paper with ribbons and labeled: "Mrs. Martin, with Christmas greetings"; "For Little Charley, with Mrs. Spencer's love"; "Mammy Sue, from the Spencer children"; and so on. And Mrs. Spencer reflected with satisfaction, as she deposited a new harness for the Martins' pug on top of the pile, that nobody was going to get ahead of *her*.

Breakfast over, and Remus, the doctor's "boy," instructed to keep himself brushed and neat, ready at an instant's notice to seize "the Martin basket," as the doctor called it, and bear it forth, Mrs. Spencer's mind was at rest. Jack was on the sidewalk, banging away, but keeping a sharp eye out toward the Martins', too; for he had scarcely been there five minutes before he called to her that Robbie Martin was playing on *his* sidewalk and watching their house like anything.

A short time passed, and Jack came running in. "Mother, I see Mammy Sue coming this way with a tray," he said.

The doctor called from his study: "How do you know she is coming here?" But Mrs. Spencer had not waited to hear him; she was already at the back door calling excitedly, "Remus, take the basket!"

"John," she cried, running back, "you see the Martins *are* sending us presents," and she got to the window in time to see Remus issuing forth with his burden. As he reached the street and turned toward the Martins', into the house rushed Robbie, calling, "Mother! Mother!" and a moment later out popped the Martins' butler, Tom, with a large basket brimming over with tissue-paper and blue ribbons on his head, and took his way toward the Spencers' at a brisk trot. It was quite a race between him and Remus; they grinned cheerfully as they passed each other half-way. Mammy Sue went by the gate with her tray, but Tom came in and set his load down in the hall, where Mrs. Spencer received it with a smile as fine as a wire.

A few minutes later the doctor came out of his study. His wife, her lips pressed together and her eyes very bright, was kneeling beside the basket, handing out be-ribboned packages to the children, who were exclaiming about her. He stood looking on in silence until she handed him one marked, "For Dr. Spencer, with Mrs. Martin's kindest wishes," which he opened.

"Beautiful!" he said. "Just what I have always needed. My office wanted only a pink china Cupid, with a gilt basket on his back, to be complete."

Mrs. Spencer made no reply, nor did she look up; her hands fluttered among the parcels. The doctor considered the top of her head for a moment.

"Ellen," he said gently, "there was just one little mistake in our calculations: we never thought of Mrs. Martin's being as clever as we are, did we?"

Mrs. Spencer looked up and laughed, but her face

quivered.

"John," she said, "I'll always love you for that 'we'."

HOW "SANDY CLAWS" TREATED POP BAKER

BY ELIZABETH CHERRY WALTZ (1866-1903)

In 1863, Thomas Nast illustrated Clement C. Moore's "A Visit from St Nicholas," and Santa Claus became widely accepted as the character of the modern Christmas. The main character in this story, Pop Baker, was too old to have heard about Santa Claus in his youth. This story describes Pop's first experience of Christmas with Santa Claus.

It is certain that Pop Baker never heard of Santa Claus in the days of his early youth. He was over seventy years old, although no one would ever have guessed it. When he was a yellow-haired urchin he was as far away from civilization as are the inhabitants of Central Africa nowadays. Louisville was a prosperous community in the early thirties of the nineteenth century,—one where the brother of the poet Keats and other scholars found polished and congenial society,—and it was only twelve miles away; but the way to it from the highlands far south of the city was over swampy morasses and through vast stretches of the "Wet Woods," forests so dense that even the Indians turned aside from them. There grew numerous ash-trees and the larger forest monarchs, and all were so thickly set together that the white man did not force his way through them for a century. Beyond then lay the hills, huge shoulders and boulders; and here Pop Baker was born, and here he lived in 1902.

Over seventy years old was he, very tall and very straight and broad-shouldered, and slightly silvered of hair and chin-beard. Also he was rosy-faced and merry-eyed. Fate had found him a hard nut to crack, and left him at the end of the span of man's life unscathed and wholesome. He had been married twice at least. He had several children, of whom "Doc" and "Jimpsey" remained on this mundane sphere, shiftless hill-billies, with none of the old man's grit or philosophy. Another, a daughter, Mahale by name, had achieved notoriety by the accumulation of nine children in a dozen years. She departed this life "'thout doin' no more dammidge," Pop said, "than ter leave seven livin'." The "seven livin'" proved for half a dozen years the old man's burden. He mothered them, and he allowed the father, Pete Mason, to live under his own roof. But when "leetle Pop" was six yeas old, his grandsire decided on a course of action, and was prompt indeed about it. He caught Pete at the rail fence one morning when the latter was mounting a mule to ride off to Pausch's Corners for an early bracer-up.

"Petey, I hear ye air goin' reg'lar-like up ter Kuykendall's. Thet air all right, but ye mought ez well be narratin', over yan, thet ye've the seven livin' ter pervide fer yit. I'm a-gittin' ter thet time o' life when I wanter hev a leetle freedom 'n' enj'yment. Ye mought ez well let on ter whichever one of them gels ye're shinin' up ter thet, ef she air bent on marryin', she must tek the hull bunch 'long wid ye."

Peter narrowed his eyes.

"Ye mought mek a sheer-up," he debated; "thar's a hull lot o' 'em."

Pop Baker shook his head decidedly.

"I'm too old ter be raisin' famblies," he said, "an' ye'll hev ter rustle a leetle more yerself from this hyah time on, Petey. They air all on their feetses now, an' rale fat an' sassy. Ef one of them Kuykendall gels hain't willin', consort elsewhar. I calkilate ter give ye a mule, a bar'l o' sorghum, an' three feather beds fer the childern. Ye must do fer yerself with yer settin' out from wherever ye marry any one."

As Peter Mason was still a strapping, swaggering fellow, he had little difficulty in persuading Georgella Kuykendall to assume the position of stepmother to the "seven livin'" and wife to himself. The family removed themselves in the springtime clear over Mitchell's Hill, and, under Georgella's thrifty and energetic reign, got on fairly well.

For the first time in his life Pop Baker enjoyed the sweets of entire freedom. He fought off Jimpsey's vehement offers to "keep house" and Doc's inclination to make his home a half-way tavern between his own cabin and Pausch's Corners. He had thirty acres to farm, two mules, and a cow. His house was part stone and part log, with a noble chimney of rough stone. He had wood and water and a garden.

All summer he reveled. He worked when he chose, he hitched up and rode around In a buckboard behind his best mule, whose name was Bully Boy. All his meat came from the woods—birds, rabbits, squirrels, racoons, and even a fat opossum now and then.

"Look at thet muscle, wull ye?" he would say to the young men pitching quoits at the picnics. "Thet thar muscle hev been made tough on work an' wild meat. Tame meat never made a man like I be."

He had his own ideas of sport.

"D' ye s'pose I'd ever kill fer the pleasure o' hearin' a noise an' seein' a creatur' die?" he said. "I live like the birds an' the varmints. I kill ter eat—the Almighty's way."

In front of him, across the rough road and over a half-cleared and enchanting woodland of old trees, rose the wildest of hills to the west; and behind him, half a mile to the east and south, were other cones and shoulders, strangely formed and freakishly upheaved, with narrow hollows between them and meandering streams tearing down, and falling down, and laughing over jagged rocks. Over the rarely trodden forests and on these hills tramped Pop Baker at will. He gave his whole soul to the delight of solitude, of falling in with nature's moods. His heart grew more tender as the days went by. He gathered a great hoard of nuts for the children. He halved the crop from his patch of pop-corn, and he traded corn for a barrel of red apples. Something was working in him that, in earlier years, had never bothered him. The "seven livin'" had brought in Christmas and "Sandy Claws" to the cabin with them, and the idea would not be swept out with their going.

All along through the fall Pop Baker was the maddest of merrymakers at the dances, the weddings, infares, and quiltings. He never heard of any social event, far or near, but he greased up his boots, tied his red comforter round his neck, and racked Bully Boy over the hills to it. He never waited for an invitation, and he was always expected. There was sure to be some congenial spirit there, either a young widow or a mischievous girl willing to spite a bashful swain, or, at the worst, one or two uproarious young blades to slap him on the shoulder.

Nothing daunted him, nothing stayed him. The cold only made his cheeks rosier; his eyes sparkled. They called him "Old Christmas hisself"; they applauded him, and egged him on to dance and flip speech. So the days and nights passed, and Christmas was at hand.

Bully Boy and The Other—for Pop Baker disdained, in his partiality, to name his less intelligent mule—pulled up over Jefferson Hill and down into Bullitt County with Pop's Christmas for Mahale's young ones in the wagon. There were the apples and the nuts, the molasses, and a big green ham. Mrs. Peter gave him a welcome, a good meal, and started him home early. To her he was only an old man who ought to be in his chimney-corner at night. The seven swarmed lovingly over him as he mounted the seat. "Leetle Pop" smeared him with molasses as he murmured:

"Wanter buss ye one, gran'dad. Ye're so dern goody, ye air!"

Then came a splendid ride homeward under the frosty starlight. Pop Baker sat on an old skin robe and rode with a bed-comfort and a horse-blanket around his legs. Straw heaped the wagon-bed in front of the empty barrel. The wagon wheels creaked over the road, broke into the forming ice on Knob Creek, and rattled down the steep slope of Mitchell's Hill. Then along the deep shadowy ways he passed through interminable woods, where sometimes there were hollows hundreds of feet below him, and sometimes there was a narrow cut under a rocky cliff where dry branches broke and crackled down. Sometimes there appeared below him, like fireflies or sparkling human eyes, half-frozen streams that ran and crossed, and reflected back the stars. Bully Boy had his master's own spirit, and literally dragged The Other up and down hill right sturdily. Pop Baker did not have to drive, Bully Boy would have resented any imputation of being driven. He knew every step of the way, and he pulled—that was his duty, Christmas or Fourth of July—without shirking. Pop took it easy, and watched the processional of the stars across the cathedral of the heavens. Now he was on the highest point of the county, on Jefferson Hill. Far, far away in the wide valley he saw glows of light. He knew that there lay the distant city, with its hundreds of shop-windows lighted up and Christmas-gay, draped with tinsels and bright colors, and full of what in his sterner moments he called "trash," in his softer moods "purties." The thick carpet of fallen leaves on the road deadened the sound of the wheels and the mules' feet. Pop Baker looked at the stars with a new awe and joy.

"Might' fine, them! Sorter hail a man ter notice. Seen 'em walkin' over thet big space many a night, but, dern it all! they never war so bright. Might' good comp'ny— the bestes' o' comp'ny fer an ol' man. Merry 'n' cheerful, 'n' deliverin' the message thet thar hain't no doin' erway with whutever air made 'n' placed—anywhar. Thet's whut I hev figgered out. I been put right here, 'n' I hev figgered out I'm in the percesslon, an' bount' ter stay,— out o' sight er in sight—perceedin' on an' never stoppin', 'ca'se I oncet war made an' do be."

No human being had ever seen the rapt face Pop Baker turned to the stars—no one but his Maker.

"Folkses thinks ez how I'd git lonesome; but when a man gits ter some age, he air got suthin' er nothin' in 'im—Dern yer buttons, Bully Boy! whut air ye stoppin' fer?"

There was a halloo, clear and high, from the bottom of the hill.

"An' ye heared that when I didn't, Boy? Waal, consarn ye! what else hev I got sech a smart mule fer? Halloo, yerself, down thar!"

"Come on down came up a stentorian sound. Then a bound barked long and loud.

"Tobey shore we wull, Bully Boy," commented Pop Baker; "for I'll bet ye yer feed it's some un thet hev been ter town an' got plumb full o' Sandy Claws, wagon-bed an' all. We air comin' down!" he hallooed merrily; then he began singing one of his own improvised songs on cider—the one that was always the chief delight of the hill folk's revels and routs:

"Ol' Unkie Doc an' the cider-pot!
He liked um col' an' he liked um hot;
Stick in the poker, an' make um sizz,
Hi! d' ye know how good thet is?

"Tetty-ti, tooty-too!
You likes me, an' I likes you;
Stick in the poker, an' make um sizz,
Hi! d' ye know how good thet is?"

He had rollicking company in the chorus long before he got to the bottom of the hill. If you had seen that hill you would have said that Bully Boy tumbled down it. As for The Other, it was his place in the order of things to fall after.

"Hi! d'ye know how good thet is?"

And there the two wagons stood side by side at a slightly widened curve in the steep road.

"Now, would ye think it!" said a sarcastic voice. Ef it hain't Pop Baker, an' not some young rake a-trapesin' after a sweetheart on a Christmas eve. But I orter 'a' knowed thet mule. Not another un in the county 'd run down Jefferson thet erway."

"He air gittin' thar, Dink Smith," retorted Pop Baker; "'sides, Bully Boy air allers cavortin' arter nightfall, goin' or comin'. The Other has plumb los' his wind, I swanny! Waal, how's Christmas?"

"Burnin' me up," replied Dink facetiously. "I sold a

hawg, an' some sorghum, an' some eggs, an' some butter, an' dried peaches. Got groceries in thet box, closes in thar, 'n' small tricks fer the kids in thet thar chip basket. Stop yer howlin', ye Dan'el Webster!"

The hound in the wagon whined and subsided.

"Wonder yet ol' woman hain't erlong with ye," observed Pop Baker.

"I guess ye hain't heared thet we got a boy yistidday," returned the young hill man. "Yes, by the great horn spoon, we got 'im, Pop! An' looky here whut I bought fer 'im—now! Jes ye wait—I'll strike a match. Ye shorely must see them that purties—jes must."

By the light of several matches a small pair of red-top boots were exhibited, handled, and commented upon. Pop Baker's face was a study.

"Waal, waal!" he said, much impressed, "thar's a thing ter grow up ter fit! Um-m-m! Dink, I'd 'a' got ye ter hev fotched me a pair o' them ef ever I'd 'a' known sech things war. War did ye git 'em?"

"Seen um in a winder," said Dink, solemnly. "Hones' Injun, Pop, I war so 'feard they'd be sold afore I got back a-sellin' my hawg. I jes went In regardless, an' ast thet storekeep' ter wrop 'em up 'n' let Dan'el Webster hyah guard 'em. He gimme jes half an hour. Dawg my buttons ef the houn' would let a pusson in the store! But I got them small boots, Pop! Ain't them beaut's, heh?"

"Them shorely air," asserted Pop Baker, solemnly. "Ye air too lucky fer it ter last, Dink—a boy, 'n' strikin' them boots. Waal, I wisht ye merry Christmas! It air gittin' cold, haint it?"

"Whut ye expectin' yerself?" quoth Dink, whose heart had opened under Pop's generous praise. "Ye orter hev suthin' fine yerself, shorely."

Pop tried to pass it off airily.

"I dunno whut Sandy Claws'll do for me," he said slowly. "I did mention ter Jimpsey thet I'd feel peart ter middlin' ef the ol' chap'd drap me a real visible houn' pup down the chimbly. Thet larst houn' I hed outen Ase Blivin's breed war thet triflin' an' cross thet the neighbers pizened him. He clumb right up inter passin' wagons. I wanter own a pup thet hev got some nateral ondertandin', an' ef he bites when he's growed up, he wull bite with reason."

"Dawgs air truly gittin' might' triflin' these days," commented Dink, leaning back. "But, Pop, I'm goin' ter give ye suthin' I got right off a rale peart Sandy Claws pack up in town, An' don't ye open it tell ye git it home, an' ye gits yer fire a-goin' good, an' air settin' roun' thar. Then ye puts yer box on a cheer 'n' ye turns on the leetle wire. Dern it all, but I wisht I war thar when ye does it! Ye're sech a sport yerself thet I hates ter miss it."

"Haint I robbin' o' ye?" asked Pop Baker, politely, although he was leaning far over and reaching out his hand in the wildest curiosity.

"Naw, naw; the feller threw thet thar trick in—an' I got some other stuff. I'll jes keep a-bustin' ter-morrer ter think o' ye an' thet box. Waal, here's ter yer Christmas in the mornin', Pop! So long, ye!"

Pop Baker clasped the small, hard parcel ecstatically to his breast while mechanically holding the reins. Bully Boy seemed to realize the importance of haste as he fairly bounded on, dragging The Other without any mercy. They rattled over the stony creek road, and finally reached the low house. In twenty minutes Pop Baker had given the mules a big feed in the barn, and was stirring up his carefully covered wood fire on the hearth with a pine stick. It struck him that the room was very nice and warm.

The pine stick flared up high, and Pop Baker looked up at the high, rough mantel-board for the one small tin lamp that he possessed. A new glare struck his eye. On the shelf sat a shining glass lamp with a clean chimney and full of oil.

"Don't thet beat anything in the hull world?" observed Pop Baker. "An' thet door hooked up ez keerful ez usual. Now I never calkilated ter own sech a 'lumination ez thet wull shorely make. Hain't that purty? Dern it! it air too fine ter dirty up. It jes does me good ter see it settin' roun'. Whar's my old one?"

He turned about, with his pine stick still blazing high. On his bed was a new patchwork quilt. In his arm-chair was a patchwork cushion. The table on which he had that morning left some very dirty dishes was spread with a new red oil-cloth, and on it were sundry parcels and covered pans.

"Sandy Claws hev gone inter the feedin' business, hit 'pears like. Waal, I'm seventy-odd, 'n' he never lit in on me afore. Shorely we live ter l'arn these hyah dayses."

Delighted, he uncovered fresh bread and pies and cake, and a cold roasted rabbit. He lighted his tin lamp, and stirred up heartsome fire of great logs. The cabin glowed and grew gloriously warm. A friendly cricket chirped upon the hearth as he ate heartily and finally set out a large stone pitcher of hard cider. He poured in some molasses and then thrust an iron poker through the red embers. On Pop Baker's face was a beautiful and tender light, in his blue eyes great love and faith in his fellow-men. The Christmas glow was in his heart, the Christmas peace brooding over him.

Then, and only then, he carefully pulled up a chair and unwrapped the little box Dink Smith had given him. It perched saucily upon the edge of the chair, and Pop sat down before it. He cut a long pine sliver carefully, and solemnly and breathlessly he touched the frail little wire fastening. *Zip!* it was open! There jumped up a rosy-faced, smiling jack-in-the-box with a fringe of gray hair and a perky chin-beard. It stared right saucily at Pop Baker and with the utmost indifference to his opinion. As for Pop, he was so amazed that he had no words. He stared and he retreated and he advanced, wholly fascinated. Then he put his hands down on his knees and he roared with laughter.

"Waal, I'm jes jee-whizzled ef hit ain't my pictur' ter a T! Sandy Claws must hev spotted me. An' I got on a blue nightgownd with posies on it. Hain't yer ol' Pop Baker dyked out fer Christmas? Waal, I never would hev b'lieved it, not ef ye'd told me fer years an' years; but thar I am, an' whut am I goin' ter do but b'lieve it? Waal, whut next? Do I shet up any more in thet box, or do I sleep a-standin'?"

He examined the toy with cautious fingers, but soon discovered the workings of the spring. At last he gently closed the box and deposited the precious thing beside the precious cheap glass lamp on the mantel-shelf.

"I couldn't stan' Sandy Claws a-doin' of much more," he said reverently, "er the Almighty thet air marchin' erlong them stars. I calkilate them two pussons air erbout the same, me not bein' up much in religion. Whut in the dickens air up? Air my house on fire? Woo-o-o!"

For a bucket or two of water was suddenly poured down his big chimney, raising a thick white steam. As this died away, a long pole let down an old basket, and, with a violent lurch from above, the contents tumbled far out on the bare floor. It was a shrieking, howling black puppy, a beautiful curly little creature that trembled like a leaf when Pop Baker jumped to its rescue and folded it in his arms.

"Dern yer buttons up yan! would ye bake the dawg a-playin' of yer Sandy Claws? This air is shorely Jimpsey's doin's. Waal, they needn't 'a' put my fire out, need they, leetle Christmas? By gum, hain't he a beauty? Sech thick ha'r! I never hev seen sech a pup. I bet he's got sense; I bet he's pure breed out o' suthin' 'sides them sneakin' ol' hill houn's. Thar, ye jes lie on my bed while I sees who air playin' Sandy Claws on ter my roof. Oh, I hears ye goin' rattlin' down my clapboards, I does! Ye means well, ye means well. Ef this here hain't a Christmas ter be marked with a stone! The Lord bless 'em all! I'm gittin' ter be ol', but ol' age air the bestes' time, the merries', free time. Sandy Claws never come a-nigh me tell now, an' I 'preciates hit. I likes the lamp, an' I likes thet pictur' of me; but this hyah leetle pup—it's a livin', breathin' thing, an' it comes right nigh ter my heart. Seems like I got 'most everything thar war in the hull world ter git, Mr. Sandy Claws er the Almighty, which air might' nigh the same thing. I thanks ye, wherever ye air."

The Christmas midnight, still solemn and holy, was on the hills. The old man slept calmly in the red light of smoldering embers. The jack-in-the-box had jumped out to see the commotion of the night before, and kept its stiff wooden arms extended toward him in benediction. Close, very close to the old man, one of whose work-worn hands lay on the thick curly fur, slept the fat little puppy that was to be his constant and faithful companion in the days to come.

WHILE THE AUTOMOBILE RAN DOWN

BY CHARLES BATTELL LOOMIS (1861-1911)

In the late nineteenth century, people in the city used cable cars, electric trolleys, and horse-drawn carriages to get around. If they could afford the cost, they called a Hansom cab, a two-wheeled cart drawn by one horse. In the 1890's, electric taxicabs were invented, and wealthy people began to use them for their city transportation. We of the twenty-first century are not the first to deal with the foibles of the electric car. The author of this story, the humorist Charles Battell Loomis, shows the pitfalls of the new technology and how people adapted to the occasional glitch.

It was a letter to encourage a hesitating lover, and certainly Orville Thornton, author of "Thoughts for Non-Thinkers," came under that head. He received it on a Tuesday, and immediately made up his mind to declare his intentions to Miss Annette Badeau that evening.

But perhaps the contents of the letter will help the reader to a better understanding of the case:

Dear Orville:

Miss Badeau sails unexpectedly for Paris on the day after Christmas, her aunt Madge having cabled for her to come and visit her. Won't you come to Christmas dinner? I've invited the Joe Burtons, and of course Mr. Marten will be there, but no others—except Miss Badeau.

Dinner will be at sharp seven. Don't be late, although I know you won't, you human timetable.

I do hope that Annette will not fall in love in Paris. I wish that she would marry some nice New-Yorker and settle near me.

I've always thought that you have neglected marriage shamefully.

Remember to-morrow night, and Annette sails on Thursday. Wishing you a Merry Christmas, I am,

Your old friend,

Henrietta Marten

Annette Badeau had come across the line of Orville's vision three months before. She was Mrs. Marten's niece, and had come from the West to live with her aunt at just about the time that the success of Thornton's book made him think of marriage.

She was pretty and bright and expansive in a Western way, and when Thornton met her at one of the few afternoon teas that he ever attended he fell in love with her. When she learned that she was the niece of his lifelong friend Mrs. Marten, he suddenly discovered various reasons why he should call at the Marten house once or twice a week.

But a strange habit he had of putting off delightful moments in order to enjoy anticipation to its fullest extent had caused him to refrain from disclosing the state of his heart to Miss Badeau, and so that young woman, who had fallen in love with him even before she knew that he was the gifted author of "Thoughts for Non-Thinkers," often wished to herself that she could in some way give him a hint of the state of her heart.

Orville received Mrs. Marten's letter on Christmas eve, and its contents made him plan a schedule for the next evening's running. No power on earth could keep him away from that dinner, and he immediately sent a telegram of regret to the Bellwether of the Wolves' Club, although he had been anticipating the Christmas gorge for a month.

He also sent a messenger with a note of acceptance to Mrs. Marten.

Then he joined the crowd of persons who always wait until Christmas eve before buying the presents that stern and unpleasant duty makes it necessary to get.

It would impart a characteristic Christmas flavor if it were possible to cover the ground with snow and to make the air merry with the sound of flashing belts of silvery sleigh bells on prancing horses; but although Christmases in stories are always snowy and frosty, and sparkling with ice-crystals, Christmases in real life are apt to be damp and humid. Let us be thankful that this Christmas was merely such a one as would not give a ghost of a reason for a trip to Florida. The mercury stood at 58, and even light overcoats were not things to be put on without thought.

Orville knew what he wished to get and where it was sold, and so he had an advantage over ninety-nine out of a hundred of the anxious-looking shoppers who were scuttling from shop to shop, burdened with bundles, and making the evening the worst in the year for tired sales -girls and -men. Orville's present was not exactly Christmassy, but he hoped that Miss Badeau would like it, and it was certainly the finest one on the velvet tray. Orville, it will be seen, was of a sanguine disposition.

He did not hang up his stocking; he had not done that for several years; but he did dream that Santa Claus brought him a beautiful doll from Paris, and just as he was saying, "There must be some mistake," the doll turned into Miss Badeau, and said: "No, I'm for you. Merry Christmas!" Then he woke up and thought how foolish and yet how fascinating dreams are.

Christmas morning was spent in polishing up an old essay on "The Value of the Summer as an Invigorator." It had long been a habit of his to work over old stuff on his holidays, and if he was about to marry he would need to sell everything he had—of a literary-marketable nature. But this morning a vision of a lovely girl who on the morrow was going to sail thousands of miles away came between him and the page, and at last he tossed the manuscript into a drawer and went out for a walk.

It was the draggiest Christmas he had ever known, and the warmest. He dropped in at the club, but there was hardly any one there; still, he did manage to play a few games of billiards, and at last the clock announced that it was time to go home and dress for the Christmas dinner.

It was half-past five when be left the club. It was twenty minutes to six when he slipped on a piece of orange-peel and measured his length on the sidewalk. He was able to rise and hobble up the steps on one foot, but the hall-boy had to help him to the elevator and thence to his room. He dropped upon his bed, feeling white about the gills.

Orville was a most methodical man. He planned his doings days ahead and seldom changed his schedule. But it seemed likely that unless he was built of sterner stuff than most of the machines called men, he would not run out of the round-house to-night. His fall had given his foot a nasty wrench.

Some engineers, to change the simile, would have argued that the engine was off the track and that therefore the train was not in running condition; but Orville merely changed engines. His own steam having been cut off, he ordered an automobile for twenty minutes to seven; and after he had bathed and bandaged his ankle he determined, with a grit worthy of the cause that brought it forth, to attend that dinner even if he paid for it in the hospital, with Annette as special nurse.

Old Mr. Nickerson, who lived across the hall, had heard of his misfortune, and called to proffer his services.

"Shall I help you get to bed?" said he.

"I am not due in bed, Mr. Nickerson, for many hours; but if you will give me a few fingers of your excellent old Scotch, with the bouquet of smoked herring, I will go on dressing for dinner."

"Dear boy," said the old gentleman, almost tearfully, "it is impossible for you to venture on your foot with such a sprain. It is badly swollen."

Mr. Nickerson, my heart has received a worse wrench than my foot has, therefore I go out to dine." At sound of which enigmatical declaration Mr. Nickerson hurried off for the old Scotch, and in a few minutes Orville's faintness had passed off, and with help from the amiable old man he got into his evening clothes—with the exception of his left foot, which was incased in a flowered slipper of sunset red.

"Now, my dear Mr. Nickerson, I'm a thousand times obliged to you, and if I can get you to help me hop downstairs I will wait for the automobile on the front stoop." (Orville had been born in Brooklyn, where they still have "stoops.") "I'm on time so far."

But if Orville was on time, the automobile was not, the driver not being a methodical man; and when it did come, it was all the motorman could do to stop it. It seemed restive.

"You ought to shut off on the oats," said Orville, gaily, from his seat on the lowest step of the "stoop."

The picture of a gentleman in immaculate evening clothes, with the exception of a somewhat rococo carpet slipper, seemed to amuse some street children who were passing. If they could have followed the "auto" they would have been even more diverted, but such was not to be their fortune. Mr. Nickerson helped his friend into the vehicle, and the driver started at a lively rate for Fifth Avenue.

Orville lived in Seventeenth Street, near Fifth Avenue; Mrs. Marten lived on Fifth Avenue, near Forty-first Street. Thirty-ninth Street and Fortieth Street were reached and passed without further incident than the fact that Orville's ankle pained him almost beyond the bearing-point; but, as it is not the history of a sprained ankle that I am writing, if the vehicle had stopped at Mrs. Marten's my pen would not have been set to paper.

But the motor-wagon did not even pause. It kept on as if the Harlem River were to be its next stop.

Orville had stated the number of his destination with distinctness, and he now rang the annunciator and asked the driver why he did not stop.

Calmly, in the even tones that clear-headed persons use when they wish to inspire confidence, the driver said: "Don't be alarmed, sir, but I can't stop. There's something out of kilter, and I may have to run some time before I can get the hang of it. There's no danger as long as I can steer."

"Can't you slacken up in front of the house, so that I can jump?"

"With that foot, sir? Impossible, and, anyway, I can't slacken up. I think we'll stop soon. I don't know when it was charged, but a gentleman had it before I was sent out with it. It won't he long, I think. I'll run around the block, and maybe I can stop the next time."

Orville groaned for a twofold reason: his ankle was jumping with pain, and he would lose the pleasure of taking Miss Badeau in to dinner, for it was a minute past seven.

He sat and gazed at his carpet slipper, and thought of the daintily shod feet of the adorable Annette, as the horseless carriage wound round the block. As they approached the house again, Orville imagined that they were slackening up, and he opened the door to be ready. It was now three minutes past seven, and dinner had begun beyond a doubt. The driver saw the door swing open, and said:

"Don't jump, sir. I can't stop yet. I'm afraid there's a good deal of run in the machine."

Orville looked up at the brownstone front of the house with an agonized stare, as if he would pull Mrs. Marten to the window by the power of his eyes. But Mrs. Marten was not in the habit of pressing her nose against the pane in an anxious search for tardy guests. In fact, it may be asserted with confidence that it is not a Fifth Avenue custom.

At that moment the purée was being served to Mrs. Marten's guests, and to pretty Annette Badeau, who really looked disconsolate with the vacant chair beside her.

"Something has happened to Orville," said Mrs. Marten, looking over her shoulder toward the hall door, "for he is punctuality itself."

Mr. Joe Burton was a short, red-faced little man,

with black mutton-chop whiskers of the style of '76, and a way of looking in the most cheerful manner upon the dark side of things. "Dessay he's been run over," said he, choppily. "Wonder any one escapes. Steam-, gasoline-, electric-, horse-flesh-, man-propelled juggernauts. Ought to be prohibited."

Annette could not repress a shudder. Her aunt saw it, and said: "Orville will never be run over. He's too wide-awake. But it is very singular."

"He may have been detained by an order for a story," said Mr. Marten, also with the amiable purpose of consoling Annette. For both of the Martens knew how she felt toward Mr. Thornton.

"Maybe he's lying on the front sidewalk, hit by a sign or bitten by a dog. Dogs ought not to be allowed in the city; they only add to the dangers of metropolitan existence," jerked out Mr. Burton, in blithe tones, totally unaware that his remarks might worry Annette.

"Dear me! I wish you'd send some one out to see, Aunt Henrietta."

"Nonsense, Annette. Mr. Burton is always an alarmist. But, Marie, you might step to the front door and look down the avenue to Fortieth Street. Mr. Thornton is always so punctual that it is peculiar."

Marie went to the front door and looked down the street just as Thornton, gesticulating wildly, disappeared around the corner of Forty-first Street.

"Oh, why didn't she come sooner!" said he aloud to himself. "At least they would know why I'm late. And she'll be gone before I come round again. Was there ever such luck? Oh for a good old horse that could stop, a dear old nag that would pause and not go round and round like a blamed carrousel! Say, driver, isn't there any way of stopping this cursed thing? Can't you run it into a fence or a house? I'll take the risk."

"But I won't, sir. These automobiles are very powerful, and one of them turned over a news-stand not long since and upset the stove in it and nearly burned up the news-man. But there's plenty of time for it to stop. I don't have to hurry back."

"That's lucky," said Orville. "I thought maybe you'd have to leave me alone with the thing. But, say, she may run all night. Here I am due at a dinner. I'm tired of riding. This is no way to spend Christmas. Slacken up, and I'll jump when I get around there again."

"I tell you I can't slacken up, and she's going ten miles an hour. You'll break your leg if you jump, and then where'll you be?"

"I might be on their sidewalk, and then you could ring their bell, and they'd take me in."

"And have you suing the company for damages? Oh, no, sir. I'm sorry, but it can't be helped. The company won't charge you for the extra time."

"No, I don't think it will," said Thornton, savagely, the more so as his foot gave a twinge of pain just then.

"There was no one in sight, ma'am," said Marie when she returned.

"Probably he had an order for a story and got absorbed in it and forgot us," said Mr. Marten; but this conjecture did not seem to suit Annette, for it did not fit what she knew of his character.

"Possibly he was dropped in an elevator," said Mr. Burton. "Strain on elevators, particularly these electrical ones, is tremendous. Some of have got to drop. And a dropping elevator is no respecter of persons. You and I may be in one when it drops. Probably he was. Sure, I hope not, but as he is known to be the soul of punctuality, we must put forward some accident to account for his lateness. People aren't always killed in elevator accidents. Are they, my dear?"

"Mr. Burton," said his wife, "I wish you would give

your morbid thoughts a rest. Don't you see that Annette is sensitive?"

"Sensitive—with half of India starving and people being shot in the Transvaal and in China every day? It's merely because she happens to know Orville that his death would be unpleasant. If a man in the Klondike were to read of it in the paper he wouldn't remember it five minutes. But I don't say he was in an elevator. Maybe some one sent him an infernal machine for a Christmas present. May have been blown up in a manhole or jumped from his window to avoid flames. Why, there are a million ways to account for his absence."

Marie had opened the parlor windows a moment before, as the house was warm, and now there came the humming of a rapidly moving automobile. Mingled with it they heard distinctly, although faintly, "Mr. Marten, here I go."

It gave them all an uncanny feeling. The fish was left untouched, and for a moment silence reigned. Then Mr. Marten sprang from the table and ran to the front door. He got there just in time to see an automobile dashing around a corner and to hear a distinctly articulated imprecation in the well-known voice of Orville Thornton.

In evening clothes and bareheaded Mr. Marten ran to Forty-first Street, and saw the vehicle approaching Sixth Avenue, its occupant still hurling strong language upon the evening air. Mr. Marten is something of a sprinter, although he has passed the fifty mark, and he resolved to solve the mystery. But before he had covered a third of the block in Forty-first Street he saw that he could not hope to overtake the runaway automobile, so he turned and ran back to the house, rightly surmising that the driver would circle the block.

When he reached his own door-step, badly winded, he saw the automobile coming full tilt up the avenue from Fortieth Street.

The rest of the diners were on the steps. "I think he's coming," he panted. "The driver must be intoxicated."

A moment later they were treated to the spectacle of Orville, still hurling imprecations as he wildly gesticulated with both arms. Several boys were trying to keep up with the vehicle, but the pace was too swift. No policeman had yet discovered its rotary course.

As Orville came near the Marten mansion he cried "Ah-h-h!" in the relieved tones of one who has been falling for half an hour and at last sees ground in sight.

"What's the matter?" shouted Mr. Marten, wonderingly, as the carriage, instead of stopping, sped along the roadway.

"Sprained foot. Can't walk. Auto out of order. Can't stop. Good-by till I come round again. Awful hungry. Merry Christmas!"

"Ah ha!" said Joe Burton. "I told you that it was an accident. Sprained his foot and lost power over vehicle. I don't see the connection, but let us be thankful that he isn't under the wheels, with a broken neck, or winding round and round the axle."

"But what's to be done?" said Mrs. Marten. "He says he's hungry."

"Tell you what!" said Mr. Burton, in his explosive way. "Put some food on a plate, and when the carriage comes round again I'll jump aboard, and he can eat as he travels."

"He loves purée of celery," said Mrs. Marten.

"Very well. Put some in a clean lard-pail or a milk-pail. Little out of the ordinary, but so is the accident, and he can't help his hunger. Hunger is no disgrace. I didn't think he'd ever eat soup again, to tell the truth. I was making up my mind whether a wreath or a harp would be better."

"Oh, you are so morbid, Mr. Burton," said his wife,

while Mrs. Marten told the maid to get a pail and put some purée into it.

When Thornton came around again he met Mr. Marten near Fortieth Street.

"Open the door, Orville, and Joe Burton will get aboard with some soup. You must be starved."

There's nothing like exercise for getting up an appetite. I'll be ready for Burton," said Orville. "Awfully sorry I can't stop and talk; but I'll see you again in a minute or two."

He opened the door as he spoke, and then, to the great delight of at least a score of people who had realized that the automobile was running away, the rubicund and stout Joe Burton, a pail of purée in one hand and some table cutlery and silverware and a napkin in the other, made a dash at the vehicle, and with help from Orville effected an entrance.

"Merry Christmas!" said Orville.

"Merry Christmas! Awfully sorry, old man, but it might be worse. Better drink it out of the pail. They gave me a knife and fork, but they neglected to put in a spoon or a dish. I thought that you were probably killed, but I never imagined this. Miss Badeau was terribly worked up. I think that she had decided on white carnations. Nice girl. You could easily jump, old man, if you hadn't sprained your foot. Hurt much?"

"Like the devil; but I'm glad it worried Miss Badeau. No, I don't mean that. But you know."

"Yes, I know," said Burton, with a sociable smile. "Mm. Marten told me. Nice girl. Let her in next time. Unusual thing, you know. People are very apt to jump *from* a runaway vehicle, but it seldom takes up passengers. Let her get in, and you can explain matters to her. You see, she sails early in the morning, and you haven't much time. You can tell her what a nice fellow you are, you know, and I'm sure you'll have Mrs. Marten's blessing. Here's where I get out."

With an agility admirable in one of his stoutness, Mr. Burton leaped to the street and ran up the steps to speak to Miss Badeau. Orville could see her blush, but there was no time for her to become a passenger that trip, and the young man once more made the circuit of the block, quite alone, but strangely happy. He had never ridden with Annette, except once on the elevated road, and then both Mr. and Mrs. Marten were of the company.

Round sped the motor, and when the Martens' appeared in sight, Annette was on the sidewalk with a covered dish in her hand and a look of excited expectancy on her face that added a hundredfold to its charms.

"Here you are—only ten cents a ride. Merry Christmas!" shouted Orville, gaily, and leaned half out of the automobile to catch her. It was a daring jump, but Annette made it without accident, and, flushed and excited, sat down in front of Mr. Thornton without spilling her burden, which proved to be sweetbreads.

"Miss Badeau—Annette, I hadn't expected it to turn out this way, but of course your aunt doesn't care, or she wouldn't have let you come. We're really in no danger. This driver has had more experience dodging teams in this last hour than he'd get in an ordinary year. They tell me you're going to Europe early tomorrow, to leave all your friends. Now, I've something very important to say to you before you go. No, thanks, I don't want anything more. That purée was very filling. I've sprained my ankle, and I need to be very quiet for a week or two, perhaps until this machine runs down, but at the end of that time would you—"

Orville hesitated, and Annette blushed sweetly. She set the sweetbreads down upon the seat beside her. Orville had never looked so handsome before to her eyes.

He hesitated. "Go on," said she.

"Would you be willing to go to Paris on a bridal trip?"

Annette's answer was drowned in the hurrah of the driver as the automobile, gradually slackening, came to a full stop in front of the Martens'.

But Orville read her lips, and as he handed his untouched sweetbreads to Mrs. Burton, and his sweetheart to her uncle, his face wore a seraphically happy expression; and when Mr. Marten and the driver helped him up the steps at precisely eight o'clock, Annette's hand sought his, and it was a jolly party that sat down to a big though somewhat dried-up Rhode Island turkey.

"Marriage also is an accident," said Mr. Burton.

A CHRISTMAS RESCUE

BY ALBERT BIGELOW PAINE (1861-1937)

Imaginative play is the subject of this, the only story in the collection that was actually written for children. In this turn-of-the-century tale, a child's wounded feelings are healed just in time for Christmas. Interestingly, the author, Albert Bigelow Paine, was employed as Mark Twain's secretary, and wrote his authorized biography in 1912.

He had never really left home before, though he had threatened to do so many times. But on the day before Christmas he felt just obliged to go. This was the way of it.

Sister Alice, who was a great deal older than he was, being sixteen and graduated from a cooking-class, was making a lot of things in the kitchen. She hadn't learned in cooking-school how to have little boys around when she was making things, so when he wanted to dig out the cake-leavings, just as he did when his mother baked, sister Alice, who of course felt very grown up, said "No!" quite severely. And when he wanted a piece of pie-crust to wad up and hammer out flat and bake on the corner of the cook-stove, she said "No!" again, not remembering that she was ever little herself, and then got quite cross, perhaps because her cake looked as if it might "fall," and told him to go out of the kitchen, and stay out until she was all through!

He *did* go out of the kitchen, and went to the nursery to play "Indians" with little Dot. But when he swooped down on little Dot's best doll, the only one that had lasted through from last Christmas, and was going to scalp her, and torture her, and burn her at the stake, little Dot screamed almost as loudly as if it were she who was to have all these things done to her, and ran to tell her mother, who was ironing in the laundry and very busy, and who sent back word that he was to put that doll down *instantly,* or he would be put to bed for two days and there would be no Christmas in *that* house for *any*body!

It was then he said that he would go. There was no place for him in that house, anyway. So he put on his thick overcoat and arctic shoes, and his cap that pulled down over his ears. Then he took his pistol, that didn't have any caps left, and his best agate taw, and told little Dot that he was going to Africa to fight tigers, and that on Christmas morning they would find him lying all dead, and that they would be *very sorry!*

Little Dot was already sorry, and began to whimper, but was afraid to tell her mother again, for fear he would go even farther than Africa, and that they would find him even deader and sooner than he had said. So she watched him through the window until she saw him go into the barn. Then she slipped out to get sister Alice to help her on with her coat and overshoes. Then she hurried after Dick, and pulled open the big slatted barn door, and found him bravely snapping his pistol at the mules.

"I'm killing tigers!" he said fiercely. I am Dick Daring, the king of the jungle! I shall be found here dead and eaten up alive on Christmas morning!"

The mules didn't know they were being killed, or that they were to have a live boy for breakfast. They kept on pulling wisps of hay from their mangers.

"Oh, Dick, isn't it *cold* in Africa!"

Little Dot shivered and doubled her mittened hands into her sleeves.

"No; Africa is a hot climate, where tigers, elephants, and poisonous serpents abound!"

"But it *is* cold here, Dick. I'm 'mos' froze! Dick, Alice is making cookies!"

Dick let at least two tigers get away. Then he said sadly:

"I won't need any cookies. I shall be dead on the Russian steppes on Christmas morning. If Africa isn't cold enough I guess Russia *is!*"

He had rushed over to the little cutter in the corner, and leaping up in the seat, began shooting wildly from the back end.

"The wolves! The wolves!" he shouted. "They are close behind, and I can't slay them all!"

"Dick! *Oh, Dick!*"

"They will eat me! They will eat me *all up!* There will be only a red stain on the snow on Christmas morning."

"Dick, Alice is making two little cakes! I saw them!"

The wolf-killing stopped for at least five seconds. Perhaps the wolves were all dead. Then the killer said tragically, and with a tremble in his voice:

"It's too late. I'm going to the North Pole. You can have the cake, Dot, and I forgive you about the doll."

Little Dot was already whimpering from the cold and from being rather scared, but she did want to see what Dick would do next. He jumped out of the cutter and ran over to a heavy post at the farther end of the barn.

"This is the north pole," he said, as he dragged bunches of hay about him. "I am in my winter hut. I shall be found dead and starved on Chr—in the spring,

I mean. It will be too late then for cakes and cookies. Dick Daring, the great explorer, will be dead!"

"Dick!" Little Dot had made her way tearfully to the north pole, and was looking at the great explorer buried in the hay. "Oh, Dick, Alice has made two little mince-pies, and they're—they're done, and she said we might *have 'em now!"*

Dick Daring, the explorer, crouched in his hut a moment longer. Then he sat straight up.

"Oh, Dot" he said, "let's play that you're a relief expedition, and that you came just in time to save me on Christmas morning!"

MERRY CHRISTMAS IN THE TENEMENTS

BY JACOB A. RIIS (1849-1914)

Jacob A. Riis, a police reporter in New York City, wrote this account of Christmas in the slums in 1897. Between 1860 and 1900, fourteen million immigrants poured into American cities to find work and found mean shelter in the dark tenements. Riis' narrative is a heart-rending journey into the lives of the Bowery's poverty stricken immigrants. Yet even in the darkest places the author finds hope and strength in his subjects' faces. Riis became a leading advocate for housing reform, writing about and photographing the terrible living conditions in the tenements in order to bring national attention to the immigrants' plight.

It was just a sprig of holly, with scarlet berries shoring against the green, stuck in, by one of the office boys probably, behind the sign that pointed the way up to the editorial rooms. There was no reason why it should have made me start when I came suddenly upon it at the turn of the stairs; but it did. Perhaps it was because that dingy hall, given over to dust and drafts all the days of the year, was the last place in which I expected

to meet with any sign of Christmas; perhaps it was because I myself had nearly forgotten the holiday. Whatever the cause, it gave me quite a turn.

I stood, and stared at it. It looked dry, almost withered. Probably it had come a long way. Not much holly
grows about Printing-House Square, except in the colored supplements, and that is scarcely of a kind to stir
tender memories. Withered and dry, this did. I thought,
with a twinge of conscience, of secret little conclaves of
my children, of private views of things hidden from
mama at the bottom of drawers, of wild flights when
papa appeared unbidden in the door, which I had allowed for once to pass unheeded. Absorbed in the business of the office, I had hardly thought of Christmas
coming on, until now it was here. And this sprig of holly
on the wall that had come to remind me,—come nobody
knew how far,—did it grow yet in the beech-wood clear-
ings, as it did when I gathered it as a boy, tracking
through the snow? "Christ-thorn" we called it in our
Danish tongue. The red berries, to our simple faith,
were the drops of blood that fell from the Saviour's brow
as it drooped under its cruel crown upon the cross.

Back to the long ago wandered my thoughts: to the
moss-grown beech in which I cut my name, and that of
a little girl with yellow curls, of blessed memory, with
the first jack-knife I ever owned; to the story-book with
the little fir-tree that pined because it was small, and
because the hare jumped over it, and would not be content though the wind and the sun kissed it, and the
dews wept over it, and told it to rejoice in its young life;
and that was so proud when, in the second year, the
hare had to go round it, because then it knew it was
getting big,—Hans Christian Andersen's story, that we
loved above all the rest; for we knew the tree right well,
and the hare; even the tracks it left in the snow we had
seen. Ah, those were the Yule-tide seasons, when the

old Domkirke shone with a thousand wax candles on Christmas eve; when all business was laid aside to let the world make merry one whole week; when big red apples were roasted on the stove, and bigger doughnuts were baked within it for the long feast! Never such had been known since. Christmas to-day is but a name, a memory.

A door slammed below, and let in the noises of the street. The holly rustled in the draft. Some one going out said, "A Merry Christmas to you all!" in a big, hearty voice. I awoke from my reverie to find myself back in New York with a glad glow at the heart. It was not true. I had only forgotten. It was myself that had changed, not Christmas. That was here, with the old cheer, the old message of good-will, the old royal road to the heart of mankind. How often had I seen its blessed charity, that never corrupts, make light in the hovels of darkness and despair! how often watched its spirit of self-sacrifice and devotion in those who had, besides themselves, nothing to give! and as often the sight had made whole my faith in human nature. No! Christmas was not of the past, its spirit not dead. The lad who fixed the sprig of holly on the stairs knew it; my reporter's notebook bore witness to it. Witness of my contrition for the wrong I did the gentle spirit of the holiday, here let the book tell the story of one Christmas in the tenements of the poor.

It is evening in Grand street. The shops east and west are pouring forth their swarms of workers. Street and sidewalk are filled with an eager throng of young men and women, chatting gaily, and elbowing the jam of holiday shoppers that linger about the big stores. The street-cars labor along, loaded down to the steps with passengers carrying bundles of every size and odd shape. Along the curb a string of peddlers hawk penny toys in push-carts with noisy clamor, fearless for once of being moved on by the police. Christmas brings a two-weeks' respite from persecution even to the friendless street-fakir. From the window of one brilliantly lighted store a bevy of mature dolls in dishabille stretch forth their arms appealingly to a troop of factory-hands passing by. The young men chaff the girls, who shriek with laughter and run. The policeman on the corner stops beating his hands together to keep warm, and makes a mock attempt to catch them, whereat their shrieks rise shriller than ever. "Them stockin's o' yourn'll be the death o' Santa Claus!" he shouts after them, as they dodge. And they, looking back, snap saucily, "Mind yer business, freshy!" But their laughter belies their words. "They gin it to ye straight that time," grins the grocer's clerk, come out to snatch a look at the crowds; and the two swap holiday greetings.

At the corner, where two opposing tides of travel form an eddy, the line of push-carts debouches down the darker side-street. In its gloom their torches burn with a fitful glare that wakes black shadows among the trusses of the railroad structure overhead. A woman, with worn shawl drawn tightly about head and shoulders, bargains with a peddler for a monkey on a stick and two cents' worth of flitter-gold. Five ill-clad youngsters flatten their noses against the frozen pane of the toy-shop, in ecstasy at something there, which proves to be a milk-wagon, with driver, horses, and cans that can be unloaded. It is something their minds can grasp. One comes forth with a penny goldfish of pasteboard clutched tightly in his hand, and casting cautious glances right and left, speeds across the way to the door of a tenement, where a little girl stands waiting. "It's yer Chris'mas, Kate," he says, and thrusts it into her eager fist. The black doorway swallows them up.

Across the narrow yard, in the basement of the rear house, the lights of a Christmas tree show against the grimy window-pane. The hare would never have gone around it, it is so very small. The two children are busily engaged fixing the goldfish upon one of its branches. Three little candles that burn there shed light upon a scene of utmost desolation. The room is black with smoke and dirt. In the middle of the floor oozes an oil-stove that serves at once to take the raw edge off the cold and to cook the meals by. Half the window-panes are broken, and the holes stuffed with rags. The sleeve of an old coat hangs out of one, and beats drearily upon the sash when the wind sweeps over the fence and rattles the rotten shutters. The family wash, clammy and gray, hangs on a clothes-line stretched across the room. Under it, at a table set with cracked and empty plates, a discouraged woman sits eying the children's show gloomily. It is evident that she has been drinking. The peaked faces of the little ones wear a famished look. There are three—the third an infant, put to bed in what was once a baby-carriage. The two from the street are pulling it around to get the tree in range. The baby sees it, and crows with delight. The boy shakes a branch, and the goldfish leaps and sparkles in the candle-light.

"See, sister!" he pipes; "see Santa Claus!" And they clap their hands in glee. The woman at the table wakes out of her stupor, gazes around her, and bursts into a fit of maudlin weeping.

The door falls to. Five flights up, another opens upon a bare attic room which a patient little woman is setting to rights. There are only three chairs, a box, and a bedstead in the room, but they take a deal of careful arranging. The bed hides the broken plaster in the wall through which the wind came in; each chair-leg stands over a rat-hole, at once to hide it and to keep the rats out. One is left; the box is for that. The plaster of the ceiling is held up with pasteboard patches. I know the story of that attic. It is one of cruel desertion. The woman's husband is even now living in plenty with the creature for whom he forsook her, not a dozen blocks away, while she "keeps the home together for the childer." She sought justice, but the lawyer demanded a retainer; so she gave it up, and went back to her little ones. For this room that barely keeps the winter wind out she pays four dollars a month, and is behind with the rent. There is scarce bread in the house; but the spirit of Christmas has found her attic. Against a broken wall is tacked a hemlock branch, the leavings of the corner grocer's fitting-block; pink string from the packing-counter hangs on it in festoons. A tallow dip on the box furnishes the illumination. The children sit up in bed, and watch it with shining eyes.

"We're having Christmas!" they say.

The lights of the Bowery glow like a myriad twinkling stars upon the ceaseless flood of humanity that surges ever through the great highway of the homeless. They shine upon long rows of lodging-houses, in which hundreds of young men, cast helpless upon the reef of the strange city, are learning their first lessons of utter loneliness; for what desolation is there like that of the careless crowd when all the world rejoices? They shine upon the tempter, setting his snares there, and upon the missionary and the Salvation Army lass, disputing his catch with him; upon the police detective going his rounds with coldly observant eye intent upon the outcome of the contest; upon the wreck that is past hope, and upon the youth pausing on the verge of the pit in which the other has long ceased to struggle. Sights and sounds of Christmas there are in plenty in the Bowery. Juniper and tamarack and fir stand in groves along the busy thoroughfare, and garlands of green embower mission and dive impartially. Once a year the old street recalls its youth with an effort. It is true that it is largely a commercial effort—that the evergreen, with an instinct that is not of its native hills, haunts saloon-corners by preference; but the smell of the pine-woods is in the air, and—Christmas is not too critical—one is grateful for the effort. It varies with the opportunity. At "Beefsteak John's" it is content with artistically embalming crullers and mince-pies in green cabbage under the window lamp. Over yonder, where the mile-post of the old lane still stands,—in its unhonored old age become the vehicle of publishing the latest "sure cure" to the world,—a florist, whose undenominational zeal for the holiday and trade outstrips alike distinction of creed and property, has transformed the sidewalk and the ugly railroad structure into a veritable bower, spanning it with a canopy of green, under which dwell with him, in neighborly good-will, the Young Men's Christian Association and the Gentile tailor next door.

In the next block a "turkey-shoot" is in progress. Crowds are trying their luck at breaking the glass balls that dance upon tiny jets of water in front of a marine view with the moon rising, yellow and big, out of a silver sea. A man-of-war, with lights burning aloft, labors under a rocky coast. Groggy sailormen, on shore leave, make unsteady attempts upon the dancing balls. One mistakes the moon for the target, but is discovered in season. "Don't shoot that," says the man who loads the guns; "there's a lamp behind it." Three scared birds in the window-recess try vainly to snatch a moment's sleep between shots and the trains that go roaring overhead on the elevated road. Roused by the sharp crack of the rifles, they blink at the lights in the street, and peck moodily at a crust in their bed of shavings.

The dime-museum gong clatters out its noisy warning that "the lecture" is about to begin. From the concert-hall, where men sit drinking beer in clouds of smoke, comes the thin voice of a short-skirted singer warbling, "Do they think of me at home?" The young fellow who sits near the door, abstractedly making figures in the wet track of the "schooners," buries something there with a sudden restless turn, and calls for another beer. Out in the street a band strikes up. A host with banners advances, chanting an unfamiliar hymn. In the ranks marches a cripple on crutches. Newsboys follow, gaping. Under the illuminated clock of the Cooper Institute the procession halts, and the leader, turning his face to the sky, offers a prayer. The passing crowds stop to listen. A few bare their heads. The devoted group, the flapping banners, and the changing torch-light on up-turned faces, make a strange, weird picture. Then the drum-beat, and the band files into its barracks across the street. A few of the listeners follow, among them the lad from the concert-hall, who slinks shamefacedly in when he thinks no one is looking.

Down at the foot of the Bowery is the "panhandlers' beat," where the saloons elbow each other at every step, crowding out all other business than that of keeping lodgers to support them. Within call of it, across the square, stands a church which, in the memory of men yet living, was built to shelter the fashionable Baptist audiences of a day when Madison Square was out in the fields, and Harlem had a foreign sound. The fashionable audiences are gone long since. To-day the church, fallen into premature decay, but still handsome in its strong and noble lines, stands as a missionary outpost in the land of the enemy, its builders would have said, doing a greater work than they planned. To-night is the Christmas festival of its English-speaking Sunday-school, and the pews are filled. The banners of United Italy, of modern Hellas, of France and Germany and England, hang side by side with the Chinese dragon and the starry flag—signs of the cosmopolitan character of the congregation. Greek and Roman Catholics, Jews and joss-worshipers, go there; few Protestants, and no Baptists. It is easy to pick out the children in their seats by nationality, and as easy to read the story of poverty and suffering that stands written in more than one mother's haggard face, now beaming with pleasure at the little ones' glee. A gaily decorated Christmas tree has taken the place of the pulpit. At its foot is stacked a mountain of bundles, Santa Claus's gifts to the school. A self-conscious young man with soap-locks has just been allowed to retire, amid tumultuous applause, after blowing "Nearer, my God, to thee" on his horn until his cheeks swelled almost to bursting. A trumpet ever takes the Fourth Ward by storm. A class of little girls is climbing upon the platform. Each wears a capital letter on her breast, and has a piece to speak that begins with the letter; together they spell its lesson. There is momentary consternation: one is missing. As the discovery is made, a child pushes past the doorkeeper, hot and breathless. "I am in 'Boundless Love,'" she says, and makes for the platform, where her arrival restores confidence and the language.

In the audience the befrocked visitor from up-town sits cheek by jowl with the pigtailed Chinaman and the dark-browed Italian. Up in the gallery, farthest from the preacher's desk and the tree, sits a Jewish mother with her three boys, almost in rags. A dingy and threadbare shawl partly hides her poor calico wrap and patched apron. The woman shrinks in the pew, fearful of being seen; her boys stand upon the benches, and applaud with the rest. She endeavors vainly to restrain them. "Tick, tick!" goes the old clock over the door through which wealth and fashion went out long years ago, and poverty came in.

Loudly ticked the old clock in time with the doxology, the other day, when they cleared the tenants out of

Gotham Court down here in Cherry Street, and shut the iron doors of Single and Double Alley against them.

Never did the world move faster or surer toward a better day than when the wretched slum was seized by the health officers as a nuisance unfit longer to disgrace a Christian city. The snow lies deep in the deserted passageways, and the vacant floors are given over to evil smells, and to the rats that forage in squads, burrowing in the neglected sewers. The wall of wrath still towers above the buildings in the adjoining Alderman's Court, but its wrath at last is wasted.

It was built by a vengeful Quaker, whom the alderman had knocked down in a quarrel over the boundary line, and transmitted its legacy of hate to generations yet unborn; for where it stood it shut out sunlight and air from the tenements of Alderman's Court. And at last it is to go, Gotham Court and all; and to the going the wall of wrath has contributed its share, thus in the end atoning for some of the harm it wrought. Tick! old clock; the world moves. Never yet did Christmas seem less dark on Cherry Hill than since the lights were put out in Gotham Court forever.

In "the Bend" the philanthropist undertaker who "buries for what he can catch on the plate" hails the Yule-tide season with a pyramid of green made of two coffins set on end. It has been a good day, he says cheerfully, putting up the shutters; and his mind is easy. But the "good days" of the Bend are over, too. The Bend itself is all but gone. Where the old pigsty stood, children dance and sing to the strumming of a cracked piano-organ propelled on wheels by an Italian and his wife. The park that has come to take the place of the slum will curtail the undertaker's profits, as it has lessened the work of the police. Murder was the fashion of the day that is past. Scarce a knife has been drawn since the sunlight shone into that evil spot, and grass and green shrubs took the place of the old rookeries. The Christmas gospel of peace and good-will moves in where the slum moves out. It never had a chance before.

The children follow the organ, stepping in the slush to the music,—bareheaded and with torn shoes, but happy,—across the Five Points and through "the Bay"— known to the directory as Baxter street,—to "the Divide," still Chatham street to its denizens though the aldermen have rechristened it Park Row. There other delegations of Greek and Italian children meet and escort the music on its homeward trip. In one of the crooked streets near the river its journey comes to an end. A battered door opens to let it in. A tallow dip burns sleepily on the creaking stairs. The water runs with a loud clatter in the sink: it is to keep it from freezing. There is not a whole window-pane in the hall. Time was when this was a fine house harboring wealth and refinement. It has neither now. In the old parlor downstairs a knot of hard-faced men and women sit on benches about a deal table, playing cards. They have a jug between them, from which they drink by turns. On the stump of a mantel-shelf a lamp burns before a rude print of the Mother of God. No one pays any heed to the hand-organ man and his wife as they climb to their attic. There is a colony of them up there—three families in four rooms.

"Come in, Antonio," says the tenant of the double flat,—the one with two rooms,—"come and keep Christmas." Antonio enters, cap in hand. In the corner by the dormer-window a "crib" has been fitted up in commemoration of the Nativity. A soap-box and two hemlock branches are the elements. Six tallow candles and a night-light illuminate a singular collection of rarities, set out with much ceremonial show. A doll tightly wrapped in swaddling-clothes represents "the Child."

Over it stands a ferocious-looking beast, easily recognized as a survival of the last political campaign,—the Tammany tiger,—threatening to swallow it at a gulp if one as much as takes one's eyes off it. A miniature Santa Claus, a pasteboard monkey, and several other articles of bric-à-brac of the kind the tenement affords, complete the outfit. The background is a picture of St. Donato, their village saint, with the Madonna, "whom they worship most." But the incongruity harbors no suggestion of disrespect. The children view the strange show with genuine reverence, bowing and crossing themselves before it. There are five, the oldest a girl of seventeen, who works for a sweater, making three dollars a week. It is all the money that comes in, for the father has been sick and unable to work eight months, and the mother has her hands full: the youngest is a baby in arms. Three of the children go to a charity school, where they are fed, a great help, now the holidays have come to make work slack for sister. The rent is six dollars—two weeks' pay out of the four. The mention of a possible chance of light work for the man brings the daughter with her sewing from the adjoining room, eager to hear. That would be Christmas indeed! "Pietro!" She runs to the neighbors to communicate the joyful tidings. Pietro comes, with his new-born baby, which he is tending while his wife lies ill, to look at the maestro, so powerful and good. He also has been out of work for months, with a family of mouths to fill, and nothing coming in. His children are all small yet, but they speak English.

"What," I say, holding a silver dime up before the oldest, a smart little chap of seven—"what would you do if I gave you this?"

"Get change," he replies promptly. When he is told that it is his own, to buy toys, his eyes open wide with wondering incredulity. By degrees he understands. The father does not. He looks questioningly from one to the other. When told, his respect increases visibly for "the rich gentleman."

They were villagers of the same community in southern Italy, these people and others in the tenements thereabouts, and they moved their patron saint with them. They cluster about his worship here, but the worship is more than an empty form. He typifies to them the old neighborliness of home, the spirit of mutual help, of charity, and of the common cause against the common enemy. The community life survives through their saint in the far city to an unsuspected extent. The sick are cared for; the dreaded hospital is fenced out. There are no Italian evictions. The saint has paid the rent of this attic through two hard months; and here at his shrine the Calabrian village gathers, in the persons of these three, to do him honor on Christmas eve.

Where the old Africa has been made over into a modern Italy, since King Humbert's cohorts struck the up-town trail, three hundred of the little foreigners are having an uproarious time over their Christmas tree in the Children's Aid Society's school. And well they may, for the like has not been en in Sullivan street in this generation. Christmas trees are rather rarer over here than on the East Side, where the German leavens the lump with his loyalty to home traditions. This is loaded with silver and gold and toys without end, until there is little left of the original green. Santa Claus's sleigh must have been upset in a snow-drift over here, and righted by throwing the cargo overboard, for there is at least a wagon-load of things that can find no room on the tree. The appearance of "teacher" with a double armful of curly-headed dolls in red, yellow, and green Mother-Hubbards, doubtful how to dispose of them, provokes a shout of approval, which is presently quieted by the principal's bell. School is "in" for the preliminary exercises. Afterward there are to be the tree and ice-cream for the good children. In their anxiety to prove their title clear, they sit so straight, with arms folded, that the whole row bends over backward. The lesson is brief, the answers to the point.

"What do we receive at Christmas?" the teacher wants to know. The whole school responds with a shout, "Dolls and toys!" To the question, "Why do we receive them at Christmas?" the answer is not so prompt. But one youngster from Thompson street holds up his hand. He knows. "Because we always get 'em," he says; and the class is convinced: it is a fact. A baby wails because it cannot get the whole tree at once. The "little mother"—herself a child of less than a dozen winters—who has it in charge coos over it, and soothes its grief with the aid of a surreptitious sponge-cake evolved from the depths of teacher's pocket. Babies are encouraged in these schools, though not originally included in their plan, as often the one condition upon which the older children can be reached. Some one has to mind the baby, with all hands out at work.

The school sings "Santa Lucia" and "Children of the Heavenly King," and baby is lulled to sleep.

"Who is this King?" asks the teacher suddenly, at the end of a verse. Momentary stupefaction. The little minds are on ice-cream just then; the lad nearest the door has telegraphed that it is being carried up in pails. A little fellow on the back seat saves the day. Up goes his brown fist.

"Well, Vito, who is he?"

"McKinley!" shouts the lad, who remembers the election just past; and the school adjourns for ice-cream.

It is a sight to see them eat it. In a score of such schools, from the Hook to Harlem, the sight is enjoyed in Christmas week by the men and women who, out of their own pockets, reimburse Santa Claus for his outlay, and count it a joy—as well they may: for their beneficence sometimes makes the one bright spot in lives that have suffered of all wrongs the most cruel—that of being despoiled of their childhood. Sometimes they are little Bohemians; sometimes the children of refugee Jews; and again, Italians, or the descendants of the Irish stock of Hell's Kitchen and Poverty Row; always the poorest, the shabbiest, the hungriest—the children Santa Claus loves best to find, if any one will show him the way. Having so much on hand, he has no time, you see, to look them up himself. That must be done for him; and it is done. To the teacher in this Sullivan-street school came one little girl, this last Christmas, with anxious inquiry if it was true that he came around with toys.

"I hanged my stocking last time, she said, a-and he didn't come at all." In the front house, indeed, he left a drum and a doll, but no message from him reached the rear house in the alley. "Maybe he couldn't find it," she said soberly. Did the teacher think he would come if she wrote to him? She had learned to write.

Together they composed a note to Santa Claus, speaking for a doll and a bell—the bell to play "go to school" with when she was kept home minding the baby. Lest he should by any chance miss the alley in spite of directions, little Rosa was invited to hang her stocking, and her sister's, with the janitor's children's in the school. And lo! on Christmas morning there was a gorgeous doll, and a bell that was a whole curriculum in itself, as good as a year's schooling any day! Faith in Santa Claus is established in that Thompson-street alley for this generation at least; and Santa Claus, got by hook or by crook into an Eighth-Ward alley, is as good as the whole Supreme Court bench, with the Court of

Appeals thrown in, for backing the Board of Health against the slum.

But the ice-cream! They eat it off the seats, half of them kneeling or squatting on the floor; they blow on it, and put it in their pockets to carry home to baby. Two little shavers discovered to be feeding each other, each watching the smack develop on the other's lips as the acme of his own bliss, are "cousins"; that is why. Of cake there is a double supply. It is a dozen years since "Fighting Mary," the wildest child in the Seventh-Avenue school, taught them a lesson there which they have never forgotten. She was perfectly untamable, fighting everybody in school, the despair of her teacher, till on Thanksgiving, reluctantly included in the general amnesty and mince-pie, she was caught cramming the pie into her pocket, after eying it with a look of pure ecstasy, but refusing to touch it. "For mother" was her explanation, delivered with a defiant look before which the class quailed. It is recorded, but not in the minutes, that the board of managers wept over Fighting Mary, who, all unconscious of having caused such an astonishing "break," was at that moment engaged in maintaining her prestige and reputation by fighting the gang in the next block. The minutes contain merely a formal resolution to the effect that occasions of mince-pie shall carry double rations thenceforth. And the rule has been kept—not only in Seventh-Avenue, but in every industrial school—since. Fighting Mary won the biggest fight of her troubled life that day, without striking a blow.

It was in the Seventh-Avenue school last Christmas that I offered the truant class a four-bladed penknife as a prize for whittling out the truest Maltese cross. It was a class of black sheep, and it was the blackest sheep of the flock that won the prize. "That awful Savarese," said Miss Haight, in despair. I thought of Fighting Mary, and bade her take heart. I regret to say that within a week the hapless Savarese was black-listed for banking up the school door with snow, so that not even the janitor could get out and at him.

Within hail of the Sullivan-street school camps a scattered little band, the Christmas customs of which I had been trying for years to surprise. They are Indians, a handful of Mohawks and Iroquois, whom some ill wind has blown down from their Canadian reservation, and left in these West-Side tenements to eke out such a living as they can weaving mats and baskets, and threading glass pearls on slippers and pincushions, until, one after another, they have died off and gone to happier hunting-grounds than Thompson street. There were as many families as one could count on the fingers of both hands when I first came upon them, at the death of old Tamenund, the basket-maker. Last Christmas there were seven. I had about made up my mind that the only real Americans in New York did not keep the holiday at all, when, one Christmas eve, they showed me how. Just as dark was setting in, old Mrs. Benoit came from her Hudson-street attic—where she was known among the neighbors, as old and poor as she, as Mrs. Ben Wah, and believed to be the relict of a warrior of the name of Benjamin Wah—to the office of the Charity Organization Society, with a bundle for a friend who had helped her over a rough spot—the rent, I suppose. The bundle was done up elaborately in blue cheese-cloth, and contained a lot of little garments which she had made out of the remnants of blankets and cloth of her own from a younger and better day. "For those," she said, in her French patois, "who are poorer than myself"; and hobbled away. I found out, a few days later, when I took her picture weaving mats in her attic room, that she had scarcely food in the house that Christmas day, and not the car-fare to take her to church! Walking was bad, and her old limbs were stiff.

She sat by the window through the winter evening, and watched the sun go down behind the western hills, comforted by her pipe. Mrs. Ben Wah, to give her her local name, is not really an Indian; but her husband was one, and she lived all her life with the tribe till she came here. She is a philosopher in her own quaint way. "It is no disgrace to be poor," said she to me, regarding her empty tobacco-pouch; "but it is sometimes a great inconvenience." Not even the recollection of the vote of censure that was passed upon me once by the ladies of the Charitable Ten for surreptitiously supplying an aged couple, the special object of their charity, with army plug, could have deterred me from taking the hint.

Very likely, my old friend Miss Sherman, in her Broome-street cellar,—it is always the attic or the cellar,—would object to Mrs. Ben Wah's claim to being the only real American in my note-book. She is from down East, and says "stun" for stone. In her youth she was lady's-maid to a general's wife, the recollection of which military career equally condones the cellar and prevents her holding any sort of communication with her common neighbors, who add to the offense of being foreigners the unpardonable one of being mostly men. Eight cats bear her steady company, and keep alive her starved affections. I found them on last Christmas eve behind barricaded doors; for the cold that had locked the water-pipes had brought the neighbors down to the cellar, where Miss Sherman's cunning had kept them from freezing. Their tin pans and buckets were even then banging against her door. "They're a miserable lot," said the old maid, fondling her cats defiantly; "but let 'em. It's Christmas. Ah!" she added, as one of the eight stood up in her lap and rubbed its cheek against hers, "they're innocent. It isn't poor little animals that does the harms. It's men and women that does it to each other." I don't know whether it was just philosophy, like

Mrs. Ben Wah's, or a glimpse of her story. If she had one, she kept it for her cats.

In a hundred places all over the city, when Christmas comes, as many open-air fairs spring suddenly into life. A kind of Gentile Feast of the Tabernacles possesses the tenement districts especially. Green-embowered booths stand in rows at the curb, and the voice of the tin trumpet is heard in the land. The common source of all the show is down by the North River, in the district known as "the Farm." Down there Santa Claus establishes headquarters early in December and until past New Year. The broad quay looks then more like a clearing in a pine-forest than a busy section of the metropolis. The steamers discharge their loads of fir-trees at the piers until they stand stacked mountain high, with foot-hills of holly and ground-ivy trailing off toward the land side. An army-train of wagons is engaged in carting them away from early morning till late at night; but the green forest grows, in spite of it all, until in places it shuts the shipping out of sight altogether. The air is redolent with the smell of balsam and pine. After nightfall, when the lights are burning in the busy market, and the homeward-bound crowds with baskets and heavy burdens of Christmas greens jostle each other with good-natured banter,—nobody is ever cross down here in the holiday season,—it is good to take a stroll through the Farm, if one has a spot in his heart faithful yet to the hills and the woods in spite of the latter-day city. But it is when the moonlight is upon the water and upon the dark phantom forest, when the heavy breathing of some passing steamer is the only sound that breaks the stillness of the night, and the watchman smokes his lonely pipe on the bulwark, that the Farm has a mood and an atmosphere all its own, full of poetry, which some day a painter's brush will catch and hold.

Into the ugliest tenement street Christmas brings something of picturesqueness as of cheer. Its message was ever to the poor and the heavy-laden, and by them it is understood with an instinctive yearning to do it honor. In the stiff dignity of the brownstone streets uptown there may be scarce a hint of it. In the homes of the poor it blossoms on stoop and fire-escape, looks out of the front window, and makes the unsightly barber-pole to sprout overnight like an Aaron's rod. Poor indeed is the home that has not its sign of peace over the hearth, be it but a single sprig of green. A little color creeps with it even into rabbinical Hester street, and shows in the shop-windows and in the children's faces. The very feather-dusters in the peddler's stock take on brighter hues for the occasion, and the big knives in the cutler's shop gleam with a lively anticipation of the impending goose "with fixin's"—a concession, perhaps, to the commercial rather than the religious holiday. Business comes then, if ever. A crowd of ragamuffins camp out at a window where Santa Claus and his wife stand in state, embodiment of the domestic ideal that has not yet gone out of fashion in these tenements, gazing hungrily at the announcement that "A silver present will be given to every purchaser by a real Santa Claus.—M. Levitsky." Across the way, in a hole in the wall, two cobblers are pegging away under an oozy lamp that makes a yellow splurge on the inky blackness about them, revealing to the passer-by their bearded faces, but nothing of the environment save a single sprig of holly suspended from the lamp. From what forgotten brake it came with a message of cheer, a thought of wife and children across the sea waiting their summons, God knows. The shop is their house and home. It was once the hall of the tenement; but to save space, enough has been walled in to make room for their bench and bed. The tenants go through the next house.

No matter if they are cramped; by and by they will have room. By and by comes the spring, and with it the steamer. Does not the green branch speak of spring and of hope? The policeman on the beat hears their hammers beat a joyous tattoo past midnight, far into Christmas morning. Who shall say its message has not reached even them in their slum?

Where the noisy trains speed over the iron highway past the second-story windows of Allen Street, a cellar-door yawns darkly in the shadow of one of the pillars that half block the narrow sidewalk. A dull gleam behind the cobweb-shrouded window-pane supplements the sign over the door, in Yiddish and English: "Old Brasses." Four crooked and moldy steps lead to utter darkness, with no friendly voice to guide the hapless customer. Fumbling along the dark wall, he is left to find the door of the shop as best he can. Not a likely place to encounter the fastidious from the Avenue! Yet ladies in furs and silk find this door and the grim old smith within it. Now and then an artist stumbles upon them, and exults exceedingly in his find. Two holiday shoppers are even now haggling with the coppersmith over the price of a pair of curiously wrought brass candlesticks. The old man has turned from the forge, at which he was working, unmindful of his callers roving among the dusty shelves. Standing there, erect and sturdy, in his shiny leather apron, hammer in hand, with the firelight upon his venerable head, strong arms bared to the elbow, and the square paper cap pushed back from a thoughtful, knotty brow, he stirs strange fancies. One half expects to see him fashioning a gorget or a sword on his anvil. But his is a more peaceful craft. Nothing more warlike is in sight than a row of brass shields, destined for ornament, not for battle. Dark shadows chase each other by the flickering light among copper kettles of ruddy glow, old-fashioned samovars, and massive andirons of tarnished brass. The bargaining goes on. Overhead the nineteenth century speeds by with rattle and roar; in here linger the shadows of the centuries long dead. The boy at the anvil listens openmouthed, clutching the bellows-rope.

In Liberty Hall a Jewish wedding is in progress. Liberty! Strange how the word echoes through these sweaters' tenements, where starvation is at home half the time. It is an all-consuming passion with these people, whose spirit a thousand years of bondage have not availed to daunt. It breaks out in strikes, when to strike is to hunger and die. Not until I stood by a striking cloak-maker whose last cent was gone, with not a crust in the house to feed seven hungry mouths, yet who had voted vehemently in the meeting that day to keep up the strike to the bitter end,—bitter indeed, nor far distant,— and heard him at sunset recite the prayer of his fathers: "Blessed art thou, 0 Lord our God, King of the world, that thou hast redeemed us as thou didst redeem our fathers, hast delivered us from bondage to liberty, and from servile dependence to redemption!"—not until then did I know what of sacrifice the word might mean, and how utterly we of another day had forgotten. But for once shop and tenement are left behind. Whatever other days may have in store; this is their day of play. The ceremony is over, and they sit at the long tables by squads and tribes. Those who belong together sit together. There is no attempt at pairing off for conversation or mutual entertainment at speechmaking or toasting. The business in hand is to eat, and it is attended to. The bridegroom, at the head of the table, with his shiny silk hat on, sets the example; and the guests emulate it with zeal, the men smoking big, strong cigars between mouthfuls. "Gosh! ain't it fine?" is the grateful comment of one curly-headed youngster, bravely attacking his third plate of chicken-stew. "Fine as silk," nods his neighbor in knickerbockers. Christmas, for once, means something to them that they can understand. The crowd of hurrying waiters make room for one bearing aloft a small turkey adorned with much tinsel and many paper flowers. It is for the bride, the one thing not to be touched until the next day—one day off from the drudgery of housekeeping; she, too, can keep Christmas.

A group of bearded, dark-browed men sit apart, the rabbi among them. They are the orthodox, who cannot break bread with the rest, for fear, though the food be kosher, the plates have been defiled. They brought their own to the feast, and sit at their own table, stern and justified. Did they but know what depravity is harbored in the impish mind of the girl yonder, who plans to hang her stocking overnight by the window! There is no fireplace in the tenement. Queer things happen over here, in the strife between the old and the new. The girls of the College Settlement, last summer, felt compelled to explain that the holiday in the country which they offered some of these children was to be spent in an Episcopal clergyman's house, where they had prayers every morning. "Oh," was the indulgent answer, "they know it isn't true, so it won't hurt them."

The bell of a neighboring church-tower strikes the vesper hour. A man in working-clothes uncovers his head reverently, and passes on. Through the vista of green bowers formed of the grocer's stock of Christmas trees a passing glimpse of flaring torches in the distant square is caught. They touch with flame the gilt cross towering high above the "White Garden," as the German residents call Tompkins Square. On the sidewalk the holy-eve fair is in its busiest hour. In the pine-board booths stand rows of staring toy dogs alternately with plaster saints. Red apples and candy are hawked from carts. Peddlers offer colored candles with shrill outcry.

A huckster feeding his horse by the curb scatters, unseen, a share for the sparrows. The cross flashes white against the dark sky.

In one of the side-streets near the East River has stood for thirty years a little mission church, called Hope Chapel by its founders, in the brave spirit in which they built it. It has had plenty of use for the spirit since. Of the kind of problems that beset its pastor I caught a glimpse the other day, when, as I entered his room, a rough-looking man went out.

"One of my cares," said Mr. Devins, looking after him with contracted brow. "He has spent two Christmas days of twenty-three out of jail. He is a burglar, or was. His daughter has brought him round. She is a seamstress. For three months, now, she has been keeping him and the home, working nights. If I could only get him a job! He won't stay honest long without it; but who wants a burglar for a watchman? And how can I recommend him?"

A few doors from the chapel an alley runs into the block. We halted at the mouth of it.

"Come in," said Mr. Devins, "and wish Blind Jennie a merry Christmas." We went in, in single file; there was not room for two. As we climbed the creaking stairs of the rear tenement, a chorus of children's shrill voices burst into song somewhere above.

"This is her class," said the pastor of Hope Chapel, as he stopped on the landing. "They are all kinds. We never could hope to reach them; Jennie can. They fetch her the papers given out in the Sunday-school, and read to her what is printed under the pictures; and she tells them the story of it. There is nothing Jennie doesn't know about the Bible."

The door opened upon a low-ceiled room, where the evening shades lay deep. The red glow from the kitchen stove discovered a jam of children, young girls mostly, perched on the table, the chairs, in each other's laps, or squatting on the floor; in the midst of them, a little old woman with heavily veiled face, and wan, wrinkled hands folded in her lap. The singing ceased as we stepped across the threshold.

"Be welcome," piped a harsh voice with a singular note of cheerfulness in it. "Whose step is that with you, pastor? I don't know it. He is welcome in Jennie's house, whoever he be. Girls, make him to home." The girls moved up to make room.

"Jennie has not seen since she was a child," said the clergyman, gently; "but she knows a friend without it. Some day she shall see the great Friend in his glory, and then she shall be Blind Jennie no more."

The little woman raised the veil from a face shockingly disfigured, and touched the eyeless sockets. "Some day," she repeated, "Jennie shall see. Not long now—not long!" Her pastor patted her hand. The silence of the dark room was broken by Blind Jennie's voice, rising cracked and quavering: "Alas! and did my Saviour bleed?" The shrill chorus burst in:

It was there by faith I received my sight,
And now I am happy all the day.

The light that falls from the windows of the Neighborhood Guild, in Delancey Street, makes a white path across the asphalt pavement. Within there is mirth and laughter. The Tenth Ward Social Reform Club is having its Christmas festival. Its members, poor mothers, scrubwomen,—the president is the janitress of a tenement near by,—have brought their little ones, a few their husbands, to share in the fun. One little girl has to be dragged up to the grab-bag. She cries at the sight of Santa Claus. The baby has drawn a woolly horse. He kisses the toy with a look of ecstatic bliss, and toddles away. At the far end of the hall a game of blindman's-buff is starting up. The aged grand-mother, who has watched it with growing excitement, bids one of the settlement workers hold her grandchild, that she may join in; and she does join in, with all the pent-up hunger of fifty joyless years. The worker, looking on, smiles; one has been reached. Thus is the battle against the slum waged and won with the child's play.

Tramp! tramp! comes to-morrow upon the stage. Two hundred and fifty pairs of little feet, keeping step, are marching to dinner in the Newsboys' Lodging-house. Five hundred pairs more are restlessly awaiting their turn upstairs. In prison, hospital, and almshouse to-night the city is host, and gives of her plenty. Here an unknown friend has spread a generous repast for the waifs who all the rest of the days shift for themselves as best they can. Turkey, coffee, and pie, with "vegetables" to fill in. As the file of eagle-eyed youngsters passes down the long tables, there are swift movements of grimy hands, and shirt-waists bulge, ragged coats sag at the pockets. Hardly is the file seated when the plaint rises: "I ain't got no pie! It got swiped on me." Seven despoiled ones hold up their hands.

The superintendent laughs—it is Christmas eve. He taps one tentatively on the bulging shirt. "What have you here, my lad?"

"Me pie," responds he, with an innocent look; "I wuz scart it would get stole."

A little fellow who has been eying one of the visitors attentively takes his knife out of his mouth, and points it at him with conviction.

"I know you," he pipes. "You're a p'lice commissioner. I seen yer picter in the papers. You're Teddy Roosevelt!"

The clatter of knives and forks ceases suddenly. Seven pies creep stealthily over the edge of the table, and are replaced on as many plates. The visitors laugh. It was a case of mistaken identity.

Farthest down-town, where the island narrows toward the Battery, and warehouses crowd the few remaining tenements, the somber-hued colony of Syrians is astir with preparation for the holiday. How comes it that in the only settlement of the real Christmas people in New York the corner saloon appropriates to itself all the outward signs of it? Even the floral cross that is nailed over the door of the Orthodox Church is long withered and dead: it has been there since Easter, and it is yet twelve days to Christmas by the belated reckoning of the Greek Church. But if the houses show no sign of the holiday, within there is nothing lacking. The whole colony is gone a-visiting. There are enough of the unorthodox to set the fashion, and the rest follow the custom of the country. The men go from house to house, laugh, shake hands, and kiss each other on both cheeks, with the salutation, "Every year and you are safe," as the Syrian guide renders it into English; and a nonprofessional interpreter amends it: "May you grow happier year by year." Arrack made from grapes and flavored with aniseed, and candy baked in little white balls like marbles, are served with the indispensable cigarette; for long callers, the pipe.

In a top-floor room of one of the darkest of the dilapidated tenements, the dusty window-panes of which the last glow in the winter sky is tingeing faintly with red, a dance is in progress. The guests, most of them fresh from the hillsides of Mount Lebanon, squat about the room. A reed-pipe and a tambourine furnish the music. One has the center of the floor. With a beer-jug filled to the brim on his head, he skips and sways, bending, twisting, kneeling, gesturing, and keeping time, while the men clap their hands. He lies down and turns over, but not a drop is spilled. Another succeeds him, stepping proudly, gracefully, furling and unfurling a handkerchief like a banner. As he sits down, and the beer goes around, one in the corner, who looks like a shepherd fresh from his pasture, strikes up a song—a far-off, lonesome, plaintive lay. "'Far as the hills,'" says the guide; "a song of the old days and the old people, now seldom heard." All together croon the refrain. The host delivers himself of an epic about his love across the seas, with the most agonizing expression, and in a shockingly bad voice. He is the worst singer I ever heard; but his companions greet his effort with approving shouts of "Yi! yi!" They look so fierce, and yet are so childishly happy, that at the thought of their exile and of the dark tenement the question arises, "Why all this joy?" The guide answers it with a look of surprise. "They sing," he says, "because they are glad they are free. Did you not know?"

The bells in old Trinity chime the midnight hour. From dark hallways men and women pour forth and hasten to the Maronite Church. In the loft of the dingy old ware-house wax candles burn before an altar of brass. The priest, in a white robe with a huge gold cross worked on the back, chants the ritual. The people respond. The women kneel in the aisles, shrouding their heads in their shawls; the surpliced acolyte swings his censer; the heavy perfume of burning incense fills the hall.

The band at the anarchists' ball is tuning up for the last dance. Young and old float to the happy strains, forgetting injustice, oppression, hatred. Children slide upon the waxed floor, weaving fearlessly in and out between the couples—between fierce, bearded men and short-haired women with crimson-bordered kerchiefs. A Punch-and-Judy show in the corner evokes shouts of laughter.

Outside the snow is falling. It sifts silently into each nook and corner, softens all the hard and ugly lines, and throws the spotless mantle of charity over the blemishes, the shortcomings. Christmas morning will dawn pure and white.

THE RAPTURE OF HETTY

BY MARY HALLOCK FOOTE (1847-1938)

During the second half of the nineteenth century, western expansion opened the frontier to people in search of jobs, money, and property. The celebration of Christmas on the frontier was very different from the celebration in the cities. This story's author, Mary Hallock Foote, lived for a few years in Idaho with her engineer husband and wrote about her experiences there. Best known as a scenic writer and illustrator of the west, she set this story near the Payette River.

The dance was set for Christmas night at Walling's, a horse-ranch where there were women, situated in a high, watered valley, shut in by foothills, sixteen miles from the nearest town. The cabin with its roof of "shakes," the sheds and corrals, can be seen from any divide between Packer's ferry and the Payette.

The "boys" had been generally invited, with one exception to the usual company. The youngest of the sons of Basset, a pastoral and nomadic house, was socially under a cloud, on the charge of having been "too handy with the frying-pan brand."

The charge could not be substantiated, but the boy's name had been roughly handled in those wide, loosely defined circles of the range, where the force of private judgment makes up for the weakness of the law in dealing with crimes that are difficult of detection and uncertain of punishment. He that has obliterated his neighbor's brand, or misapplied his own, is held as in the age of tribal government and ownership was held the remover of his neighbor's landmarks. A word goes forth against him potent as the Levitical curse, and all the people say amen.

As society's first public and pointed rejection of him, the slight had rankled with the son of Basset; and grievously it wore on him that Hetty Rhodes was going with the man who had been his earliest and most persistent accuser—Hetty, prettiest of all the bunch-grass belles, who never reproached nor quarreled, but judged people with her smile and let them go. He had not complained, though he had her promise,—one of her promises,— nor asked a hearing in his own defense. The sons of Basset were many and poor; their stock had dwindled upon the range; her men-folk condemned him, and Hetty believed, or seemed to believe, as the others.

Had she forgotten the night when two men's horses stood at her father's fence—the Basset boy's and his that was afterward his accuser, and the other's horse was unhitched when the evening was but half spent, and furiously ridden away, while the Basset boy's stood at the rails till close upon midnight? Had the coincidence escaped her that from this night, of one man's rage and another's bliss, the ugly charge had dated? Of these things a girl may not testify.

They met in town on the Saturday before the dance, Hetty buying her dancing-shoes at the back of the store, where the shoe-cases framed in a snug little alcove for the exhibition of a "fit," the boy, in his belied spurs and "chaps" of goat-hide, lounging disconsolate and sulky against one of the front counters. She wore a striped Ulster—an enchanted garment his arm had pressed—and a pink crocheted Tam-o'-Shanter cocked bewitchingly over her dark eyes. Her hair was ruffled, her cheeks were red with the wind she had faced two hours on the spring-seat of her father's "dead ax" wagon. Critical feminine eyes might have found her a trifle blowzy; the sick-hearted Basset boy looked once—he dared not look again.

Hetty coquetted with her partner in the shoe-bargain, a curly-headed young Hebrew, who flattered her familiarly and talked as if he had known her from a child, but always with an eye to business. She stood, holding back her skirts and rocking her instep from right to left while she considered the effect of the new style—patent-leather foxings and tan-cloth tops, and heels that came under the middle of her foot, and narrow toes with tips of stamped leather; but what a price! More than a third of her chicken-money gone for that one fancy's satisfaction. But who can know the joy of a really distinguished choice in shoe-leather as one that in her childhood has trotted barefoot through the sage-brush and associated shoes only with cold weather or going to town? The Basset boy tried to fix his strained attention upon anything rather than upon that tone of high jocosity between Hetty and the shiny-haired clerk. He tried to summon his own self-respect and leave the place.

What was the tax, he inquired, on those neck-handkerchiefs, and he pointed with the loaded butt of his braided leather "quirt" to a row of dainty silk mufflers signaling custom from a cord stretched above the gentlemen's furnishing-counter.

The clerk explained that the goods in question were first class, all silk, brocaded, and of an extra size.

Plainly he expected that a casual mention of the price would cool the inexperienced customer's curiosity, especially as the colors displayed in the handkerchiefs were not those commonly affected by the cowboy cult. The Basset boy threw down his last half-eagle and carelessly called for the one with a blue border. The delicate "baby blue" attracted him by its perishability, its suggestion of impossible refinements beyond the soilure and dust of his grimy circumstances. Yet he pocketed his purchase as though it were any common thing, not to show his pride in it before the patronizing salesman.

He waited foolishly for Hetty, not knowing if she would even speak to him. When she came at last loitering down the shop, with her eyes on the gay Christmas counters, her arms filled with bundles, he silently fell in behind her and followed her to her father's wagon, where he helped her unload her purchases.

"Been buying out the store?" he opened the conversation.

"Buying more than father'll want to pay for," she drawled, glancing at him sweetly. Those entoiling looks of Hetty's dark-lashed eyes had grown to a habit with her; even now the little Jewish salesman was smiling over his brief portion in them. Her own coolness made her careless, as children are, in playing with fire.

"Here's some Christmas the old man won't have to pay for." A soft paper parcel was crushed into her hand.

"Who is going to pay for it I'd like to know? If it's some of your doings, Jim Basset, I can't take it—so there!"

She thrust the package back upon him. He tore off the wrapper and let the wind carry his rejected token into the trampled mud and slush of the street.

Hefty screamed, and pounced to the rescue. "What a shame! It's a beauty of a handkerchief: It must have cost a lot of money. I sha'n't let you use it so."

She shook it, and wiped away the spots from its delicate sheen, and folded it into its folds again.

"*I* don't want the thing." He spurned it fiercely.

"Then give it to some one else." She endeavored coquettishly to force it into his hands or into the pockets of his coat. He could not withstand her thrilling little liberties in the face of all the street.

"I'll wear it Monday night," said he. "Maybe you think I won't be there?" he added hoarsely, for he had noted her look of surprise mingled with an infuriating touch of pity. "You kin bank on it I'll be there."

Hetty toyed with the thought that after all it might be better that she should not go to the dance. There might be trouble, for certainly Jim Basset had looked as if he meant it when he had said he would be there; and Hetty knew the temper of the company, the male portion of it, too well to doubt what their attitude would be toward an inhibited guest who disputed the popular verdict and claimed social privileges which, it had been agreed, he had forfeited. But it was never really in her mind to deny herself—at least the excitement. She and her escort were among the first couples to cross the snowy pastures stretching between her father's claim and the lights of the lonely horse-ranch.

It was a cloudy night, the air soft, chill, and spring like. Snow had fallen early and frozen upon the ground; the stockmen welcomed the "Chinook wind" as the promise of a break in the hard weather. Shadows came out and played on the pale slopes as the riders rose and dropped past one long swell and another of dim country, falling away like a ghostly land seeking a ghostly sea. And often Hetty looked back, fearing yet half hoping that the interdicted one might be on his way, among the dusky, straggling shapes behind.

The company was not large, nor up to nine o'clock particularly merry. The women were engaged in cooking supper, or up in the roof-room brushing out their crimps by the light of an unshaded kerosene-lamp placed on the pine washstand which did duty as a dressing-table. The men's voices came jarringly through the loose boards of the floor from below.

About that hour came the unbidden guest, and like the others he had brought his "gun." He was stopped at the door and told that he could not come in among the girls to make trouble. He denied that he had come with any such intention. There were persons present—he mentioned no names—who were no more eligible, socially speaking, than himself, and he ranked himself low in saying so; where such as these could be admitted, he proposed to show that he could. He offered, in evidence of his good faith and peaceable intentions, to give up his gun; but on condition that he be allowed one dance with the partner of his choosing, regardless of her previous engagements.

This unprecedented proposal was referred to the girls, who were charmed with its audacity. But none of them spoke up for the outcast till Hetty said she could not think what they were all afraid of. A dozen to one, and that one without his weapon! Then the other girls chimed in, and added their timid suffrages. There may have been some twinges of disappointment, there could hardly have been surprise, when the black sheep directed his choice without a look elsewhere to Hetty. She stood up, smiling but rather pale, and he rushed her to the head of the room, securing the most conspicuous place before his rival, who with his partner took the place of second couple opposite.

"Keep right on!" the fiddler chanted, in sonorous cadence to the music, as the last figure of the set ended with "Promenade all! He swung into the air of the first figure again, smiling, with his cheek upon his instrument and his eyes upon the floor. Hetty fancied that his smile meant more than merely the artist's pleasure in the joy he evokes.

"Keep your places!" he shouted again, after the "Promenade all!" a second time had raised the dust and made the lamps flare, and lighted with smiles of sympathy the rugged faces of the elders ranged against the walls. The side couples dropped off exhausted, but the tops held the floor, and neither of the men was smiling.

The whimsical fiddler invented new figures, which he "called off" in time to his music, to vary the monotony of a quadrille with two couples missing.

The opposite girl was laughing hysterically; she could no longer dance or stand. The rival gentleman looked about him for another partner. One girl jumped up, then, hesitating, sat down again. The music passed smoothly into a gallop, and Hetty and her bad boy kept the floor, regardless of shouts and protests warning the trespasser that his time was up and the game in other hands.

Thrice they circled the room. They looked neither to right nor left; their eyes were upon each other. The men were all on their feet, the music playing madly. A group of half-scared girls were huddled, giggling and whispering, near the door of the dimly lighted shed-room. Into the midst of them Hetty's partner plunged with his breathless, smiling dancer in his arms, passed into the dim outer place to the door where his horse stood saddled, and they were gone.

They crossed the little valley known as Seven Pines, they crashed through the thin ice of the creek, they rode double sixteen miles before midnight—Hetty wrapped in her lover's "slicker," with the blue-bordered handkerchief, her only wedding-gift, tied over her blowing hair.

THEIR CHRISTMAS MEETING

BY FLORENCE WATTERS SNEDEKER (d. 1893)

This story is about a Methodist preacher and his son. In the early nineteenth century, circuit preachers went from town to town visiting church members and emphasizing strict rules of conduct and discipline. By the second half of the nineteenth century, church activity was extended to include missionary work—to the poor people of the cities, to Native Americans, to former slaves, and to people in other countries. This story, written in 1892, shows how the expanded scope of the church's work affected two generations of the faithful.

I

The Reverend Ezra Leal came to the pulpit in the saddle-bag days of Methodism. Pure, fervent, he rode the wilderness; appeared in the clearing with a smile that was heaven's light to the godly, though to the ungodly it was heaven's light of scathing; and melted all men's hearts, while mightily he preached of sin, of righteousness, and of judgment to come.

In time he was sent to congregations the largest, even to the wrestle with Mammon in big cities. He was heard, too, in the councils of the church; was presiding elder; was even delegate to General Conference. And honor followed him still in his later days, when the people's ears dulled to his preaching, and he went, contented, to the smaller charges.

In his sixty-eighth year Denham-on-the-River received him and his family, his sister Hannah and Robert, his only child. It was then that Robert entered college.

"Don't look so down-hearted, father," the lad begged, on his knees before his trunk that last evening. He was a tall fellow, with broader shoulders than his father's, with fuller lips, too, and a wider brow. "It's only twelve weeks to Christmas. And you shall have a Christmas present of a record that will make you smile. See if you don't."

"No doubt, Rob. I look to be proud of your scholarship. That does not trouble me. It is the dangers, the temptations—"

"Father, I'll behave myself. Can't you trust me?"

"'That maketh flesh his arm; whose heart departeth from the Lord,'" quoted Aunt Hannah, where she sat sewing beside the lamp.

"I'm not a heathen!"

"That is it, Rob! That is the worst of it!" exclaimed the father. "It might be better if you were. You have heard the gospel message so often it has an uncertain sound. It does not convict. You trust in yourself. And you need to be broken by the Lord—at his altar. O Rob, there is where I wanted to see you before you went!"

"Gospel-hardened." Hannah Leal said it solemnly. Then she rolled her work up tight, tucked it into the trunk, and left the room. In her chamber tears fell upon the white pillow-shams she folded away.

When she was gone, her nephew looked up with a hot face, and cried almost fiercely:

"Would you have me at the altar just to please you—and Aunt Hannah? I'm no hypocrite. I can't whine to order. My soul's my own—"

"Robert!"

"Anyhow, it isn't any other man's—not even my own father's."

Speechless, the two gazed at each other; then arose, and the son, with a broken word, put his arms around his father. Together they went up-stairs; and as they separated they kissed, though it was not their custom.

Yet Robert Leal, for the first time, went to bed prayerless.

As for the tale of prayers, that was more than made up. Until dawn the Reverend Ezra Leal wrestled with the Lord, like Jacob at the brook Jabbok. But the father forgot how easily a mettlesome spirit may be pricked beyond its natural leap. In the morning young Leal went away sore-hearted under his condemnation. And during this journey, before ever he began his college life, there grew upon him an unfortunate new estimate of his life at home.

The Saturday before Christmas Robert was expected back from college. But his father brought from the evening train only the conviction, stated often for comfort of Hannah Leal, that "Robert is sure to come bright and early Monday; and there is not the slightest reason in the world to fret."

The Sabbath was a day of light. Light filled the sky, and glistened on the bare, brown trees, and on the snow-fields round about the little village, and on the frozen river as one saw it from the church-porch. Before the church-bells rang, sleighs began to wind down from the hills, and to draw up before the door with an eager jingle. The men hurried back from the horse-sheds.

While they stood about the porch, and blinked in the light, they talked of Robert's coming. So did the women, scorching their faces at the wood-stoves within the church. When the minister appeared, there was an expectant hubbub.

"Where's Rob, Dominie? Where's the boy?"

Disappointed, they scattered to their seats. The choir around the small melodeon arose, with dampened ardor, to the most intricate anthem in the book. And since enthusiasm was needed for the deft leaping in and out at strange places, and for the steady sticking of each one to his clue with yet a side thought for his neighbor, they came out straggling, and sat down flushed. Vexation had burned among them had not the minister quenched it, smiling down his approval, and saying,

"Let us all sing as heartily the one hundred and thirtieth hymn."

They were no over-devout saints, this branch of the church militant. Their supreme warfare was with the frosts, the droughts, the devouring insects that made their living hard. Their God was oftenest the fearsome mystery at the center of the havoc of things. When times were good, they gave him feeble thanks. When times were bad, they tried, in their grumbling, not to pass beyond the bounds of submission.

And yet this house, with its square white walls and its green blinds, was to them the gate of heaven. When they sat in the straight-backed pews of their fathers, and heard the sweep of the wind; and saw, through the windows, the branches sway above the graves; and caught, through their reverie, holy words, they were dimly stirred: faintly their horizon lifted. So, now, they swelled the hymn. Ancient voices quavered with a sense of ecstasy:

"And wo-on, and wo-o-onders of his love!"

In his high pulpit arose the minister. To-day his pale cheeks glowed, his blue eyes sparkled. "And—they—shall—call—his—name—Immanuel," he read, each word dropping slower. As his sermon advanced, and the spirit within him burned, he stood on tiptoe, his head thrown back, his eyes upon the ceiling. Then the bright eyes came down, peering over their gold-rimmed spectacles for an answering brightness in the faces below—

What was that?

A door noisily opening, an unsteady step, some one stumbling up the aisle, and staggering drunkenly into the minister's pew.

There was not a sound, not a motion. Here and there a face paled, a sob was stifled. All eyes went mutely from that abject figure to the face leaning from the pulpit in awful tension, its light dashed out.

At last there came a change. The minister drew his narrow shoulders back. He turned, stepped firmly down the pulpit-stairs, down the aisle, and laid his hand upon his son's shoulder.

"Come home!"

The youth lifted his heavy eyes. Without a word he rose. Arm-and-arm the two passed from the house. Outside, their steps upon the walk came back to the motionless people.

The congregation broke up very quietly. There was little comment now upon what, to-morrow, would be town-talk.

To Robert Leal the shame and sin of it were not for easy explanation or excuse. He was frightened from his self-confidence; and that Christmas-tide he made the abiding choice of his father's righteousness and of his father's God. But his choice was like a woman's, of the heart. Doctrine might or might not follow. Then, later, there came to his analytical mind a growing fear lest doctrinal details should make a second separation between himself and his father. After his college course, he entered upon his profession of the law, and was prospered in it, and honored. But still he remained without the pale of his father's church.

II

The shock that made the son unmade the father. When next the Reverend Ezra Leal stood in his high pulpit, he felt a change in himself—a break, as it were, between his spirit and its instrument of expression. Thereafter, each Sunday, he felt it more keenly. And when his time was up in Denham-on-the-River he bowed his meek head in a final benediction, went to Conference, and had his name written in the list of the superannuated.

Then he bought, high on the river-bank near Denham, a cottage with a large garden and many fruit-trees. He still preached at times, and especially at funerals. No Denham man, nor, indeed, any of the countryside, could quite think his dead laid away in fitting and sure triumph unless Dominie Leal stretched up his thin arms and talked of heaven. For then the crowding people almost saw the dead man rise from his lidded box to his place in glory, and stand there in the white ranks with a palm in his hand, a golden crown upon his head, and on his face the last, perfect smile.

But chiefly the old man went his loving rounds of the village houses, and worked in his garden, and read papers and books, light-hearted, not overburdened now with the conduct of the world. More and more his face, which withered, took on an almost mystic shining under his silver hair, and he grew to a oneness with the children he loved. And more and more—but most when he prepared the brown mold, and watched the seed in its springing—it seemed as though, for very joy, his spirit must burst its feeble bonds, and flutter forth upon its rapturous quest of God. And Denham people said, "The old Dominie would go straight up, if he didn't keep on fretting about his boy."

Most men would have felt only pride in a son such as Robert Leal. But this care for "temporalities"—literature, art, social and political reform—was to the Reverend Ezra Leal the following of an age that "thought more of the loaves and fishes than of the Lord." When Robert gave money for such things, his father calculated how much the sum would have done for the heathen. And when his boy married, though the old man's beautiful courtliness grew into pride and fondness while he welcomed his new daughter, pain sharper than he had felt since that sad Sunday lay for him in the fact that "poor Alice" was an Episcopalian.

Hannah Leal's disapproval of this marriage was none the lighter in that she could not have defined her own creed. Still, she came to admit that "Alice was a good woman." And when Robert received his children, their Aunt Hannah deliberately broke every rule rigorous in their father's day, and pampered them to the damage of both soul and body. Especially at Christmas time did their Aunt Hannah spend herself for them. From which fact arose the trouble in the heart of her brother, one November evening.

"For mercy's sake, Ezra," she suddenly exclaimed, "don't sit there peeking at me over that letter. It fairly sends cold chills down my back. If anything is wrong, I have got to know it, first or last."

"Nothing wrong, Hannah. But there is something—something new."

"What has Alice been doing now?"

"Nothing. It is something they are planning to do."

"Not Christmas?"

"Well, yes, it is Christmas, Hannah. Here is just what Alice writes. She says—she says—ah, here it is—she says here: 'And now I must tell you something very beautiful of your grandchildren.' I did hope they might have experienced religion," sighed the Reverend Ezra Leal. "'They came to me in a body, reckless Rob for spokesman, and they said this year they didn't want any Christmas presents, except for Dot and Baby. But they wanted to give a dinner at Christmas to the *newsboys!* Grandfather, it was purely their own thought! You should have seen Robert when I told him. Of course we must meet the sweet impulse. So this year you and Aunt Hannah will come to us. And very early, because Christmas would not be Christmas without Aunt Hannah's cakes and pies, that shame our cooks and bakers. Tell her she shall have the kitchen all to herself, for her mysteries, quite as at home. Robert says'—but that is all of that. Well, Hannah?"

Miss Leal was slow in collecting herself.

"Newsboys!" she said at last. "But it's only what might be expected, Ezra Leal. We didn't use to think of bringing the off-scouring of the earth into our houses, and setting them up with dinners and compliments. But nowadays, actually, the poorer, and the raggedier, and the dirtier a man is, the better for him, and the more people will fuss over him!"

"I think myself," her brother said sadly, "there is too much attention paid to the body, and too little to the soul."

"That is just what I said. What those boys want is a sense of sin. And once a sound thrashing was thought likelier for that than a dinner. It is all nonsense. Positively, it is a shame—and a disgrace. And Alice Leal needn't ask me to uphold her in it."

"What? Not go, Hannah? But what will Alice say? And Robert? And the children, Hannah?"

"It is their own doings. I am sure I have always stood ready to work and to do the best I could for those poor children; but missions I set my face against from the first. I said then, there are the churches. I won't mention unkindness," she continued more faintly, "though Alice knows—or she might if she thought—how I have been busy ever since September getting things ready, and stoves in every room, and the crib down for the baby, which hasn't been up since Dot, and all the new little sheets and pillow-cases—" Miss Leal closed her lips; nor, from that moment, would she speak or hear more of Christmas.

From day to day her brother hoped that her mood would change, and fidgeted in his packing, and still lingered at home after forwarding his trunk. So that it was not until the day before Christmas that, satchel in hand, he received his sister's parting charge.

"You will see I haven't forgotten the children. The wafers are in the biggest box. Rob says he has never had enough yet, poor child. The waffles are in the next, and the crullers in the smallest. I expect they will be dry as chips. The plum-cake for Robert, Alice will find I haven't stinted. The other things are all marked, so there will be no excuse for getting them mixed up, though I haven't an idea the baby's will fit. I meant to finish them after he came. But I am not likely to know now whether he is fat or thin, or blue eyes or black eyes—"

The door shut. The turning of the key was a melancholy sound to the Reverend Ezra Leal. He walked to the station, and climbed into the car, downcast and remorseful.

But the afternoon sun was bright upon the river, and the car was full of children fain to frolic, and granted more than their usual license. So that one little tot cried to him, 'Mewy Cwismas, Gwampa!' at which a laugh went round, and people beamed upon one another in exceeding good fellowship. And when, presently, he grew drowsy, each time he roused, the flash of the river came like "Merry Christmas!"

Alighting in New York, he was astonished at the holiday multitude. He felt enlarged at the sight, as though he were become a citizen of the world; even as though he were returned from stereotyped old age to big-hearted, big-thoughted youth. And he squared his shoulders, and stepped on lithely.

When he entered the Brooklyn ferry-boat, with the great hurrying throng, and managed to look out over his spectacles at the tangle of shipping, and the twinkling span of the great bridge, and the answering lights of the two cities, his heart leaped up, for he thought it was like the end of time, and "all nations bringing their glory and their honor." And he longed to lift up a Methodist shout of "Bless the Lord!" So that at sight of his face the woman next to him laughed aloud, and said: "Goin' to the childer? So am oy. Faix an' it's worth the hard work the rest of the year to see the day; isn't it, sor?"

The woman was so short and stout that she had trouble with her many bundles and big basket. He carried the basket off the boat, and delivered it to her at the horse-car with a stately bow. And now, as he drew near his son's house, his heart beat so excitedly that he stepped into an open church, and sat down to steady himself.

The church was a solemn pile, lifting high a cross. It was wreathed with greens, and with flowers among the carved work and the gold and the colors of flame. And in the far front, near the altar whereon candles burned like stars, beings like angels were echoing back and forth, "Alleluia! Alleluia!" as though it were "before the Throne." He had been wont to call it heathen mummery; but now he cried softly "Amen! Bless the Lord!" and went out so uplifted that, after all, he came unexpectedly to his son's house.

He saw the high front all ablaze. He discovered that the chief illumination, together with a humming confusion, came from the lower windows. He stooped and looked in. He beheld a long and loaded table; pressing turbulently around it, shabby boys; waiting upon them, his grandchildren; at the near end, Alice in a bright gown; at the far end, mustering the guests into something like order, his son Robert. And at that instant, in the dazzle, while his son smiled upon the circle, the momentary, dim, yet answering smile on each marred face smote upon the sight of the Reverend Ezra Leal as strange, as beyond human, as tarnished, but divine, as meaning, "Ye have done it unto ME!"

He stumbled to the door. He motioned the servant who admitted him to leave him unannounced. He sat down upon a hall chair, put his satchel upon the floor, took off his hat, and leaned his head against the wall. And sitting with closed eyes, he said to himself: "Flesh and blood have not revealed it to him. This is the way he has seen the Lord! He has been serving him this way for years and years. I've been unjust to my boy. I've been set to drive him my way into the kingdom. 'And many shall come from the east and west.... But the children of the kingdom'—"God forgive me! Bigotry is an awful thing!" Faint, almost, as though his poor body must crumble then and there, and deliver up his humbled yet satisfied soul, he whispered, "Lord, now lettest thou thy servant depart in peace!"

Meanwhile, beyond the door that stood ajar, Robert Leal was saying:

"Now, boys, what does Christmas mean to us tonight?"

"Grub!" "Boots and shoes!" "Larks!" were in the buzzing response. One thin voice raised itself and chirped, "We'd all ought to be good!"

He smiled down on the puny speaker. "I couldn't preach to you if I wanted to. I expected my father to be here to talk to you. He hasn't come—"

Sounds of "Bully for him!" "Solid old chap!" "He's all right!"

"So I'll just tell you what Christmas means to me."

His mind went back to that one dark Christmas. He looked into these pathetic faces, whose darkness was always with them; and suddenly it was to Robert Leal as though, for the first time, he was really looking into human sin and its divine despair. The horror of it was at his throat. He choked upon it. God! what words had he now, he, the easy theorizer upon life? While yet, burdened, tortured, in that moment he would have given all—even himself, like Christ—to save.

He looked across to the windows, and cried thinly, "Father!"

And he seemed to see his father's face, wasted, lifelong, in this same struggle. He understood it now. In this revelation moment he saw clearly. Another thing he saw: that fancies, speculations, had had their day for him; that for him, with his childhood's bent and faith, there could henceforth be no working theory of helping men like the old, thorough-going one of his father's.

Then he opened his lips. And to the dulling ears of that veteran in the hall the words he spoke came like old war-cries.

But they were meaningless to the boys. A minute had not elapsed when all the itching eyes and fingers were let loose. The confusion that before had only rippled low began to mount tumultuously. Fear came into the faces of Alice Leal and her children. A plate crashed. Two of the guests shot up to grapple each other—

The door swung in. The radiant old man on the threshold, roused from weakness of the flesh, and unmindful of all his late-born fear of bigotry, lifted up his voice and cried:

"That's it! That's it! Put that doctrine to them straight, Rob! Why, bless the Lord! My boy, that's better Methodism—straighter-laced—than ever your old father preached in his best days!"

THE CHRISTMAS SHADRACH

BY FRANK R. STOCKTON (1834-1902)

The characters in this story are well-to-do. They have country estates and domestic help, and they have precise rules of decorum. In the Gilded Age, this was not an unusual circumstance. Industrialization and commerce made many people millionaires. Frank R. Stockton was known for his ambiguous humor, and in this story he employs it to poke a little fun at a proper young gentleman.

Whenever I make a Christmas present I like it to mean something, not necessarily my sentiments toward the person to whom I give it, but sometimes an expression of what I should like that person to do or to be. In the early part of a certain winter not very long ago I found myself in a position of perplexity and anxious concern regarding a Christmas present which I wished to make.

The state of the case was this. There was a young lady, the daughter of a neighbor and old friend of my father, who had been gradually assuming relations toward me which were not only unsatisfactory to me, but were becoming more and more so. Her name was Mildred Bronce. She was between twenty and twenty-five years of age, and as fine a woman in every way as one would be likely to meet in a lifetime. She was handsome, of a tender and generous disposition, a fine intelligence, and a thoroughly well-stocked mind. We had known each other for a long time, and when fourteen or fifteen Mildred had been my favorite companion. She was a little younger than I, and I liked her better than any boy I knew. Our friendship had continued through the years, but of late there had been a change in it; Mildred had become very fond of me, and her fondness seemed to have in it certain elements which annoyed me.

As a girl to make love to no one could be better than Mildred Bronce; but I had never made love to her,—at least not earnestly,—and I did not wish that any permanent condition of loving should be established between us. Mildred did not seem to share this opinion, for every day it became plainer to me that she looked upon me as a lover, and that she was perfectly willing to return my affection.

But I had other ideas upon the subject. Into the rural town in which my family passed the greater part of the year there had recently come a young lady, Miss Janet Clinton, to whom my soul went out of my own option. In some respects, perhaps, she was not the equal of Mildred, but she was very pretty, she was small, she had a lovely mouth, was apparently of a clinging nature, and her dark eyes looked into mine with a tingling effect that no other eyes had ever produced. I was in love with her because I wished to be, and the consciousness of this fact caused .me a proud satisfaction. This affair was not the result of circumstances, but of my own free will.

I wished to retain Mildred's friendship, I wished to make her happy; and with this latter intent in view I wished very much that she should not disappoint herself in her anticipations of the future.

Each year it had been my habit to make Mildred a Christmas present, and I was now looking for something to give her which would please her and suit my purpose.

When a man wishes to select a present for a lady which, while it assures her of his kind feeling toward. her, will at the same time indicate that not only has he. no matrimonial inclinations in her direction, but that it would be entirely unwise for her to have any such inclinations in his direction; that no matter with what degree of fondness her heart is disposed to turn toward him, his heart does not turn toward her, and that, in spite of all sentiments induced by long association and the natural fitness of things, she need never expect to be to him anything more than a sister, he has, indeed, a difficult task before him. But such was the task which I set for myself.

Day after day I wandered through the shops. I looked at odd pieces of jewelry and bric-a-brac, and at many a quaint relic or bit of art work which seemed to have a meaning, but nothing had the meaning I wanted. As to books, I found none which satisfied me; not one which was adapted to produce the exact impression that I desired.

One afternoon I was in a little basement shop kept by a fellow in a long overcoat, who, so far as I was able to judge, bought curiosities but never sold any. For some minutes I had been looking at a beautifully decorated saucer of rare workmanship for which there was no cup to match, and for which the proprietor informed me no cup could now be found or manufactured. There were some points in the significance of an article of this sort, given as a present to a lady, which fitted to my purpose, but it would signify too much: I did not wish to suggest to Mildred that she need never expect to find a cup. It would be better, in fact, if I gave her anything of this kind, to send her a cup and saucer entirely unsuited to each other, and which could not, under any conditions, be used together.

I put down the saucer, and continued my search among the dusty shelves and cases.

"How would you like a paper-weight?" the shop-keeper asked. "Here is something a little odd," handing me a piece of dark-colored mineral nearly as big as my fist, flat on the under side and of a pleasing irregularity above. Around the bottom was a band of arabesque work in some dingy metal, probably German silver. I smiled as I took it.

"This is not good enough for a Christmas present," I said. "I want something odd, but it must have some value."

"Well," said the man, "that has no real value, but there is a peculiarity about it which interested me when I heard of it, and so I bought it. This mineral is a piece of what the iron-workers call shadrach. It is a portion of the iron or iron ore which passes through the smelting-furnaces without being affected by the great heat, and so they have given it the name of one of the Hebrew youths who was cast into the fiery furnace by Nebu-chadnezzar, and who came out unhurt. Some people think there is a sort of magical quality about this shad-rach, and that it can give out to human beings something of us power to keep their minds cool when they are in danger of being overheated. The old gentleman who had this made was subject to fits of anger, and he thought this piece of shadrach helped to keep him from giving way to them. Occasionally he used to leave it in the house of a hot-tempered neighbor, believing that the testy individual would be cooled down for a time, without knowing how the change had been brought about I bought a lot of things of the old gentleman's widow, and this among them. I thought I might try it some time, but I never have."

I held the shadrach in my hand, ideas concerning it rapidly flitting through my mind. Why would not this be a capital thing to give to Mildred? If it should, indeed, possess the quality ascribed to it; if it should be able to cool her liking for me, what better present could I give her? I did not hesitate long.

"I will buy this," I said; "but the ornamentation must be of a better sort. It is now too cheap- and tawdry-looking."

"I can attend to that for you," said the shopkeeper. "I can have it set in a band of gold or silver filigree-work like this, if you choose."

I agreed to this proposition, but ordered the silver, the cool tone of that metal being more appropriate to the characteristics of the gift than the warmer hues of gold.

When I gave my Christmas present to Mildred she was pleased with it; its oddity struck her fancy.

"I don't believe anybody ever had such a paper-weight as that," she said, as she thanked me. "What is it made of?"

I told her, and explained what shadrach was but I did not speak of its presumed influence over human beings, which, after all, might be nothing but the wildest fancy. I did not feel altogether at my ease, as I added that it was merely a trifle, a thing of no value except as a reminder of the season.

"The fact that it is a present from you gives it value," she said, as she smilingly raised her eyes to mine.

I left her house—we were all living in the city then— with a troubled conscience. What a deception I was practicing upon this noble girl, who, if she did not already love me, was plainly on the point of doing so. She had received my present as if it indicated a warmth of feeling on my part, when, in fact, it was the result of a desire for a cooler feeling on her part.

But I called my reason to my aid, and showed myself that what I had given Mildred—if it should prove to possess any virtue at all—was, indeed, a most valuable boon. It was something which would prevent the waste of her affections, the wreck of her hopes. No kindness could be truer, no regard for her happiness more sincere, than the motives which prompted me to give her the shadrach.

I did not soon again see Mildred, but now as often as possible I visited Janet. She always received me with a charming cordiality, and if this should develop into warmer sentiments I was not the man to wish to cool them. In many ways Janet seemed much better suited to me than Mildred. One of the greatest charms of this beautiful girl was a tender trustfulness, as if I were a being on whom she could lean and to whom she could look up. I liked this; it was very different from Mildred's manner: with the latter I had always been well satisfied if I felt myself standing on the same plane.

The weeks and months passed on, and again we were all in the country; and here I saw Mildred often. Our homes were not far apart, and our families were very intimate. With my opportunities for frequent observation I could not doubt that a change had come over her. She was always friendly when we met, and seemed as glad to see me as she was to see any other member of my family, but she was not the Mildred I used to know. It was plain that my existence did not make the same impression on her that it once made. She did not seem to consider it important whether I came or went; whether I was in the room or not; whether I joined a party or stayed away. All this had been very different. I knew well that Mildred had been used to consider my presence as a matter of much importance, and I now felt sure that my Christmas shadrach was doing its work. Mildred was cooling toward me. Her affection, or, to put it more modestly, her tendency to affection, was gently congealing into friendship. This was highly gratifying to my moral nature, for every day I was doing my best to warm the soul of Janet. Whether or not I succeeded in this I could not be sure. Janet was as tender and trustful and charming as ever, but no more so than she had been months before.

Sometimes I thought she was waiting for an indication of an increased warmth of feeling on my part before she allowed the temperature of her own sentiments to rise. But for one reason and another I delayed the solution of this problem. Janet was very fond of company, and although we saw a great deal of each other, we were not often alone. If we two had more frequently walked, driven, or rowed together, as Mildred and I used to do, I think Miss Clinton would soon have had every opportunity of making up her mind about the fervor of my passion.

The summer weeks passed on, and there was no change in the things which now principally concerned me, except that Mildred seemed to be growing more and more indifferent to me. From having seemed to care no more for me than for her other friends, she now seemed to care less for me than for most people. I do not mean that she showed a dislike, but she treated me with a sort of indifference which I did not fancy at all. This sort of thing had gone too far, and there was no knowing how much further it would go. It was plain enough that the shadrach was overdoing the business.

I was now in a state of much mental disquietude. Greatly as I desired to win the love of Janet, it grieved me to think of losing the generous friendship of Mildred—that friendship to which I had been accustomed for the greater part of my life, and on which, as I now discovered, I had grown to depend.

In this state of mind I went to see Mildred. I found her in the library writing. She received me pleasantly, and was sorry her father was not at home, and begged that I would excuse her finishing the note on which she was engaged, because she wished to get it into the post-office before the mail closed. I sat down on the other side of the table, and she finished her note, after which she went out to gave it to a servant.

Glancing about me, I saw the shadrach. It was partly under a litter of papers, instead of lying on them. I took it up, and was looking at it when Mildred re-turned. She sat down and asked me if I had heard of the changes that were to be made in the time-table of the railroad. We talked a little on the subject, and then I spoke of the shadrach, saying carelessly that it might he interesting to analyze the bit of metal; there was a little knob which might be filed off without injuring it in the least.

"You may take it," she said, "and make what ex-periments you please. I do not use it much; it is unnec-essarily heavy for a paper-weight."

From her tone I might have supposed that she had forgotten that I had given it to her. I told her that I would he very glad to borrow the paper-weight for a time, and, putting it into my pocket, I went away, leav-ing her-arranging her disordered papers on the table, and giving quite as much regard to this occupation as she had given to my little visit.

I could not feel sure that the absence of the shad-rach would cause any diminution in the coolness of her feelings toward me, but there was reason to believe that it would prevent them from growing cooler. If she should keep that shadrach she might in time grow to hate me. I was very glad that I had taken it from her.

My mind easier on this subject, my heart turned more freely toward Janet, and, going to her house, the next day I was delighted find her alone. She was as lovely as ever, and as cordial, but she was flushed and evidently annoyed.

"I am in a bad humor to-day," she said, "and I am glad you came to talk to me and quiet me. Dr. Gilbert promised to take me to drive this afternoon, and we were going over to the hills where they find the wild rhododendron. I am told that it is still in blossom up there, and I want some flowers ever so much—I am going to paint them. And besides, I am crazy to drive with his new horses; and now he sends me a note to say that he is engaged."

This communication shocked me, and I began to talk to her about Dr. Gilbert. I soon found that several times she had been driving with this handsome young physician, but never, she said, behind his new horses, nor to the rhododendron hills.

Dr. Hector Gilbert was a fine young fellow, beginning practice in town, and one of my favorite associates. I had never thought of him in connection with Janet, but I could now see that he might make a most dangerous rival. When a young and talented doctor, enthusiastic in his studies, and earnestly desirous of establishing a practice, and who, if his tune were not fully occupied, would naturally wish that the neighbors would think that such were the case, deliberately devotes some hours on I know not how many days to driving a young lady into the surrounding country, it may be supposed that he is really in love with her. Moreover, judging from Janet's present mood, this doctor's attentions were not without encouragement.

I went home; I considered the state of affairs; I ran my fingers through my hair; I gazed steadfastly upon the floor. Suddenly I rose. I had had an inspiration; I would give the shadrach to Dr. Gilbert.

I went immediately to the doctor's office, and found him there. He too was not in a very good humor.

"I have had two old ladies here nearly all the afternoon, and they have bored me to death," he said. "I could not get rid of them because I found they had made an appointment with each other to visit me to-day and talk over a hospital plan which I proposed some time ago and which is really very important to me, but I wish they had chosen some other time to come here. What is that thing?"

"That is a bit of shadrach," I said, "made into a paper-weight." And then I proceeded to explain what shadrach is, and what peculiar properties it must possess to resist the power of heat, which melts other metal apparently of the same class; and I added that I thought it might be interesting to analyze a bit of it and discover what fire-proof constituents it possessed.

"I should like to do that," said the doctor, attentively turning over the shadrach in his hand. "Can I take off a piece of it?"

I will give it to you," said I," and you can take what use of it you please. If you do analyze it I shall be very glad indeed to hear the results of your investigations."

The doctor demurred a little at taking the paper-weight with such a pretty silver ring around it, but I assured him that the cost of the whole affair was trifling, and I should he gratified if he would take it. He accepted the gift, and was thanking me, when a patient arrived, and I departed.

I really had no right to give away this paper-weight, which, in fact, belonged to Mildred, but there are times when a man must keep his eyes on the chief good, and not think too much about other things. Besides, it was evident that Mildred did not care in the least for the bit of metal, and she had virtually given it to me.

There was another point which I took into consideration. It might be that the shadrach might simply cool Dr. Gilbert's feelings toward me, and that would be neither pleasant nor advantageous. If I could have managed matters so that Janet could have given it to him, it would have been all right. But now all that I could do was to wait and see what would happen. If only the thing would cool the doctor in a general way, that would help. He might then give more thought to his practice and his hospital ladies, and let other people take Janet driving.

About a week after this I met the doctor; he seemed in a hurry, but I stopped him. I had a curiosity to know if he had analyzed the shadrach, and asked him about it.

"No," said he; "I haven't done it. I haven't had time. I knocked off a piece of it, and I will attend to it when I get a chance. Good day."

Of course if the man was busy he could not be expected to give his mind to a trifling matter of that sort, but I thought that he need not have been so curt about it. I stood gazing after him as he walked rapidly down the street. Before I resumed my walk I saw him enter the Clinton house. Things were not going on well. The shadrach had not cooled Dr. Gilbert's feelings toward Janet.

But because the doctor was still warm in his attentions to the girl I loved, I would not in the least relax my attentions to her. I visited her as often as I could find an excuse to do so. There was generally some one else there, but Janet's disposition was of such gracious expansiveness that each one felt obliged to be satisfied with what he got, much as he may have wished for something different.

But one morning Janet surprised me. I met her at Mildred's house, where I had gone to borrow a book of reference. Although I had urged her .not to put herself to so much trouble, Mildred was standing on a little ladder looking for the book, because, she said, she knew exactly what I wanted, and she was sure she could find the proper volume better than I could. Janet had been sitting in a window-seat reading, but when I came in she put down her book and devoted herself to conversation with me. I was a little sorry for this, because Mildred was very kindly engaged in doing me a service, and I really wanted to talk to her about the book she was looking for. Mildred showed so much of her old manner this morning that I would have been very sorry to have her think that I did not appreciate her returning interest in me. Therefore, while under other circumstances I would have been delighted to talk to Janet, I did not wish to give her so much of my attention then. But Janet Clinton was a girl who insisted on people attending to her when she wished them to do so, and, having stepped through an open door into the garden, she present called me to her. Of course I had to go.

"I will not keep you a minute from your fellow student," she said, "but I want to ask a favor of you." And into her dark, uplifted eyes there came a look of tender trustfulness clearer than any I had yet seen there. "Don't you want to drive me to the rhododendron hills?" she said. "I suppose the flowers are all gone by this time, but I have never been there, and I should like ever so much to go."

I could not help remarking that I thought Dr. Gilbert was going to take her there.

"Dr. Gilbert, indeed!" she said with a little laugh. "He promised once, and didn't come, and the next day he planned for it, it rained. I don't think doctors make very good escorts, anyway, for you can't tell who is going to be sick just as you are about to start on a trip. Besides there is no knowing how much botany I should have to hear, and when I go on a pleasure-drive I don't care very much about studying things. But of course I don't want to trouble you."

"Trouble!" I exclaimed. "It will give me the greatest delight to take you that drive or any other, and at whatever time you please."

"You are always so good and kind," she said, with her dark eyes again upraised. "And now let us go in and see if Mildred has found the book."

I spoke the truth when I said that Janet's proposition delighted me. To take a long drive with that charming girl, and at the same time to feel that she had chosen me as her companion, was a greater joy than I had yet had reason to expect; but it would have been a more satisfying joy if she had asked me in her own house and not in Mildred's; if she had not allowed the love which I hoped was growing up between her and me to interfere with the revival of the old friendship between Mildred and me.

But when we returned to the library Mildred was sitting at a table with a book before her, opened at the passage I wanted.

"I have just found it," she said with a smile. "Draw up a chair, and we will look over these snaps together. I want you to show me how he traveled when he left his ship."

"Well, if you two are going to the pole," said Janet, with her prettiest smile, "I will go back to my novel."

She did not seem in the least to object to my geographical researches with Mildred, and if the latter had even noticed my willingness to desert her at the call of Janet, she did not show it. Apparently she was as much a good comrade as she had ever been. This state of things was gratifying in the highest degree.

If I could be loved by Janet and still keep Mildred as my friend, what greater earthly joys could I ask?

The drive with Janet was postponed by wet weather. Day after day it rained, or the skies were heavy, and we both agreed that it must be in the bright sunshine that we would make this excursion. When we should make it, and should be alone together on the rhododendron hill, I intended to open my soul to Janet.

It may seem strange to others, and at the time it also seemed strange to me, but there was another reason besides the rainy weather which prevented my declaration of love to Janet. This was a certain nervous anxiety in regard to my friendship for Mildred. I did not in the least waver in my intention to use the best endeavors to make the one my wife, but at the same time I was oppressed by a certain alarm that in carrying out this project I might act in such a way as to wound the feelings of the other.

This disposition to consider the feelings of Mildred became so strong that I began to think that my own sentiments were in need of control. It was not right that while making love to one woman I should give so much consideration to my relations with another. The idea struck me that in a measure I had shared the fate of those who had thrown the Hebrew youths into the fiery furnace. My heart had not been consumed by the flames, but in throwing the shadrach into what I supposed were Mildred's affections it was quite possible that I had been singed by them. At any rate my conscience told me that under the circumstances my sentiments toward Mildred were too warm; in honestly making love to Janet I ought to forget them entirely.

It might have been a good thing, 1 told myself, if I had not given away the shadrach, but kept it as a gift from Mildred. Very soon I reached this conclusion it became evident to me that Mildred was again cooling in my direction as rapidly as the mercury falls after sunset on a September day. This discovery did not make my mercury fall; in fact, it brought it for a time nearly to the boiling-point. I could not imagine what had happened. I almost neglected Janet, so anxious was I to know what had made this change in Mildred.

Weeks passed on, and I discovered nothing, except that Mildred had now become more than indifferent to me. She allowed me to see my companionship did not give her pleasure.

Janet had her drive to the rhododendron hills, but she took it with Dr. Gilbert and not with me. When I heard of this it pained me, though I could not help admitting that I deserved the punishment; but my surprise was almost as great as my pain, for Janet had recently given me reason to believe that she had a very small opinion of the young doctor. In fact, she had criticized him so severely that I had been obliged to speak in his defense. I now found myself in a most doleful quandary, and there was only one thing of which I could be certain—I needed cooling toward Mildred if I still allowed myself to hope to marry Janet.

One afternoon I was talking to Mr. Bronce in his library, when, glancing toward the table used by his daughter for writing purposes, I was astounded to see, lying on a little pile of letters, the Christmas shadrach. As soon as I could get an opportunity I took it in my hand and eagerly examined it. I had not been mistaken. It was the paper-weight I had given Mildred. There was the silver band around it, and there was the place where a little piece had been knocked off by the doctor. Mildred was not at home, but I determined that I would wait and see her. I would dine with the Bronces; I would spend the evening; I would stay all night; I would not leave the house until I had had this mystery explained. She returned in about half an hour and greeted me in the somewhat stiff manner she had adopted of late; but when she noticed my perturbed expression and saw that I held the shadrach in my hand, she took a seat by the table, where for some time I had been waiting for her, alone.

"I suppose you want to ask me about that paper-weight," she remarked. "Indeed I do," I replied. "How in the world did you happen to get it again?"

"Again?" she repeated satirically. "You may well say that. I will explain it to you. Some little time ago I called on Janet Clinton, and on her writing-desk I saw that paper-weight. I remembered it perfectly. It was the one you gave me last Christmas and afterward borrowed of me, saying that you wanted to analyze it, or something of the sort. I had never used it very much, and of course was willing that you should take it, and make experiments with it if you wanted to, but I must say that the sight of it on Janet Clinton's desk both shocked and angered me. I asked her where she got it, and she told me a gentleman had given it to her. I did not need to waste any words in inquiring who this gentleman was, but I determined that she should not rest under a mistake in regard to its proper ownership, and told her plainly that the person who had given it to her had previously given it to me; that it was mine, and he had no right to give it to any one else. 'Oh, if that is the case,' she exclaimed, 'take it, I beg of you. I don't care for it, and, what is more, I don't care any more for the man who gave it to me than I do for the thing itself.' So I took it and brought it home with me. Now you know how I happened to have it again."

For a moment I made no answer. Then I asked her how long it had been since she had received the shadrach from Janet Clinton.

"Oh, I don't remember exactly," she said; "it was several weeks ago."

Now I knew everything; all the mysteries of the past were revealed to me. The young doctor, fervid in his desire to please the woman he loved, had given Janet this novel paper-weight. Front that moment she had begun to regard his attentions with apathy, and finally—her nature was one which was apt to go to extremes—to dislike him. Mildred repossessed herself of the shadrach, which she took, not as a gift from Janet, but as her rightful property, presented to her by me. And this horrid little object, probably with renewed power, had cooled, almost frozen indeed, the sentiments of that dear girl toward me. Then, too, had the spell been taken from Janet's inclinations, and she had gone to the rhododendron hills with Dr. Gilbert.

One thing was certain. I must have that shadrach.

"Mildred," I exclaimed, "will you not give me this paper-weight? Give it to me for my own?"

"What do you want to do with it?" she asked sarcastically. "Analyze it again?"

"Mildred," said I, "I did not give it to Janet. I gave it to Dr. Gilbert, and he must have given it to her: I know I had no right to give it away at all, but I did not believe that you would care; but now I beg that you will let me have it. Let me have it for my own. I assure you solemnly I will never give it away. It has caused trouble enough already."

"I don't exactly understand what you mean by trouble," she said, 'But take it if you want it. You are perfectly welcome." And picking up her gloves and hat from the table she left me.

As I walked home my hatred of the wretched piece of metal in my hand increased with every step. I looked at it with disgust when I went to bed that night, and when my glance lighted upon it the next morning I involuntarily shrank from it, as if it had been an evil thing. Over and over again that day I asked myself why I should keep in my possession something which would make my regard for Mildred grow less and less; which would eventually make me care for her not at all? The very thought of not caring for Mildred sent a pang through my heart.

My feelings all prompted me to rid myself of what I looked upon as a calamitous talisman, but my reason interfered. If I still wished to marry Janet it was my duty to welcome indifference to Mildred.

In this mood I went out, to stroll, to think, to decide; and that I might be ready to act on my decision I put the shadrach into my pocket. Without exactly intending it I walked toward the Bronce place, and soon found myself on the edge of a pretty pond which lay at the foot of the garden. Here, in the shade of a tree there stood a bench, and on this lay a book, an ivory paper-cutter in its leaves as marker.

I knew that Mildred had left that book on the bench; it was her habit to come to this place to read. As she had not taken the volume with her, it was probable that she intended soon to return. But then the sad thought came to me that if she saw me there she would not return. I picked up the book; I read the pages she had been reading. As I read I felt that I could think the very thoughts that she thought as she read. I was seized with a yearning to be with her, to read with her, to think with her. Never had my soul gone out to Mildred as at that moment, and yet heavily dangling in my pocket, I carried—I could not bear to think of it. Seized by a sudden impulse, I put don the book; I drew out the shadrach, and, tearing off the silver band, I tossed the vile bit of metal into the pond.

"There!" I cried. "Go out of my possession, out of my sight! You shall work no charm on me. Let nature take its course, and let things happen as they may." Then, relieved from the weight on my heart and the weight in my pocket, I went home.

Nature did take its course, and in less than a fortnight from that day the engagement of Janet and Dr. Gilbert was announced. I had done nothing to prevent this, and the news did not disturb my peace of mind; but my relations with Mildred very much disturbed it. I had hoped that, released from the baleful influence of the shadrach, her friendly feelings toward me would return, and my passion for her had now grown so strong that I waited and watched, as a wrecked mariner waits and watches for the sight of a sail, for a sign that she had so far softened toward me that I might dare to speak to her of my love. But no such appeared.

I now seldom visited the Bronce house; none of that family, once my best friends, seemed to care to see me. Evidently Mildred's feelings toward me had extended themselves to the rest of the household. This was not surprising, for her family had long been accustomed to think as Mildred thought.

One day I met Mr. Bronce at the post-office, and, some other gentlemen coming up, we began to talk of a proposed plan to introduce a system of water-works into the village, an improvement much desired by many of us.

"So far as I am concerned," said Mr. Bronce, "I am not now in need of anything of the sort. Since I set up my steam-pump I have supplied my house from the pond at the end of my garden with all the water we can possibly want for every purpose."

"Do you mean," asked one of the gentlemen, "that you get your drinking-water in that way?"

"Certainly," replied Mr. Bronce "The basin of the pond is kept as clean and in as good order as any reservoir can be, and the water comes from an excellent, rapid-flowing spring. I want nothing better."

A chill ran through me as I listened. The shadrach was in that pond. Every drop of water which Mildred drank, which touched her, was influenced by that demonic paper-weight, which, without knowing what I was doing, I had thus bestowed upon the whole Bronce family.

When I went home I made diligent search for a stone which might be about the size and weight of the shadrach, and having repaired to a retired spot I practiced tossing it as I had tossed the bit of metal into the pond. In each instance I measured the distance which I had thrown the stone, and was at last enabled to make a very fair estimate of the distance to which I had thrown the shadrach when I had buried it under the waters of the pond.

That night there was a half-moon, and between eleven and twelve o'clock, when everybody in our village might be supposed to be in bed and asleep, I made my way over the fields to the back of the Bronce place, taking with me a long fish-cord with a knot in it, showing the average distance to which I had thrown the practice stone. When I reached the pond I stood as nearly as possible in the place by the bench from which I had hurled the shadrach and to this spot I pegged one end of the cord. I was attired in an old tennis suit, and, having removed my shoes and stockings, I entered the water, holding the roll of cord in my hand. This I slowly unwound as I advanced toward the middle of the pond, and when I reached the knot I stopped, with the water above my waist.

I had found the bottom of the pond very smooth, and free from weeds and mud, and I now began feeling about with my bare feet, as I moved from side to side, describing a small arc; but I discovered nothing more than an occasional pebble no larger than a walnut.

Letting out some more of the cord, I advanced a little farther into the center of the pond, and slowly described another arc. The water was now nearly up to my armpits, but it was not cold, though if it had been I do not think I should have minded it in the ardor my search. Suddenly I put my foot on something hard and as big as my fist, but in an instant it moved away from under my foot; it must have been a turtle. This occurrence made me shiver a little, but I did not swerve from my purpose, and, loosing the string a little more, I went farther into the pond. The water was now nearly up to my chin, and there was something weird, mystical, and awe-inspiring in standing thus in the depths of this silent water, my eyes so near its gently rippling surface, fantastically lighted by the setting moon, and tenanted by nobody knew what cold and slippery creatures. But from side to side I slowly moved, reaching out with my feet in every direction, hoping to touch the thing for which I sought.

Suddenly I set my right foot upon something hard and irregular. Nervously I felt it with my toes. I patted it with my bare sole. It was as big as the shadrach! It felt like the shadrach. In a few moments I was almost convinced that the direful paper-weight was beneath my foot.

Closing my eyes, and holding my breath, I stooped down into the water, and groped on the bottom with my hands. In some way I had moved while stooping, and at first I could find nothing. A sensation of dread came over me as I felt myself in the midst of the dark solemn water,—around me, above me, everywhere,—almost suffocated, and apparently deserted even by the shadrach. But just as I felt that I could hold my breath no longer my fingers touched the thing that had been under my foot, and, clutching it, I rose and thrust my head out of the water. I could do nothing until I had taken two or three long breaths; then, holding up the object in my hand to the light of the expiring moon, I saw that it was like the shadrach; so like, indeed, that I felt that it must be it.

Turning, I made my way out of the water as rapidly as possible, and, dropping on my knees on the ground, I tremblingly lighted the lantern which I had left on the bench, and turned its light on the thing I had found. There must be no mistake, if this was not the shadrach I would go in again. But there was no necessity for reentering the pond; it was the shadrach.

With the extinguished lantern in one hand and the lump of mineral evil in the other, I hurried home. My wet clothes were sticky and chilly in the night air. Several times in my haste I stumbled over clods and briers, and my shoes, which I had not taken time to tie, flopped up and down as I ran. But I cared for none of these discomforts; the shadrach was in my power.

Crossing a wide field I heard, not far away, the tramping of hoofs, as of a horseman approaching at full speed. I stopped and looked in the direction of the sound. My eyes had now become so accustomed to the dim light that I could distinguish objects somewhat plainly, and I quickly perceived that the animal that was galloping toward me was a bull. I well knew what bull it was; this was Squire Starling's pasture-field, and that was his great Alderney bull, Ramping Sir John of Ramapo II.

I was well acquainted with that bull, renowned throughout the neighborhood for his savage temper and his noble pedigree—son of Ramping Sir John of Ramapo I, whose sire was the Great Rodolphin, son of Prince Maximus of Granby, one of whose daughters averaged eighteen pounds of butter a week, and who, himself, had killed two men.

The bull, who had not perceived me when I crossed the field before, for I had then made my way with as little noise as possible, was bent on punishing my intrusion upon his domains, and bellowed as he came on. I was in a position of great danger. With my flopping shoes it was impossible to escape by flight; I must stand and defend myself. I turned and faced the furious creature, who was not twenty feet distant, and then, with all my strength, I hurled the shadrach, which I held in my right hand, directly at his shaggy forehead. My ability to project a missile was considerable, for I had held, with credit, the position of pitcher in a base-ball nine, and as the shadrach struck the bull's head with a great thud he stopped as if he had suddenly run against a wall.

I do not know that actual and violent contact with the physical organism of a recipient accelerates the influence of a shadrach upon the mental organism of said recipient, but I do know that the contact of my projectile with that bull's skull instantly cooled the animal's fury. For a few moments he stood and looked at me, and then his interest in me as a man and trespasser appeared to fade away, and, moving slowly from me, Ramping Sir John of Ramapo II began to crop the grass.

I did not stop to look for the shadrach; I considered it safely disposed of. So long as Squire Starling used that field for a pasture connoisseurs in mineral fragments would not be apt to wander through it, and when it should be plowed, the shadrach, to ordinary eyes no more than a common stone, would be buried beneath the sod. I awoke the next morning refreshed and happy, and none the worse for my wet walk.

"Now," I said to myself, "nature shall truly have her own way. If the uncanny comes into my life and that of those I love, it shall not be brought in by me."

About a week after this I dined with the Bronce family. They were very cordial, and it seemed to me the most natural thing in the world to be sitting at their table. After dinner Mildred and I walked together in the garden. It was a charming evening, and we sat down on the bench by the edge of the pond. I spoke to her of some passages in the book I had once seen there.

"Oh, have you read that?" she asked with interest.

"I have seen only two pages of it," I said, "and those I read in the volume you left on this bench, with a paper-cutter in it for a marker. I long to read more and talk with you of what I have read."

"Why, then, didn't you wait? You might have known that I would come back."

I did not tell her that I knew that because I was there she would not have come. But before I left the bench I discovered that hereafter, wherever I might be, she was willing to come and to stay.

Early in the next spring Mildred and I were married, and on our wedding-trip we passed through a mining district in the mountains. Here we visited one of the great iron-works, and were both much interested in witnessing the wonderful power of man, air, and fire over the stubborn king of metals.

"What is this substance?" asked Mildred of one of the officials who was conducting us through the works.

"That," said the man, "is what we call shad—"

"My dear," I cried, "we must hurry away this instant or we shall lose the train. Come; quick; there is not a moment for delay." And with a word of thanks to the guide I seized her hand and led her, almost running, into the open air.

Mildred was amazed.

"Never before," she exclaimed, "have I seen you in such a hurry. I thought the train we decided to take did not leave for at least an hour."

"I have changed my mind," I said, "and think it will be a great deal better for us to take the one which leaves in ten minutes."

THE KID HANGS UP HIS STOCKING

BY JACOB A. RIIS

There were thousands of homeless children in American cities in the second half of the nineteenth century. Lodging houses run by the Children's Aid Society sheltered boys who needed a place to stay. For a fee, boys could have a bed, food, and a locker; most of the boys worked for their money as shoe shines or newsboys. The person in charge—the superintendent—often kept a "bank," where boys could keep their money and gain interest on it. This is an endearing story of Christmas spirit and boyhood camaraderie in a turn-of-the-century lodging house.

The clock in the West-Side Lodging-house ticked out the seconds of Christmas eve as slowly and methodically as if six fat turkeys were not sizzling in the basement kitchen against the morrow's spread, and as if two-score boys were not racking their brains to guess what kind of pies would go with them. Out on the avenue the shop-keepers were barring doors and windows, and shouting "Merry Christmas!" to one another across the street as they hurried to get home. The drays ran

133

over the pavement with muffled sounds; winter had set in with a heavy snow-storm. In the big hall the monotonous click of checkers on the board kept step with the clock. The smothered exclamations of the boys at some unexpected, bold stroke, and the scratching of a little fellow's pencil on a slate, trying to figure out how long it was yet till the big dinner, were the only sounds that broke the quiet of the room. The superintendent dozed behind his desk.

A door at the end of the hall creaked, and a head with a shock of weather-beaten hair was stuck cautiously through the opening.

"Tom!" it said in a stage-whisper. "Hi, Tom! Come up an' git on ter de lay of de Kid."

A bigger boy in a jumper, who had been lounging on two chairs by the group of checker-players, sat up and looked toward the door. Something in the energetic toss of the head there aroused his instant curiosity, and he started across the room. After a brief whispered conference the door closed upon the two, and silence fell once more on the hall.

They had been gone but a little while when they came back in haste. The big boy shut the door softly behind him and set his back against it. "Fellers," he said, "what d' ye t'ink? I'm blamed if de Kid ain't gone an' hung up his sock fer Chris'mas!"

The checkers dropped, and the pencil ceased scratching on the slate, in breathless suspense.

"Come up an' see," said Tom, briefly, and led the way.

The whole band followed on tiptoe. At the foot of the stairs their leader halted.

"You don't make no noise," he said, with a menacing gesture. "You, Savoy!"—to one in a patched shirt and with a mischievous twinkle,—"you don't come none o' yer monkey-shines. If you scare de Kid you'll get it in de neck, see!"

With this admonition they stole upstairs. In the last cot of the double tier of bunks a boy much smaller than the rest slept, snugly tucked in the blankets. A tangled curl of yellow hair strayed over his baby face. Hitched to the bedpost was a poor, worn little stocking, arranged with much care so that Santa Claus should have as little trouble in filling it as possible. The edge of a hole in the knee had been drawn together and tied with a string to prevent anything falling out. The boys looked on in amazed silence. Even Savoy was dumb.

Little Willie, or, as he was affectionately dubbed by the boys, "the Kid," was a waif who had drifted in among them some months before. Except that his mother was in the hospital, nothing was known about him, which was regular and according to the rule of the house. Not as much was known about most of its patrons; few of them knew more themselves, or cared to remember. Santa Claus had never been anything to them but a fake to make the colored supplements sell. The revelation of the Kid's simple faith struck them with a kind of awe. They sneaked quietly down-stairs.

"Fellers," said Tom, when they were all together again in the big room,—by virtue of his length, which had given him the nick-name of "Stretch," he was the speaker on all important occasions,—"ye seen it yerself. Santy Claus is a-comin' to this here joint to-night. I wouldn't 'a' believed it. I ain't never had no dealin's wid de ole guy. He kinda forgot I was around, I guess. But de Kid says he is a-comin' to-night, an' what de Kid says goes."

Then he looked round expectantly. Two of the boys, "Gimpy" and Lem, were conferring aside in an undertone. Presently Gimpy, who limped, as his name indicated, spoke up.

"Lem says, says he—"

"Gimpy, you chump! you'll address de chairman," interrupted Tom, with severe dignity, "or you'll get yer jaw broke, if yer leg *is* short, see!"

"Cut it out, Stretch," was Gimpy's irreverent answer. "This here ain't no regular meetin', an' we ain't goin' to have none o' yer rot. Lem he says, says he, let's break de bank an' fill de Kid's sock. He won't know but it wuz ole Santy done it."

A yell of approval greeted the suggestion. The chairman, bound to exercise the functions of office in season and out of season, while they lasted, thumped the table.

"It is regular motioned an' carried," he announced, "that we break de bank fer de Kid's Chris'mas. Come on, boys!"

The bank was run by the house, with the superintendent as paying-teller. He had to be consulted, particularly as it was past banking hours; but the affair having been succinctly put before him by a committee, of which Lem and Gimpy and Stretch were the talking members, he readily consented to a reopening of business for a scrutiny of the various accounts which represented the boys' earnings at selling papers and blacking boots, minus the cost of their keep and of sundry surreptitious flings at "craps" in secret corners. The inquiry developed an available surplus of three dollars and fifty cents. Savoy alone had no account; the run of craps had recently gone heavily against him. But in consideration of the season, the house voted a credit of twenty-five cents to him. The announcement was received with cheers. There was an immediate rush for the store, which was delayed only a few minutes by the necessity of Gimpy and Lem stopping on the stairs to "thump" one another as the expression of their entire satisfaction.

The procession that returned to the lodging-house later on, after wearing out the patience of several belated storekeepers, might have been the very Santa's supply-train itself. It signalized its advent by a variety of discordant noises, which were smothered on the stairs by Stretch, with much personal violence, lest they wake the Kid out of season. With boots in hand and bated breath, the midnight band stole up to the dormitory and looked in. All was safe. The Kid was dreaming, and smiled in his sleep. The report roused a passing suspicion that he was faking, and Savarese was for pinching his toe to find out. As this would inevitably result in disclosure, Savarese and his proposal were scornfully sat upon. Gimpy supplied the popular explanation.

"He's a-dreamin' that Santy Claus has come," he said, carefully working a base-ball bat past the tender spot in the stocking.

"Hully Gee!" commented Shorty, balancing a drum with care on the end of it, "I'm thinkin' he ain't far out. Looks's ef de hull shop'd come along."

It did when it was all in place. A trumpet and a gun that had made vain and perilous efforts to join the bat in the stocking leaned against the bed in expectant attitudes. A picture-book with a pink Bengal tiger and a green bear on the cover peeped over the pillow, and the bedposts and rail were festooned with candy and marbles in bags. An express-wagon with a high seat was stabled in the gangway. It carried a load of fir-branches that left no doubt from whose livery it hailed. The last touch was supplied by Savoy in the shape of a monkey on a yellow stick, that was not in the official bill of lading.

"I swiped it fer de Kid," he said briefly in explanation.

When it was all done the boys turned in, but not to sleep. It was long past midnight before the deep and regular breathing from the beds proclaimed that the last had succumbed.

The early dawn was tingeing the frosty window-panes with red when from the Kid's cot there came a shriek that roused the house with a start of very genuine surprise.

"Hello!" shouted Stretch, sitting up with a jerk and rubbing his eyes. "Yes, sir! in a minute. Hello, Kid, what to—"

The kid was standing barefooted in the passageway, with a base-ball bat in one hand and a trumpet and a pair of drumsticks in the other, viewing with shining eyes the wagon and its cargo, the gun and all the rest. From every cot necks were stretched, and grinning faces watched the show. In the excess of his joy the Kid let out a blast on the trumpet that fairly shook the building. As if it were a signal, the boys jumped out of bed and danced a breakdown about him in their shirt-tails, even Gimpy joining in.

"Holy Moses!" said Stretch, looking down, "if Santy Claus ain't been here an' forgot his hull kit, I'm blamed!"

THE CURIOUS VEHICLE
A MIDNIGHT STORY

BY ALEXANDER W. DRAKE (1843-1916)

This is an unusual, magical love story. Its supernatural elements have their origins in the nineteenth-century fascination with mathematics, specifically the study of optics. The author, Alexander W. Drake, even includes a footnote about an actual (though questionable) mathematical discovery as part of his story. This not-so-subtle blend of science and fiction lends a curious quality to this Christmas story.

It was midnight in early December. A dense silver mist hid the sleeping city, the street-lamps gave a faint yellow glimmer through the almost impenetrable gloom, the air was like the cold breath from the dying, the fog hanging in great drops on my clothing. Stray policemen had taken refuge in sheltering doorways, and my own footsteps echoed with unfamiliar and uncanny sound down the long street—the only sound that broke the midnight stillness, save the hoarse whistles of wandering and belated ferry-boats on the distant river.

As I emerged from a narrow street into the main thoroughfare, my shivering attention was attracted to a

139

curious covered vehicle standing in the bright glare of an electric light. It was neither carriage nor wagon, but an odd, strongly made affair, painted olive green, with square windows in the sides, reaching from just above the middle to the roof, and a smaller window in the back near the top. On each side of the middle window were two panels of glass. From the middle window only a dim light shone, like the subdued light from a nurse's lamp. On the seat in front, underneath a projecting hood, sat a little old black man wrapped in a buffalo-robe and a great fur coat partly covered with a rubber cape or mackintosh, and with a fur cap pulled down over his ears. The horse was heavily blanketed, arid also well protected with rubber covers. Both man and beast waited with unquestioning patience. Both seemed lost in reverie or sleep.

With chattering teeth I stood, wondering what could be going on in that queer box-like wagon at that time of night. The silence was oppressive. There stood the dimly lighted wagon; there stood the horse; there sat the Negro—and I the only observer of this queer vehicle.

I stepped cautiously to the side of the wagon, and listened. Not a sound from within. Shivering and benumbed, I, too, like the policemen, took refuge in a doorway, and waited and watched for some sound or sign from that mysterious interior. I was too fond of adventure to give it up. It seemed to me that hours passed and I stood unrewarded. Just as I was reluctantly leaving, much chagrined to find that I had waited in vain, I saw, thrown against the window for a few moments only, a curious enlarged shadow of a man's head. It seemed to wear a kind of tam-o'-shanter, below which was a shade or visor sticking out beyond the man's face like the gigantic beak of a bird. A mass of wavy hair and beard showed underneath the cap. Suddenly the shadow disappeared, much to my disappointment, and although I watched in the fog and dampness for half an hour longer, it did not again appear.

I wandered home, puzzled and speculating, but determined that I would wait until morning if I were ever fortunate enough to come across the vehicle again. Weeks passed before the opportunity occurred, and even then, had it not been for a very singular incident, I doubt if I should ever have fathomed the mystery of the curious vehicle.

It was Christmas eve, the night bitterly cold. I had clothed myself in my thickest Ulster. My feet were incased in arctics, my hands in warm fur gloves, and with rough Scotch cap I felt sure I could brave the coldest night. Thus equipped, I started out, and when I returned at midnight in the beginning of a whirling, almost blinding snow-storm, the Christmas chimes were ringing, and the whole air seemed filled with Christmas cheer.

Turning a corner, I discovered the vehicle in the same place and position. This time, as I had before resolved, I would wait until morning if necessary. So I began pacing up and down the sidewalk in front of the vehicle taking strolls of five or ten minutes apart, and then returning. I walked until I was almost exhausted. In spite of my heavy Ulster I began to feel chilly, so I again took refuge in the doorway of a building opposite.

Should I give it up, I asked myself after waiting so long? I stood debating the question. No, I would wait a little longer; so, puffing my pipe, I shivered, and watched for developments. At last I was about determined that I must go or perish, when suddenly I saw through the blinding snow the shadow of a pair of hands appear at the dimly lighted window, adjusting a frame or inner sash. You can imagine my interest in the proceedings.

Just at this moment a street sparrow, numb with the cold, and crowded from a window-blind by its companions, dropped, half falling, half flying, to the sidewalk directly in front of the window of the vehicle. It sat blinking in the bright rays of the electric light, quite bewildered, turning its little head first one way, then the other. In the mean time the shadows of the two hands were still visible. The sparrow, probably attracted by the light and the movement of the hands, suddenly flew up, not striking the glass, but hovering with a quick motion of the wings directly in front of the window, its magnified shadow thrown on it by the rays of the electric light. Then the bird dropped to the ground. The occupant was evidently much startled by the large shadow coming so suddenly and at such a time of night. The shadow of his hands quickly disappeared, and so did the frame. In another moment the door of the vehicle opened, giving me a glimpse of a cozy and remarkable interior. It seemed, in contrast with the cold and storm without, filled with warmth and sunshine. It was like a pictorial little room rather than the inside of a wagon or carriage. The occupant looked out in a surprised, excited, and questioning way, as much as to say, "What could that have been?" His whole manner implied that he had been disturbed.

This was my opportunity, and, seizing it instantly, I walked boldly to the door of the vehicle, and said, "It was a little sparrow benumbed with the cold, that fluttered down to the sidewalk, where it lay for a moment, until, probably attracted by the light, it hovered for a few seconds before your window, then fell to the ground again."

I felt the man eying me intently, studying me with a most searching glance. Was he in doubt as to my sincerity? Was it a hidden bond of sympathy between us that made him suddenly relent and invite me to enter his vehicle? What else could have prompted him? For my own part, I instinctively felt for the man, without knowing why, a deep pity.

"Please step inside," he said; "it is cold."

And so, at last, I was really admitted, invited into the little interior—that little interior which had piqued my curiosity for so long a time. Yes, I was admitted at last, and now had a chance to look about, and to study the general appearance of the occupant as he moved over for me to sit beside him on the roomy, luxurious seat. What a curious personality! He was a tall, raw-boned man of strong character. His soft gray beard and hair made a marked contrast to the dark surroundings. Now I understood the shadow which I had seen thrown on the window for a few seconds. He wore a tam-o'-shanter cap, and beneath it, to protect his eyes from the lamp-light, a large visor, or shade, which threw his entire face into deep shadow, giving him the look of a painting by an old master.

He had on a loose coat of some rough material.

Surely the interior of no conveyance could be more interesting than this. In the front, just back of the driver, were two square windows with sliding wooden shutters, and between the two was a little square mirror. Above these was a rod, from which hung a dark-green cloth curtain which could be drawn at will. Underneath was a chest, or cabinet, of shallow drawers filling the entire width of the carriage, with small brass rings by which to pull them out. On top of this cabinet stood several clear glass jars half filled with pure water. There were two or three oil-lamps with large shades hung in brackets with sockets like steamer-lamps, only one of which was lighted. Underneath the seat was a locker. On the floor of the conveyance, along its four sides, were oblong bars of iron, and in the center was a warm fur rug. One side only of the carriage opened. On the side opposite the door was a rack reaching from the window to the floor, in which stood six or eight light but strongly made frames, over which was stretched the thinnest parchment-like paper. The top of the vehicle was tufted and padded. The prevailing color was dark green. In shape it was somewhat longer and broader than the usual carriage. There was a small revolving circular ventilator in front, over the mirror, which could be opened or closed at will, and which could also be used by the occupant for conversing with the driver.

The man arose, and, opening the ventilator, told the coachman to drive on. Meanwhile I enjoyed the wonderful effect of the little interior—its rich gloom, the strong light from the shaded lamp which was thrown over the floor; the bright electric light gleaming through the falling snow into the window on my left.

The night, being so disagreeable, made the interior seem very bright and comfortable by contrast, as the man closed the sliding wooden shutters, separating us entirely from the snow-storm without. There was an artificial warmth which I could not understand, and with it all a sense of security and coziness. The stranger's manner was both gentle and reassuring. We rode in silence over the rough pavement until we reached the smooth asphalt. Then he began:

"I do not consider myself superstitious, but somehow I don't like it—that little bird hovering in front of my window. It seems like a bad omen, and it was a shadow which startled me. My life seems haunted with shadows, and they always bring misfortune to me."

We were both silent for a time, when he went on:

"How curious life is! Here am I riding with you, a total stranger, long past midnight. You are the first I have ever admitted into this wagon, with the exception of my faithful Cato, who is driving. If one could only see from the beginning how strangely one's life is to be ordered."

The stranger's voice was rich and deep. I hoped he would continue so that I might get some idea of him and his peculiar mode of life, and what was going on night after night in this interior. I waited for him to proceed.

"Have you known trouble or sorrow in your life?" he asked.

"Yes," I replied; "I have lost nearly all who were dear to me in this round world."

"Then," said he, "I will tell you my story with the hope that it will be both understood and appreciated. I loved from childhood a charming girl, sweet and pure. I need not go into the detail of all that boyish love, but in my early manhood and her early womanhood we were married—and what a sweet bride she was!

"We lived in an old white farm-house in a village near the great city—a beautiful place, a long, low, two-story-and-attic farm-house, probably fifty or sixty years old. How well I can see it—its sloping roof, the extension, the quaint doorway with side-lights and with a window over the top, the front porch with gracefully shaped newels, the long piazza running the entire length of the extension, great chimneys at each end, and enormous pine-trees in front of the house! The house stood on a little elevation, with terraced bank, and with a pretty fence inclosing it. Beyond was an old well with lattice-work sides and door, and a pathway trodden by the feet of former occupants, long since dead. In front of the house were circular beds of old-time flowers—sweet-williams, lady's-slippers, larkspur, and foxglove. At the rear, great banks of tiger-lilies threw their delicate blue shadows against the white surface of our little home. In one corner of our garden we had left the weeds to grow luxuriantly, like miniature forest trees, and found much pleasure in studying their beautiful forms. How fine they looked in silhouette against the sunset sky! On one side of the old-fashioned doorway were shrubs and a rose-of-Sharon tree, and on the other, honeysuckle and syringa-bushes. There were also many kinds of fruit- and shade-trees.

"How happily we walked up and down the shady lanes of that little village! For us the birds sang sweetly. We took delight in our flowers, and everything about us. In the evening we would enjoy the sunsets, returning home arm in arm in the afterglow, to sit in the cool of the evening on the piazza and to listen to the wind as it sighed through the pines. What music they made for us! We compared it with what poets of all ages had sung of them, and went to sleep, lulled to rest by the wind through their soft boughs."

He paused again, evidently thinking of the happy time.

"How can I tell you," he resumed, "of the life that went on in that simple old farm-house? Our pleasant wood-fire on the hearth; a few photographs from the old masters on the walls; our favorite books of poetry and fiction, which we read together during the long winter evenings, while the pine-trees sighed outside, and all was so comfortable and cozy within; or the lovely walks in spring and summer, through the byways of the pretty little village, with its hedgerows, blackberries, and wild flowers. How we watched for the first violets, and what joy the early blossoms gave us! What pleasure we took in those delightful years, and how smoothly our lives ran on! Each day I went to the city, and was always cheered by the thought that my sweet wife would be at the station to meet me. How pure she looked in the summer evenings, clad in her thin white dresses, with a silver fan and brooch, her dark hair and eyes like those of a startled fawn!

"Well, I need not dwell longer on all this. It was only for a few short years, when one cruel cold day about the happy Christmas-time she was taken ill, and grew steadily worse, and all that could be done for her would not save her. She died. I can see her now—her dark hair laid back on the pillow, and the peaceful, happy smile on her face. We buried her beneath the snow, in the old graveyard overlooking the river, and I went home broken-hearted."

I heard the poor fellow sigh, and for a time he was silent as the carriage went on through the snow. "What can be the connection of this queer craft with what he is telling me?" I thought. When he resumed, he said:

"For months I tried to live on in the little house, but life became terrible. In the evenings, as I sat by the pleasant log-fire, I would imagine I heard her footsteps on the stairs, and her voice calling me. I did my best to conquer my grief, but it was of no use. The light seemed gone out of my life. At last I could stand it no longer, and I moved all my worldly possessions to another house in the same village. I could not bear to think of going away from the place entirely.

"When the springtime came again, and the lovely flowers were in bloom, and the birds were singing their sweet songs; when the wind breathed softly through the pine-trees, and she was gone, the sunsets were in vain, and all nature seemed mourning. After this I busied myself with all kinds of occupation, but without success. Life became sadder and sadder, until finally in despair I took a foreign trip. I traveled far and wide, but always with the same weary despondency and gloom. The image of my loved one was always with me. Nothing in life satisfied me. I wandered through country after country, looking at old masters, grand churches, listening to cathedral music, but always before me was the same picture—the old white farm-house, the great mournful pines, and with it all the memory of the sweet life now departed, for which nothing could make amends."

Then he was silent, and as we drove over the soft, snow-covered asphalt, he became absorbed in thought.

"After a year or so of restless foreign travel I drifted back to my own country and to the little village. Night after night I wandered around the empty house where we had lived, and through the little garden, and would stand at midnight listening to the sad sighing of the wind through the pine-trees, which to me sounded like a requiem for the dead. Many a moonlight night have I stood gazing into the windows, and imagined her looking out at me as in the happy days of old, and I would walk up and down the path thinking, oh, how sadly! of the times we used to return by it from our evening walks.

"Finally the little village became hateful to me. I could endure it no longer, and I shook its dust from my feet. With reluctance I moved away into the heart of the great city, but with the same longing in my heart—the same despair. I hunted up my two faithful black servants who had lived with us for several years. I bought a house in the old part of the city, and there we now live, and I am well cared for by them. Let me read you portions of a letter from her—one of the last she wrote," and he took from his pocket a little morocco book with monogram in silver script letters. He rose and asked the driver to stop, and, tuning the light up, said: "This will give you some idea of the sweet life, with its love of nature, that went on in and about that little cottage. The letter was written to me when I was in another city." He read as follows:

"My dear, I can hardly tell you how lovely the shadows looked as I strolled around our little house this evening, and was filled with delight by their beautiful but evasive forms. To begin with, you remember the exquisite, almost silhouette, shadow of the rose-of-Sharon bush by the front door. I gave it a long study tonight. Its fine, decorative character reminded me of a Japanese drawing, only it is far more delicate and subtle. If this could be painted in soft gray on the door-posts and around the little side windows, how it would beautify our plain dwelling, and what a permanent reminder it would be of our delightful summer days!

"But if I spend too much time on a single shadow, I shall have no room left to tell you of the greater ones we have enjoyed together. From the path near the gate, and looking toward the house, I saw tonight, and seemed to feel for the first time, the wonderful tenderness of the great shadow which nearly covers the end and side of our home. How mysterious our kitchen became, with its shed completely enclosed in velvety gloom suggesting both sorrow and tragedy; while the other end of the house was covered with fantastic forms, soft and ethereal, and with a delicacy indescribable. But when the moon came up, and the soft shadows of the pines were cast on the pure white weather-boards of our little home,—the shadows of our own pines, the pines we love so well, and through whose branches we have heard music sweet and low, soft and sad,—then I thought of you as I studied their masses tossing so gently, their movement almost imperceptible, and I longed for you as I studied their moving forms, their richness, variety, and texture—for you to tell me of their artistic beauty— your delicate, poetic appreciation of their loveliness. And at last, may the sun and moon shine brightly and cast beautiful shadows among and over the tombstones for you and for me, my dear, and may a blessed hope make the sunset of life glorious for us both."

When he had finished reading, and had asked the driver to drive on, he became absorbed and silent, and I thought, "How strange to be riding through the streets of the city after midnight in a whirling snow-storm with a stranger, in a vehicle so remarkable, listening to such a pathetic love-story, such a beautiful description of quiet domestic life." It was a charming idyll.

"You can get an idea from this," he said, "of the delightful, contented life which went on in the little cottage," and he sat holding the book in his bands as though he were living it all over again, while the bright silver script monogram gleamed and glistened on the cover until he turned down the light, and for a time we drove over the smooth asphalt in utter silence.

"Do you wonder," he suddenly asked, "that the shadow of that little bird has caused me uneasiness, and yet do you not see that almost the last letter she wrote to me was filled with omens, shadows? It is but natural that I should have some feeling about it—and yet, why should I care? I have only myself and my two old servants who could be affected by it, bad or good. For myself, my only desire is to live long enough to complete my work; then I am both ready and willing to go. I shall welcome death with delight."

I had become so absorbed in his story that I had forgotten all about my surroundings; but now as he paused I again asked myself what strange connection had this sad story, and the letter, and all that he had been telling me, with the wagon; for I was sure that in some queer way the story would help to explain it all.

"While in Europe," he went on, "I studied the old masters a great deal, particularly the halos and nimbuses surrounding the heads of the saints. I cannot begin to tell you how interesting they became to me. I was struck with the exquisite workmanship bestowed on many of them, but fine as they were, they never came up to my idea of what a halo should be. As my loved one was so pure and gentle, I always thought of her as a saint (and indeed she is such), and I would become in-

terested and imagine what kind of halo I would surround her with if I were painting her—not one of the halos of the old masters seemed fine enough or ethereal
enough for her. I had always been fond of art, and had
been considered a fair amateur artist. One evening after
I had moved to the city, and while riding in a cab (oh,
how gloomy!) on a snowy evening something like this
very night, I looked through the window at an electric
light, and there I saw the loveliest halo, in miniature.
Such tints! A heavenly vision! I thought of the old masters, of the beautiful Siena Madonnas, and with sudden
joy I thought: 'Why should I not paint the image of her I
love? Why should I not clothe her in Madonna-like
robes, with a halo which could come only out of the
nineteenth century? Why should she not have a halo far
outshining and far surpassing in beauty halo ever
painted by mortal man?' I rode nearly the whole night
through, evidently to the despair of the driver, as I re-
peatedly asked him to stop opposite electric lights and
street-lamps.

"From that day I had a new purpose in life. I had
this wagon built just as you see it. For months I
thought of it. Over and over again I drew my plans before the vehicle was actually constructed. Then I began
my work. Old Cato, who is driving, sits night after night,
unmindful of the cold, wrapped in his great fur coat,
and he waits and I work through the midnight hours to
conceive and make real the new Madonna."

What a strange, subtle connection the whole thing
had, as he suddenly tapped on the small window and
we stopped directly in front of an electric light! As he
opened the sliding shutter I saw, through the frosted
window and the feathery snow, such a vision of loveliness—a little halo that could scarcely be described in
words. It was like a miniature circular rainbow, intensi-

fied and glorified by the glittering rays of the penetrating electric light.

"What could be more beautiful than that? Isn't it exquisite?" he asked. "Did ever painted saint have a halo like that?"

I held thy breath, for I had never seen anything so beautiful.

"I have worked at it for a long time. I have not yet accomplished it, but I hope to. I am coming nearer to it every night in which I can work. There are not many during the winter; the conditions of atmosphere and temperature must be just right. On foggy nights, or when the air is filled with light, flying snow—these are the nights in which the little halos glow around the electric lights, street-lamps, and lights in show-windows. "Oh," he said, "they fill me with a happiness and delight I cannot describe, as I try all kinds of experiments to transfix the beautiful colors of their delicate rays!

"Let me show you," he went on, and he lifted one of the frames which I have already described, covered with a thin parchment-like paper. This he carefully buttoned to a groove in the window. On the surface of the stretched parchment the little halo glowed with its prismatic tints, and again I held my breath at the beauty of it. I too was becoming a halo-worshiper. Then he lifted from the rack on the side, and held up to the light, first one and then another of the frames, on the parchment surface of which he had actually traced with lines of color, against the gloom beyond, radiating lines crossing and re-crossing, glowing with rainbow tints seen through and against the window.

"Do you know anything of Frankenstein's wonderful Magic Reciprocals, sometimes called Harmonic Responses?"[1] he asked. "How I longed for his marvelous power, so that I might experiment with them. But they were far beyond my skill, and also, perhaps, too scientific and geometrical for my purpose; and so I was forced to discard them and begin afresh in my own way. I have had reasonable success, although I have not yet reached the purity of color nor the brilliancy that I wish. I do not know that mortal man ever can. I have tried all sorts of experiments—lines of silver crossed with lines of gold; prismatic threads of silk; and now I have abandoned them all, and am beginning again, perhaps for the fortieth time. But if I am only able to do it, nothing

---

[1] The Magic Reciprocals, or Harmonic Responses, were discovered by Gustavus Frankenstein, and are properly drawn in color. The following are extracts from letters received from Mr. Frankenstein: "To-morrow morning I shall send them. They are transcendently lovely. They are halos, if ever there was a halo. So wonderfully magical are they that I think thou wilt modify thy language, and perhaps say that Frankenstein produces halos almost, if not quite, to the very perfection. Why, they seem to dazzle and bewilder like the very sun itself. They do not actually emit light, but they look like the *soul* of light. More like beautiful thoughts are they, spirits of loveliness, than like anything tangible."... "I was a long time working out the mathematical problem of the perfectly balanced and completely symmetrical circular harmonic responses; and then the drawings were executed with the greatest care as to perfect precision and accuracy."... "The little round white spot in the center imparts an animating expression to the whole Response; and now, as I write, it occurs to me very forcibly that the whole Response looks something like—and very much like—the iris of the eye, and the little round spot in the center is the pupil. If the iris were all iris, having no pupil in the center, it would appear expressionless and not vividly suggestive of the soul of life. The spot in the center may be looked upon as the tangible existence or thing which is the source of the surrounding halo. Again: The true and complete Response—the mathematical assertion—has the animating spot in the center."

can give me greater happiness. I can close my eyes in peace at last."

After he had shown me his experiments, he removed the little frame from the window, closed the sliding shutter on the side, and, turning the circular ventilator, asked the driver to drive on.

"Now for an extended view," he said, and he opened the shutter of one of the front windows, and then of the other on each side of the mirror. What a vista of loveliness! A long perspective of glowing halos, vanishing down the street through the flying snow, until they were mere specks of light in the distance. The whole atmosphere was filled with circular rainbows, and again he dwelt on their beauty. They glowed with ultramarine, with delicate green, with gold and silver, and like light from burnished copper, and our little vehicle seemed a moving palace of delight, as we drove on through the blinding storm. Turning into one of the narrower streets, away from the electric lights, we saw the long line of receding gas-lamps, each with its softly subdued nimbus, and he said in a low and gentle voice, almost a whisper, "The street of halos."

When he had closed the shutters again he said, "Let me show you my cabinet of colors and working tools." He pulled out a shallow drawer, and there on small porcelain plaques (the kind used by water-color painters) side by side, in regular order, was every shade of red, from the faintest pink to the deepest crimson. He opened the next drawer, and instead of the red was an arrangement of blues, from delicate turquoise to deepest ultramarine. In the third drawer was an arrangement of yellows, running from Naples to deepest cadmium.

"I deal in primary colors," he said, "for what would you paint rainbows in but red, blue, and yellow?"

Then he opened the fourth drawer, and there, laid with precision, were long-handled brushes from the finest sable (mere pin-points) up to thick ones as large as one's finger. There were flat ones and round ones, short ones and long ones. As he opened the fifth drawer, "For odds and ends," he said. This was a little deeper than the others, and in it were sponges fine and coarse, erasers, scrapers, and boxes of drawing-tacks of various sizes. In the last drawer were soft white rags and sheets of blotting-paper of assorted sizes.

After he had shown me the contents of the cabinet, he said, "I have been quite disturbed by the shadow of that little bird. Will you join me in a glass of old sherry?" He opened the locker underneath the seat, and brought out an odd-shaped bottle, which he unscrewed, handing me a small, thistle-shaped glass and a tin box containing crackers.

"It is a bad night," he said, "a very bad night. I feel it, even with the warmth of this interior. Those long bars of iron are filled with hot water, which usually keeps me very warm."

Then he passed through the ventilator, to the driver, some crackers and sherry. After he had closed it, and put away the bottle, box, and glasses, we both mused a long time, the halo-painter completely lost in reverie, and I thinking of the undying love of such a man—a man who could love but one, and for whom no other eyes or voice could ever mean so much. With him love was an all-absorbing passion. He had given his heart without reserve, and for him no other love could ever bloom again. I thought of him sitting, night after night, in his solitary vehicle working at the halo—the new halo which should surround the head of her he loved. I thought of him in the lonely early morning hours, working at a nimbus which was far to outshine in beauty and delicacy any painted or dreamed of by God-fearing saint-painters of old.

He opened the shutters, and the light from the lamp began to grow dimmer as the early morning light shone faintly through the windows. I noticed the deep furrows of care and sorrow which marked his strong, pathetic face, purified by suffering and lighted by divine hope—the face of one who lived in another world, and for whom all of life was centered in his ideal—one who was in the world, but not of it.

As be bade me good-by, his face beamed in the early Christmas morning light with indescribable tenderness; and as the little wagon its faithful old black driver disappeared through the snow, I thought again and again of the beautiful, touching love of the man who would sit night after night trying to realize his dream of beauty, to clothe in the garb of a saint the form of her he loved.

MY COUSIN FANNY

BY THOMAS NELSON PAGE (1853-1922)

Gilded Age society idealized marriage and woman's place in the home. People in most social circles felt sorry for unmarried women and, in fact, often joked about them. This humorous story illustrates the absurdity of measuring a woman's worth by her marital status. Why do you suppose Christmas always reminds the narrator of Cousin Fanny?

Christmas always brings up to me my cousin Fanny; I suppose because she always was so foolish about Christmas.

My cousin Fanny was an old maid; indeed, to follow St. Paul's turn of phrase, she was an old maid of the old maids. No one who saw her a moment could have doubted it. Old maids are a peculiar folk. They have from most people a feeling rather akin to pity—a hard heritage. They very often have this feeling from the young. This must be the hardest part of all—to see around them friends, each "a happy mother of children," little ones responding to affection with the sweet caresses of childhood, while any advances that they, their aunt or cousin, may make are met with indifference or condescension. My cousin Fanny was no exception. She was as proud as Lucifer yet she went through life—the part that 1 knew of—bearing the pity of the great majority of the people who knew her. This seemed to be quite natural.

She lived at an old place called "Woodside," which had been in the family for a great many years; indeed, ever since before the Revolution. The neighborhood dated back to the times of the colony, and Woodside was one of the old places. My cousin Fanny's grandmother had stood in the door of her chamber with her large scissors in her hand, and defied Tarleton's red-coated troopers to touch the basket of old communion-plate which she had hung on her arm.

The house was a large brick edifice, with a pyramidal roof, covered with moss, small windows, porticos with pillars somewhat out of repair, a big, high hall, and a staircase wide enough to drive up it a gig if it could have turned the corners. A grove of great forest oaks and poplars densely shaded it, and made it look rather gloomy, and the garden, with the old graveyard covered with periwinkle at one end, was almost in front, while the side of the wood—a primeval forest, from which the place took its name—came up so close as to form a strong, dark background. During the war the place, like most others in that neighborhood, suffered greatly, and only a sudden exhibition of spirit on Cousin Fanny's part saved it from a worse fate. After the war it went down; the fields were poor, and grew up in briers and sassafras, and the house was too large and out of repair to keep from decay, the ownership of it being divided between Cousin Fanny and other members of the family. Cousin Fanny had no means whatever, so that it soon was in a bad condition. The rest of the family, as they grew up, went off, compelled by necessity to seek some means of livelihood, and would have taken Cousin Fanny too if she would have gone; but she would not go.

They did all they could for her, but she preferred to hang around the old place, and to do what she could with her "mammy," and "old Stephen," her mammy's husband, who alone remained in the quarters. She lived in a part of the house, locking up the rest, and from time to time visited among her friends and relatives, who always received her hospitably. She had an old piece of a mare (which I think she had bought from Stephen), with one eye, three legs, and no mane or tail to speak of, and on which she lavished, without the least perceptible result, care enough to have kept a stable in condition. In a freak of humor she named this animal "Fashion," after a noted racer of the old times, which had been raised in the county, and had beaten the famous Boston in a great race. She always spoke of Fash with a tone of real tenderness in her voice, and looked after her, and discussed her ailments, which were always numerous, as if she had been a delicate child. Mounted on this beast, with her bags and bundles, and shawls and umbrella, and a long stick or pole, she used occasionally to make the tour of the neighborhood, and was always really welcomed; because, notwithstanding the trouble she gave, she always stirred things up. As was said once, you could no more have remained dull where she was than you could have dozed with a chinkapin burr down your back. Her retort was that a chinkapin bur might be used to rouse people from a lethargy (she had an old maid's tongue). By the younger members of the family she was always welcomed, because she furnished so much fun. She nearly always fetched some little thing to her host,—not her hostess,—a fowl, or a pat of butter from her one old cow, or something of the kind, because, she said, "Abigail had established the precedent, and she was 'a woman of good understanding'—she understood that feeding and flattery were the way to win men." She would sometimes have a chicken in a basket hung on the off pommel of her old saddle, because at times she fancied she could not eat anything but chicken soup, and she did "not wish to give trouble." She used to give trouble enough; for it generally turned out that she had heard some one was sick in the neighborhood, and she wanted the soup carried to her. I remember how mad Joe got because she made him go with her to carry a bucket of soup to old Mrs. Ronquist.

Cousin Fanny had the marks of an old maid. She was thin ("scrawny" we used to call her, though I remember now she was quite erect until she grew feeble); her features were sharp; her nose was inclined to be a little red (it was very straight); her hair was brown; and her eyes, which were dark, were weak, so that she had often to wear a green shade. She used to say herself that they were "bad eyes." They had been so ever since the time when she was a young girl, and there had been a very bad attack of scarlet fever at her home, and she had caught it. I think she caught a bad cold with it— sitting up nursing some of the younger children, per- haps,—and it had settled in her eyes. She was always very liable to cold.

I believe she had a lover then or about that time; but her mother had died not long before, and she had some notion of duty to the children, and so discarded him. Of course, as every one said, she'd much better have married him. I do not suppose he ever could have addressed her. She never would admit that he did, which did not look much like it. I think we used to speak of her as "sore-eyed"; I know she was once spo- ken of in my presence as "a sore-eyed old maid"—I have forgotten who said it. Yet I can now recall occasions when her eyes, being "better," appeared unusually soft, and, had she not been an old maid, would sometimes have been beautiful—as, for instance, occasionally, when she was playing at the piano in the evenings before the candles were lighted.

I recollect particularly once when she was singing an old French love-song. Another time was when on a certain occasion some one was talking about marriages and the reasons which led to or prevented them. She sat quite still and silent, looking out of the window, with her thin hands resting in her lap. Her head was turned away from most of the people but I was sitting where I could see her, and the light of the evening sky was on her face. It made her look very soft. She lifted up her eyes, and looked far off toward the horizon. I remember it recalled to me, young as I was, the speech I had heard some one once make when I was a little boy, and which I had thought so ridiculous, that "when she was young, before she caught that cold, she was almost beautiful." There was an expression on her face that made me think she ought always to sit looking out of the window at the evening sky. I believe she had brought me some apples that day when she came, and that made me feel kindly toward her. The light on her hair gave it a reddish look, quite auburn. Presently she withdrew her eyes from the sky, and let them fall into her lap with a sort of long, sighing breath, and slowly interlaced her fingers. The next second some one jocularly fired this question at her: "Well, Cousin Fanny, give us your views," and her expression changed back to that which she ordinarily wore.

"Oh, my views, like other people's, vary from my practice," she said. "It is not views, but experiences, which are valuable in life. When I shall have been married twice I will tell you."

"While there's life there's hope, eh?" hazarded some one; for teasing an old maid like her, in any way, was held perfectly legitimate.

"Yes, indeed," and she left the room, smiling, and

went upstairs.

This was one of the occasions when her eyes looked well. There were others that I remember, as sometimes when she was in church; sometimes when she was playing with little children; and now and then when, as on that evening, she was sitting still, gazing out of the window. But usually her eyes were weak, and she wore the green shade which gave her face a peculiar pallor, making her look old, and giving her a pained, invalid expression.

Her dress was one of her peculiarities. Perhaps it was because she made her clothes herself, without being able to see very well. I suppose she did not have much to dress on. I know she used to turn her dresses, and change them around several times. When she had any money she used to squander it, buying dresses for Scroggs's girls or for some one else. She was always scrupulously neat, being quite old-maidish. She said that cleanliness was next to godliness in a man, and in a woman it was on a par with it. I remember once seeing a picture of her as a young girl, as young as Kitty, dressed in a soft white dress, with her hair down over her ears, and some flowers in her dress (that is, it was said to be she; but I did not believe it). To be sure, the flowers looked like it. She always would stick flowers or leaves in her dress, which was thought quite ridiculous. The idea of associating flowers with an old maid! It was as hard as believing she ever was the young girl. It was not, however, her dress, old and often queer and ill-made as it used to be, that was the chief grievance against her. There was a much stronger ground of opposition; she had *nerves!* The word used to be strung out in pronouncing it, with a curve of the lips, as "ner-erves." I don't remember that she herself ever mentioned them; that was the exasperating part of it. She would never say a word; she would just close her thin lips tight, and wear a sort of ill look, as if she were in actual pain. She used to go up-stairs, and shut the door and windows tight, and go to bed, and have mustard-plasters on her temples and the back of her neck; and when she came down, after a day or two, she would have bright red spots burnt on her temples and neck, and would look ill. Of course it was very hard not to be exasperated at this. Then she would creep about as if merely stepping jarred her; would put on a heavy blue veil, and wrap her head up in a shawl, and feel along by the chairs till she got to a seat, and drop back in it, gasping. Why, I have even seen her sit in the room, all swathed up, and with an old parasol over her head to keep out the light, or some such nonsense, as we used to think. It was too ridiculous to us, and we boys used to walk heavily and stumble over chairs,—"accident-tally," of course,—just to make her jump. Sometimes she would even start up and cry out. We had the incon-testable proof that it was all "put on"; for if you began to talk to her, and got her interested, she would forget all about her ailments, and would run on and talk and laugh for an hour, until she suddenly remembered, and sank back again in her shawls and pains.

She knew a great deal. In fact, I recall now that she seemed to know more than any woman I have ever been thrown in with, and if she had not been an old maid, I am bound to admit that her conversation would have been the most entertaining I ever knew. She lived in a sort of atmosphere of romance and literature; the old writers and their characters were as real to her as we were, and she used to talk about them to us whenever we would let her. Of course, when it came from an old maid, it made a difference. She was not only easily the best French scholar in our region, where the ladies all knew more or less of French, but she was an excellent Latin scholar, which was much less common. I have often lain down before the fire when I was learning my Latin lesson, and read to her, line by line, Cesar or Ovid or Cicero, as the book might be; and had her render it into English as fast as I read. Indeed, I have even seen Horace read to her as she sat in the old rocking-chair after one of her headaches, with her eyes bandaged, and her bead swathed in veils and shawls, and she would turn it into not only proper English, but English with a glow and color and rhythm that gave the very life of the odes. This was an exercise we boys all liked and often engaged in,—Frank, and Joe, and Doug, and I, and even old Blinky,—for, as she used to admit herself, she was always worrying us to read to her (I believe I read all of Scott's novels to her). Of course this translation helped us as well as gratified her. I do not remember that she was ever too unwell to help us in this way except when she was actually in bed. She was very fond of us boys, and was always ready to take our side and to further our plans in any way whatever. We would get her to steal off with us, and translate our Latin for us by the fire. This, of course, made us rather fond of her. She was so much inclined to take our part and to help us that I remember it used to be said of her as a sort of reproach, "Cousin Fanny always sides with the boys." She used to say it was because she knew how worthless women were. She would say this sort of thing herself, but she was very touchy about women, and never would allow any one else to say anything about them. She had an old maid's temper. I remember that she took Doug up short once for talking about "old maids." She said that for her part she did not mind it the least bit; but she would not allow him to speak so of a large class of her sex which contained some of the best women in the world; that many of them performed work, and made sacrifices, that the rest of the world knew nothing about. She said the true word for them was the old

Saxon term "spinster"; that it proved that they performed the work of the house, and that it was a term of honor of which she was proud. She said that Christ had humbled himself to be born of a Virgin, and that every woman had this honor to sustain. Of course such lectures as that made us call her an old maid all the more. Still, I don't think that being mischievous or teasing her made any difference with her. Frank used to worry her more than any one else, even than Joe, and I am sure she liked him best of all. That may perhaps have been because he was the best looking of us. She said once that he reminded her of some one she used to know a long time before, when she was young. That must have been a long time before, indeed. He used to tease the life out of her.

She was extraordinarily credulous—would believe anything on earth any one told her, because, although she had plenty of humor, she herself never would deviate from the absolute truth a moment even in jest. I do not think she would have told an untruth to save her life. Well, of course we used to play on her to tease her. Frank would tell her the most unbelievable and impossible lies, such as that he thought he saw a mouse yesterday on the back of the sofa she was lying on (this would make her bounce up like a ball), or that he believed he heard—he was not sure—that Mr. Scroggs (the man who had rented her old home) had cut down all the old trees in the yard, and pulled down the house because he wanted the bricks to make brick ovens. This would worry her excessively (she loved every brick in the old house, and often said she would rather live in the kitchen there than in a palace anywhere else), and she would get into such a state of depression, that Frank would finally have to tell her that he was just "fooling her."

She used to make him do a good deal of waiting on

her in return, and he was the one she used to get to dress old Fashion's back when it was raw, and to put drops in her eyes. He got quite expert at it. She said it was a penalty for his worrying her so.

She was the great musician of the connection. This is in itself no mean praise; for it was the fashion for every musical gift among the girls to be cultivated, and every girl played or sang more or less, some of them very well. But Cousin Fanny was not only this. She had a way of playing that used to make the old piano sound different from itself; and her voice was almost the sweetest I ever heard except one or two on the stage. It was particularly sweet in the evenings, when she sat down at the piano and played. She would not always do it; she either felt "not in the mood," or "not sympathetic," or some such thing. None of the others were that way; the rest could play just as well in the glare of day as in the twilight, and before one person as another; it was, we all knew, just one of Cousin Fanny's old-maid crochets. When she sat down at the piano and played, her fussiness was all forgotten; her first notes used to be recognized through the house, and the people used to stop what they were doing, and come in. Even the children would leave off playing, and come straggling in, tiptoeing as they crossed the floor. Some of the other performers used to play a great deal louder, but we never tiptoed when they played. Cousin Fanny would sit at the piano looking either up or right straight ahead of her, or often with her eyes closed (she never looked at the keys), and the sound used to rise from under her long, thin fingers, sometimes rushing and pouring forth like a deep roar, sometimes ringing out clear like a band of bugles, making the hair move on the head and giving strange tinglings down the back. Then we boys wanted to go forth in the world on fiery, black chargers, like the olden knights, and fight giants and rescue beautiful ladies and poor women. Then again, with her eyes shut, the sound would almost die away, and her fingers would move softly and lingeringly as if they loved the touch of the keys, and hated to leave them; and the sound would come from away far off, and everything would grow quiet and subdued, and the perfume of the roses out of doors would steal in on the air, and the soft breezes would stir the trees, and we were all in love, and wanted to see somebody that we didn't see. And Cousin Fanny was not herself any longer, but we imagined some one else was there. Sometimes she suddenly began to sing (she sang old songs, English or French); her voice might be weak (it all depended on her whims; *she* said, on her health), in that case she always stopped and left the piano; or it might be "in condition." When it was, it was as velvety and mellow as a bell far off, and the old ballads and *chansons* used to fill the twilight. We used even to forget then that she was at old maid. Now and then she sang songs that no one else had ever heard. They were her own; she had composed both the words and the air. At other times she sang the songs of others to her own airs. I remember the first time I ever heard of Tennyson was when, one evening in the twilight, she sang his echo song from "The Princess." The air was her own, and in the chorus you heard perfectly the notes of the bugle, and the echoes answering, "Dying, dying, dying." Boy as I was, I was entranced, and she answered my enthusiasm by turning and repeating the poem. I have often thought since how musical her voice was as she repeated,

Our echoes roll from soul to soul,
And grow forever and forever.

She had a peculiarly sentimental temperament. As I look back at it all now, she was much given to dwelling upon old-time poems and romances, which we thought very ridiculous in any one, especially in a spinster of forty odd. She would stop and talk about the branch of a tree with the leaves all turning red or yellow or purple in the common way in which, as every one knows, leaves always turn in the fall, or even about a tangle of briers, scarlet with frost, in a corner of an old worm-fence, keeping us waiting while she fooled around a brier patch with old Blinky, who would just as lief have been in one place as another, so it was out of doors; and even when she reached the house she would still carry on about it, worrying us by telling over again just how the boughs and leaves looked massed against the old gray fence, which she could do till you could see them precisely as they were. She was very aggravating in this way. Sometimes she would even take a pencil or pen and a sheet of paper for old Blinky, and reproduce it. She could not draw, of course, for she was not a painter; all she could do was to make anything look almost just like it was.

There was one thing about her which excited much talk; I suppose it was only a piece of old-maidism. Of course she was religious.

She was really very good. She was considered very high church. I do not think from my recollection of her that she really was, or, indeed, that she could have been; but she used to talk that way, and it was said that she was. In fact, it used to be whispered that she was in danger of becoming a Catholic. I believe she had an aunt that was one, and she had visited several times in Norfolk and Baltimore, where it was said there were a good many. I remember she used to defend them, and say she knew a great many very devout ones. And she admitted that she sometimes went to the Catholic church, and found it devotional; the choral service, she said, satisfied something in her soul. It happened to be in the evening that she was talking about this. She sat down at the piano, and played some of the Gregorian chants she had heard, and it had a soothing influence on every one. Even Joe, the fidgetiest of all, sat quite still through it. She said that some one had said it was the music that the angels sing in heaven around the great white throne, and there was no other sacred music like it. But she played another thing that evening which she said was worthy to be played with it. It had some chords in It that I remembered long afterward. Years afterward I heard it played the same way in the twilight by one who is a blessed saint in heaven, and may be playing it there now. It was from Chopin. She even said that evening, under the impulse of her enthusiasm, that she did not see, except that it might be abused, why the crucifix should not be retained by all Christian churches, as it enabled some persons not gifted with strong imaginations to have a more vivid realization of the crucified Saviour. This, of course, was going too far, and it created considerable excitement in the family, and led to some very serious talk being given her, in which the second commandment figured largely. It was considered as carrying old-maidism to an extreme length. For some time afterward she was rather discountenanced. In reality, I think what some said was true: it was simply that she was emotional, as old maids are apt to be. She once said that many women have the nun's instinct largely developed, and sigh for the peace of the cloister.

She seemed to be very fond of artists. She had the queerest tastes, and had, or had had when she was young, one or two friends who, I believe, claimed to be something of that kind; she used to talk about them to old Blinky. But it seemed to us from what she said that artists never did any work; just spent their time lounging around, doing nothing, and daubing paint on their canvas with brushes like a painter, or chiseling and chopping rocks like a mason. One of these friends of hers was a young man from Norfolk who had made a good many things. He was killed or died in the war; so he had not been quite ruined; was worth something anyhow as a soldier. One of his things was a Psyche, and Cousin Fanny used to talk a good deal about it; she said it was fine, was a work of genius. She had even written some verses about it. She repeated them to me once, and I wrote them down. Here they are:

LINES TO GALT'S PSYCHE

Well art thou called the soul;
For as I gaze on thee,
My spirit, past control,
Springs up in ecstasy.

Thou canst not be dead stone;
For o'er thy lovely face,
Softer than music's tone,
I see the spirit's grace.

The wild Aeolian lyre
Is but a silken string,
Till summer winds inspire,
And softest music bring.

Psyche, thou wast but stone
Till his inspiring came:
The sculptor's hand alone,
Made not that soul-touched frame.

They have lain by me for years, and are pretty good for an old maid. I think, however, she was young when she addressed them to the "soul-touched" work of the young sculptor, who laid his genius and everything at Virginia's feet. They were friends, I believe, when she was a girl, before she caught that cold, and her eyes got bad.

Among her eccentricities was her absurd cowardice. She was afraid of cows, afraid of horses, afraid even of sheep. And bugs, and anything that crawled, used to give her a fit. If we drove her anywhere, and the horses cut up the least bit, she would jump out and walk, even in the mud; and I remember once seeing her cross the yard, where a young cow that had a calf asleep in the weeds, over in a corner beyond her, started toward it at a little trot with a whimper of motherly solicitude. Cousin Fanny took it into her head that the cow was coming at her, and just screamed, and sat down flat on the ground, carrying on as if she were a baby. Of course we boys used to tease her, and tell her the cows were coming after her. You could not help teasing an old maid like that.

I do not see how she managed to do what she did when the enemy got to Woodside in the war. That was quite remarkable, considering what a coward she was. During 1864 the Yankees on a raid got to her house one evening in the summer. As it happened, a young soldier, one of her cousins (she had no end of cousins), had got a leave of absence, and had come there sick with fever just the day before (the house was always a sort of hospital). He was in the boys' room in bed when the Yankees arrived, and they were all around the house before she knew it. She went downstairs to meet them. They had been informed by one of the Negroes that Cousin Charlie was there, and they told her that they wanted him.

She told them they could not get him. They asked her, "Why? Is he not there?" (I heard her tell of it once.) She said:

"You know, I thought when I told them they could not get him that they would go away, but when they asked me if he was not there, of course I could not tell them a story; so I said I declined to answer impertinent questions. You know poor Charlie was at that moment lying curled up under the bed in the boys' room with a roll of carpet a foot thick around him, and it was as hot as an oven. Well, they insisted on going through the house, and I let them go all through the lower stories; but when they started up the staircase I was ready for them. I had always kept, you know, one of papa's old horse-pistols as a protection.

Of course it was not loaded. I would not have had it loaded for anything in the world. I always kept it safely locked up, and I was dreadfully afraid of it even then. But you have no idea what a moral support it gave me, and I used to unlock the drawer every afternoon to see that it still was there all right, and then lock it again, and put the key away carefully.

Well, as it happened, I had just been looking at it— which I called inspecting my garrison. I used to feel just like *Lady Margaret* in Tillieludlam Castle. Well, I had just been looking at it that afternoon when I heard the Yankees were coming, and by a sudden inspiration—I cannot tell for my life how I did it—I seized the pistol, and hid it under my apron. I held on to it with both hands, I was so afraid of it, and all the time those wretches were going through the rooms downstairs I was quaking with terror. But when they started up the stairs I had a new feeling. I knew they were bound to get poor Charlie if he had not melted and run away,—no, he would never have run any; I mean evaporated,—and I suddenly ran up the stairway a few steps before them, and, hauling out my big pistol, pointed it at them, and told them that if they came one step higher I would cer-tainly pull the trigger. I could not say I would shoot, for it was not loaded. Well, do you know, they stopped! They stopped dead still. I declare I was so afraid the old pistol would go off, though, of course, I knew it was not loaded, that I was just quaking. But as soon as they stopped I began to attack. I remembered my old grandmother and her scissors, and, like General Jackson, I followed up my advantage. I descended the steps, brandishing my pistol with both hands, and abusing them with all my might. I was so afraid they might ask if it was loaded. But they really thought I would shoot them (you know men have not liked to be slain by a woman since the time of Abimelech), and they actually ran down the steps, with me after them, and I got them all out of the house. Then I locked the door and barred it, and ran up-stairs and had such a cry over Charlie. (That was like an old maid.) Afterward they were going to burn the house, but I got hold of their colonel, who was not there at first, and made him really ashamed of himself; for I told him we were nothing but a lot of poor, defenseless women and a sick boy. He said he thought I was right well defended, as I had held a company at bay. He finally promised that if I would give him some music he would not go up-stairs. So I paid that for my ransom, and a bitter ransom it was too, I can tell you, singing for a Yankee! But I gave him a dose of Confederate songs, I promise you. He asked me to sing the 'Star-spangled Banner'; but I told him I would not do it if he burnt the house down with me in it. Then he asked me to sing 'Home, sweet Home,' and I did that, and he actually had tears in his eyes—the hypocrite! He had very fine eyes too. I think I did sing it well, though. I cried a little myself thinking of the old house being so nearly burnt. There was a young doctor there, a surgeon, a really nice-looking fellow for a Yankee; I made him feel ashamed of himself, I tell you. I told him I had no doubt he had a good mother and sister up at home, and to think of his coming and warring on poor women. And they really placed a guard over the house for me while they were there."

This she actually did. With her old empty horse-pistol she cleared the house of the mob, and then vowed that if they burned the house she would burn up in it, and finally saved it by singing "Home, sweet Home" for the colonel. She could not have done much better even if she had not been an old maid.

I did not see much of her after I grew up. I moved away from the old county. Most others did the same. It had been desolated by the war, and got poorer and poorer. With an old maid's usual crankiness and inability to adapt herself to the order of things, Cousin Fanny remained behind. She refused to come away; said, I believe, she had to look after the old place, mammy, and Fash, or some such nonsense. I think she had some idea that the church would go down, or that the poor people around would miss her, or something equally unpractical. Anyhow, she stayed behind, and lived for quite a while the last of her connection in the county. Of course all did the best they could for her, and had she gone to live around with her relatives, as they wished her to do, they would have borne with her and supported her, though it would have been right hard on them. But she said no; that a single woman ought never to live in any house but her father's or her own; and we could not do anything with her. She was so proud she would not take money as a gift from any one, not even from her nearest relatives.

Her health got rather poor—not unnaturally, considering the way she divided her time between doctoring herself and fussing after sick people in all sorts of weather. With the fancifulness of her kind, she finally took it into her head that she must consult a doctor in New York for her ailments. Of course no one but an old maid would have done this; the home doctors were good enough for every one else. Nothing would do, however, but she must go to New York; so, against the advice of every one, she wrote to a cousin who was living there to meet her, and with her old wraps, and cap, and bags, and bundles, and old stick, and umbrella, she started. The lady met her; that is, went to meet her, but failed to find her at the station, and, supposing that she had not come, or had taken some other railroad, which she was likely to do, returned home, to find her in bed, with her "things" piled up on the floor. Some gentleman had come across her in Washington, holding the right train while she insisted on taking the Pittsburg route, and had taken compassion on her, and not only escorted her to New York, but had taken her and all her parcels, and brought her to her destination, where she had at once retired.

"He was a most charming man, my dear," she said to her cousin, who told me of it afterward, in narrating her eccentricities, "and, to think of it, I don't believe I had looked in a glass all day, and when I got here, my cap had somehow got twisted around and was perched right over my left ear, making me look a perfect fright. He told me his name, but I have forgotten it, of course. But he was such a gentleman, and to think of his being a Yankee! I told him I hated all Yankees, and he just laughed, and did not mind my stick, nor old umbrella, nor bundles a bit. You'd have thought my old cap was a Parisian bonnet. I will not believe he was a Yankee."

Well, she went to see the doctor, the most celebrated in New York—at the infirmary, of course, for she was too poor to go to his office; one consultation would have taken every cent she had. Her cousin went with her, and told me of it. She said that when she came downstairs to go, she never saw such a sight. On her head she had her blue cap, and her green shade, and her veil, and her shawl; and she had the old umbrella and long stick, which she had brought from the country, and a large pillow under her arm, because she "knew she was going to faint." So they started out, but it was a slow procession. The noise and bustle of the street dazed her, her cousin fancied, and every now and then she would clutch her companion and declare she must go back or she should faint. At every street-crossing she insisted upon having a policeman to help her over, or, in default of that, she would stop some man and ask him to escort her across, which, of course, he would do, thinking her crazy.

Finally they reached the infirmary, where there were already a large number of patients, and many more came in afterward. Here she shortly established an acquaintance with several strangers. She had to wait an hour or more for her turn, and then insisted that several who had come in after her should go in before her, because she said the poor things looked so tired. This would have gone on indefinitely, her cousin said, if she had not finally dragged her into the doctor's room. There the first thing that she did was to insist that she must lie down, she was so faint, and her pillow was brought into requisition. The doctor humored her, and waited on her. Her friend started to tell him about her, but the doctor said, "I prefer to have her tell me herself." She presently began to tell, the doctor sitting quietly by listening, and seeming to be much interested. He gave her some prescription, and told her to come again next day; and when she went he sent for her ahead of her turn, and after that made her come to his office at his private house, instead of to the infirmary as at first. He turned out to be the surgeon who had been at her house with the Yankees during the war. He was very kind to her. I suppose he had never seen anyone like her. She used to go every day, and soon dispensed with her friend's escort, finding no difficulty in getting about. Indeed, she came to be known on the streets she passed through, and on the cars she traveled by, and people guided her. Several times as she was taking the wrong car men stopped her; and said to her, "Madam, yours is the red car." She said, sure enough it was, but she never could divine how they knew. She addressed the conductors as "My dear sir," and made them help her not only off, but quite to the sidewalk, when she thanked them, and said "Good-by," as if she had been at home. She said she did this on principle, for it was such a good thing to teach them to help a feeble woman. Next time they would expect to do it, and after a while it would become a habit. She said no one knew what terror women had of being run over and trampled on.

She was, as I have said, an awful coward. She used to stand still on the edge of the street, and look up and down both ways ever so long; then go out in the street and stand still, look both ways and then run back; or as like as not, start on and turn and run back after she was more than half-way across, and so get into real danger. One day, as she was passing along, a driver had in his cart an old bag-of-bones of a horse, which he was beating to make him pull up the hill, and Cousin Fanny, with an old maid's meddlesomeness, rushed out in the street and caught hold of him and made him stop, which of course collected a crowd, and, just as she was coming back, a little cart came rattling along, and, though she was in no earthly danger, she ran so to get out of the way of the horse that she tripped and fell down in the street and hurt herself. So much for cowardice.

The doctor finally told her that she had nothing the matter with her, except something with her nerves and, I believe, her spine, and that she wanted company (you see she was a good deal alone). He said it was the first law of health ever laid down, that it was not good for man to be alone; that loneliness is a specific disease. He said she wanted occupation, some sort of work to interest her, and make her forget her aches and ailments. He suggested missionary work of some kind. This was one of the worst things he could have told her, for there was no missionary work to be had where she lived. Besides, she could not have done missionary work; she had never done anything in her life; she was always wasting her time pottering about the county on her old horse, seeing sick old darkies or poor people in the pines. No matter how bad the weather was, nor how deep the roads, she would go prowling around to see some old "aunty" or "uncle," in their out-of-the-way cabins, or somebody's sick child. I have met her on old Fashion in the rain, toiling along in roads that were knee-deep to get the doctor to come to see some sick person, or to get a dose of physic from the depot. How could she have done any missionary work?

I believe she repaid the doctor for his care of her by sending him a charity patient to look after—Scroggs's eldest girl, who was bedridden or something. Cousin Fanny had a fancy that she was musical. I never knew how it was arranged. I think the doctor sent the money down to have the child brought on to New York for him to see. I suppose Cousin Fanny turned beggar, and asked him. I know she told him the child was the daughter of "a friend" of hers (a curious sort of friend Scroggs was, a drunken reprobate, who had done everything he could to cheat her), and she took a great deal of trouble to get her to the train, lending old Fashion to haul her, which was a good deal more than lending herself; and the doctor treated her in New York for three months without any charge, till, I believe, the child got better. Old maids do not mind giving people trouble.

She hung on at the old place as long as she could, but it had to be sold, and finally she had to leave it; though, I believe, even after it was sold she tried boarding for awhile with Scroggs, the former tenant, who had bought it. He cheated her, in one way or another, out of all of her part of the money, claiming offsets for services rendered her, and treated her so badly that finally she had to leave, and boarded around. I believe the real cause was she caught him plowing with old Fashion.

After that I do not know exactly what she did. I heard that though the parish was vacant she had a Sunday school at the old church, and so kept the church open, and that she used to play the wheezy old organ and teach the poor children the chants; but as they grew up they all joined the Baptist church; they had a new organ there. I do not know just how she got on. I was surprised to hear finally that she was dead— had been dead since Christmas. It had never occurred to me that she would die. She had been dying so long that I had almost come to regard her as immortal, and as a necessary part of the old county and its associations.

I fell in some time afterward with a young doctor from the old county, who, I found, had attended her, and I made some inquiries about her. He told me that she died Christmas night. She came to his house on her old mare, in the rain and snow the night before, to get him to go to see some one, some "friend" of hers who was sick. He said she had more sick friends than any one he ever knew; he told her that he was sick himself and could not go; but she was so importunate that he promised to go next morning (she was always very worrying). He said she was wet and shivering then (she never had any idea about really protecting herself; her resources being exhausted in her fancies), and that she appeared to have a wretched cold. She had been riding all day seeing about a Christmas tree for the poor children. He urged her to stop and spend the night, but she insisted that she must go on, though it was quite dark and raining hard, and the roads would have mired a cat (old maids are so self-willed). Next day he went to see the sick woman, and when he arrived he found her in one bed and Cousin Fanny in another, in the same room. When he had examined the patient, he turned and asked Cousin Fanny what was the matter with her. "Oh, just a little cold, a little trouble in the chest, as Theodore Hook said," she replied. "But I know how to doctor myself." Something about her voice struck him. He went over to her and looked at her, and found her suffering from acute pneumonia. He at once set to work on her. He took the other patient up in his arms and carried her into another room, where he told her that Cousin Fanny was a desperately ill woman. "She was actually dying then, sir," he said to me, "and she died that night. When she arrived at the place the night before, which was not until after nine o'clock, she had gone to the stable her-self to put up her old mare, or rather to see that she was fed,—she always did that,— so when she got into the house she was wet and chilled through, and she had to go to bed. She must have had on wet clothes," he said.

I asked him if she knew she was going to die. He said he did not think she did; that he did not tell her, and she talked about nothing except her Christmas tree and the people she wanted to see. He heard her praying in the night, "and, by the way," he said, "she mentioned you. She shortly became rather delirious, and wandered a good deal, talking of things that must have happened when she was young; spoke of going to see her mother somewhere. The last thing she ever said was something about fashion, which," he said, "showed how ingrained is vanity in the female mind." The doctor knows something of human nature. He concluded what he had to say with, "She was in some respects a very remarkable woman—if she had not been an old maid. I do not suppose that she ever drew a well breath in her life. Not that I think old maids cannot be very acceptable women," he apologized. "They are sometimes very useful." The doctor was a rather enlightened man.

Some of her relatives got there in time for the funeral, and a good many of the poor people came; and she was carried in a little old spring wagon, drawn by Fashion, through the snow, to the old home place, where Scroggs very kindly let them dig the grave, and was buried there in the old graveyard in the garden, in a vacant space just beside her mother, with the children around her. I really miss her a great deal. The other boys say they do the same. I suppose it is the trouble she used to give us.

The old set are all doing well. Doug is a professor. He says the word "spinster" gave him a twist to philology. Old Blinky is in Paris. He had a picture in the salon last year, an autumn landscape, called *Le Cote du Bois.* I believe the translation of that is "The Woodside." His coloring is said to be nature itself. To think of old Blinky being a great artist! Little Kitty is now a big girl, and is doing finely at school. I have told her she must not be an old maid. Joe is a preacher with a church in the purlieus of a large city. I was there not long ago. He had a choral service. The Gregorian music carried me back to old times. He preached on the text, "I was sick, and ye visited me." It was such a fine sermon, and he had such a large congregation, that I asked why he did not go to a finer church. He said he was "carrying soup to Mrs. Ronquist." By the way, his organist was a splendid musician. She introduced herself to me. It was Scroggs's daughter! She is married, and can walk as well as I can! She had a little girl with her that I think she called

"Fanny." I do not think that was Mrs. Scroggs's name. Frank is now a doctor, or rather a surgeon, in the same city with Joe, and becoming very distinguished. The other day he performed a great operation, saving a woman's life, which was in all the papers. He said to an interviewer that he became a surgeon from dressing a sore on an old mare's back. I wonder what he was talking about. He is about to start a woman's hospital for poor women. Cousin Fanny would have been glad of that; she was always proud of Frank. She would as likely as not have quoted that verse from Tennyson's song about the echoes. She sleeps now under the myrtle at Scroggs's. I have often thought of what that doctor said about her: that she would have been a very remarkable woman, if she had not been an old maid—I mean, a spinster.

A NEIGHBOR'S LANDMARK

A WINTER STORY WITH A CHRISTMAS ENDING

BY SARAH ORNE JEWETT (1849-1909)

The American wilderness was ravaged by the industrialization of the nineteenth century. Old ways of life were often thrust aside in favor of "progress." Many writers observed and commented on the profound consequences of industrialization. The author of this story, Sarah Orne Jewett, offers a cautionary tale about the timber industry. This is a graceful account of the guardianship of nature and the powerful bond of community.

I

The timber-contractor took a long time to fasten his horse to the ring in the corner of the shed; but at last he looked up as if it were a matter of no importance to him that John Packer was coming across the yard. "Good day," said he; "good day, John." And John responded by an inexpressive nod.

"I was goin' right by, an' I thought I'd stop an' see if you want to do anything about them old pines o' yourn."

"I don't know's I do, Mr. Ferris," said John, stiffly.

"Well, that business is easy finished," said the contractor, with a careless air and a slight look of disappointment. "Just as you say, sir. You was full of it a spell ago, and I kind o' kep' the matter in mind. It ain't no plot o' mine, 'cept to oblige you. I don't want to move my riggin' nowhere for the sake o' two trees—one tree, you might say: there ain't much o' anything but firewood in the sprangly one. I shall end up over on the Foss lot next week, an' then I'm goin' right up country quick 's I can, before the snow begins to melt."

John Packer's hands were both plunged deep into his side pockets, and the contractor did not fail to see that he was moving his fingers nervously.

"You don't want 'em blowin' down, breakin' all to pieces right onto your grass-land. They'd spile pretty near an acre fallin' in some o' them spring gales. Them old trees is awful brittle. If you're ever calc'latin' to sell 'em, now's your time; the sprangly one's goin' back a'ready. They take the goodness all out o' that part o' your field, anyway," said Ferris, casting a sly glance as he spoke.

"I don't know's I care; I can maintain them two trees," answered Packer, with spirit; but he turned and looked away, not at the contractor.

"Come, I mean business. I'll tell you what I'll do: if you want to trade, I'll give you seventy-five dollars for them two trees, and it's an awful price. Buyin' known trees like them's like tradin' for a tame calf; you'd let your forty-acre piece go without no fuss. Don't mind what folks say. They're yourn, John; or ain't they?"

"I'd just as soon be rid on 'em; they've got to come down some time," said Packer, stung by this bold taunt.

"I ain't goin' to give you a present o' half their value, for all o' that."

"You can't handle 'em yourself, nor nobody else about here; there ain't nobody got proper riggin' to handle them butts but me. I've got to take 'em down for ye, fur's I can see," said Ferris, looking sly, and proceeding swiftly from persuasion to final arrangements. "It's some like gittin' a tooth hauled; you kind o' dread it, but when't is done you feel like a man. I ain't said nothin' to nobody, but I hoped you'd do what you was a-mind to with your own property. You can't afford to let all that money rot away; folks won't thank ye."

"What you goin' to give for 'em?" asked John Packer, impatiently. "Come, I can't talk all day."

"I'm a-goin' to give you seventy-five dollars in bank-bills," said the other man, with an air of great spirit.

"I ain't a-goin' to take it, if you be," said John, turning round, and taking a hasty step or two toward the house. As he turned he saw the anxious faces of two women at one of the kitchen windows, and the blood flew to his pinched face.

"Here, come back here and talk man-fashion!" shouted the timber-dealer. "You couldn't make no more fuss if I come to seize your farm. I'll make it eighty, an' I'll tell you jest one thing more: if you're holdin' out, thinkin' I'll give you more, you can hold out till dooms-day."

"When'll you be over?" said the farmer, abruptly; his hands were clenched now in his pockets. The two men stood a little way apart, facing eastward, and away from the house. The long, wintry fields before them sloped down to a wide stretch of marshes covered with ice, and dotted here and there with an abandoned haycock. Beyond was the gray sea less than a mile away; the far horizon was like an edge of steel. There was a small fishing-boat standing in toward the shore, and far off were two or three coasters.

"Looks cold, don't it?" said the contractor. "I'll be over middle o' the week some time, Mr. Packer." He unfastened his horse, while John Packer went to the unsheltered wood-pile and began to chop hard at some sour, heavy-looking pieces of red-oak wood. He stole a look at the window, but the two troubled faces had disappeared.

II

Later that afternoon John Packer came in from the barn; he had lingered out-of-doors in the cold as long as there was any excuse for born and passed away, and still these landmark pines lived their long lives, and were green and vigorous yet.

III

There was a fishing-boat coming into the neighboring cove, as has already been said, while Ferris and John Packer stood together talking in the yard. In this fishing-boat were two other men, younger and lighter-hearted if it were only for the reason that neither of them had such a store of petty ill deeds and unkindnesses to remember in dark moments. They were in an old dory, and there was much ice clinging to her, inside and out, as if the fishers had been out for many hours. There were only a few cod lying around in the bottom, already stiffened in the icy air. The wind was light, and one of the men was rowing with short, jerky strokes, to help the sail, while the other held the sheet and steered with a spare oar that had lost most of its blade. The wind came in flaws, chilling, and mischievous in its freaks. "I ain't goin' out any more this year," said the younger man, who rowed, giving a great shudder. "I ain't goin' to perish myself for a pinch o' fish like this"— pushing them with his heavy boot. "Generally it's some warmer than we are gittin' it now 'way into January. I've got a good chance to go into Otis's shoe-shop; Bill Otis was tellin' me he didn't know but he should go out West to see his uncle's folks,—he done well this last season, lobsterin',—an' I can have his bench if I want it. I do' know but I may make up some lobster-pots myself, eve- nin's an' odd times, and take to lobsterin' another sea- son—I know a few good places that Bill Otis ain't struck; and then the scarcer lobsters git to be, the more you git for 'em, so now a poor ketch's 'most better 'n a good one."

"Le' me take the oars," said Joe Banks, without at- tempting a reply to such deep economical wisdom.

"You hold that sheet light," grumbled the other man, "or these gusts'll have us over. An' don't let that old oar o' yourn range about so. I can't git no hold o' the water." The boat lifted suddenly on a wave and sank again in the trough, the sail flapped, and a great cold splash of salt water came aboard, floating the fish to the stern, against Banks's feet. Chauncey, grumbling heartily, be- gan to bail with a square-built wooden scoop for which he reached far behind him in the bow.

"They say the sea holds its heat longer than the land, but I guess summer's about over out here." He shivered again as he spoke. "Come, le's say this is the last trip, Joe."

Joe looked up at the sky, quite unconcerned. "We may have it warmer after we git more snow," he said. "I'd like to keep on myself until after the first o' the year, same's usual. I've got my reasons," he added. "But don't you go out no more, Chauncey."

"What you goin' to do about them trees o' Packer's?" asked Chauncey, suddenly, and not without effort. The question had been on his mind all the afternoon. "Old Ferris has laid a bet that he'll git 'em anyway. I signed the paper they've got down to Fox'l Berry's store to the Cove. A number has signed it, but I shouldn't want to be the one to carry it up to Packer. They all want your name, but they've got some feelin' about how you're situated. Some o' the boys made me promise to speak to you, bein' 's were keepin' together."

"You can tell 'em I'll sign it," said Joe Banks, flushing a warm, bright color under his sea-chilled skin. "I don't know what set him out to be so poor-behaved. He's a quick-tempered man, Packer is, but quick over. I never knew him to keep no such a black temper as this."

"They always say that you can't drive a Packer," said Chauncey, tugging against the uneven waves. "His mother came o' that old fightin' stock up to Boston; 't was a different streak from his father's folks—they was different-hearted an' all pleasant. Ferris has done the whole mean business. John Packer'd be madder 'n he is now if he knowed how Ferris is makin' a tool of him. He got a little too much aboard long ago's Thanksgivin' Day, and bragged to me an' another fellow when he was balmy how he'd rile up Packer into sellin' them pines, and then he'd double his money on 'em up to Boston; he said there wa'n't no such a timber pine as that big one left in the State that he knows on. Why, 't is 'most five foot through high's I can reach."

Chauncey stopped rowing a minute, and held the oars with one hand while he looked over his shoulder. "I should miss them old trees," he said; "they always make me think of a married couple. They ain't no common growth, be they, Joe? Everybody knows 'em. I bet you if anything happened to one of 'em t'other would go an' die. They say ellums has, mates, an' all them big trees."

Joe Banks had been looking at the pines all the way in; he had steered by them from point to point. Now he saw them just over Fish Rock, where the surf was whitening, and over the group of fish-houses, and began to steer straight inshore. The sea was less rough now, and after getting well into the shelter of the land he drew in his oar. Chauncey could pull the rest of the way without it. A sudden change in the wind filled the three-cornered sail, and they moved faster.

She'll make it now, herself, if you'll just keep her straight, Chauncey; no, 't wa'n't nothin' but a flaw, was it? Guess I'd better help ye"; and he leaned on the oar once more, and took a steady sight of the familiar harbor marks.

"We're right over one o' my best lobster rocks," said Chauncey, looking warm-blooded and cheerful again. "I'm satisfied not to be no further out; it's beginnin' to snow; see them big flakes a-comin'? I'll tell the boys about your signin' the paper; I d'know 's you'd better resk it, either."

"Why not?" said Joe Banks, hastily. "I suppose you refer to me an' Lizzie Packer; but she wouldn't think no more o' me for leavin' my name off a proper neighborhood paper, nor her father, neither. You git them two pines let alone, and I'll take care o' Lizzie. I've got all the other boats and men to think of besides me, an' I've got some pride anyway. I ain't goin' to have Boston folks an' all on 'em down to the Centre twittin' us, nor twittin' Packer he'll turn sour toward everybody the minute he does it. I know Packer; he's rough and ugly, but he ain't the worst man in town by a good sight. Anybody'd be all worked up to go through so much talk, and I'm kind o' 'fraid this minute his word's passed to Ferris to have them trees down. But you show him the petition; 't will be kind of formal, and if that don't do no good, I do' know what will. There, you git the sail in while I hold her stiddy, Chauncey."

IV

After a day or two of snow that turned to rain, and was followed by warmer weather, there came one of the respites which keep up New England hearts in December. The short, dark days seemed shorter and darker than usual that year, but one morning the sky had a look of Indian summer, the wind was in the south, and the cocks and hens of the Packer farm came boldly out into the sunshine, to crow and cackle before the barn. It was Friday morning, and the next day was the day before Christmas.

John Packer was always good-tempered when the wind was in the south. The milder air, which relaxed too much the dispositions of less energetic men, and made them depressed and worthless only softened and tempered him into reasonableness. As he and his wife and daughter sat at breakfast, after he had returned from feeding the cattle and horses, he wore a pleasant look, and finally leaned back and said the warm weather made him feel boyish, and he believed that he would take the boat and go out fishing.

"I can haul her out and fix her up for winter when I git ashore," he explained. "I've been distressed to think it wa'n't done before. I expect she's got some little ice in her now, there where she lays just under the edge of Joe Banks's fish-house. I spoke to Joe, but he said she'd do till I could git down. No; I'll turn her over, and make her snug for winter, and git a small boat o' Joe. I ain't goin' out a great ways; just so's I can git a cod or two. I always begin to think of a piece o' new fish quick's these mild days come; feels like the Janooary thaw."

"'Twould be a good day for you to ride over to Bolton, too," said Mrs. Packer. "But I'd like to go with you when you go there, an' I've got business here today. I've put the kettle on some time ago to do a little colorin'. We can go to Bolton some day next week."

"I've got to be here next week," said Packer, ostentatiously; but at this moment his heart for the first time completely failed him about the agreement with Ferris. The south wind had blown round the vane of his determination. He forgot his wife and daughter, laid down his knife and fork, and quite unknown to himself began to hang his head. The great trees were not so far from the house that he had not noticed the sound of the southerly breeze in their branches as he came across the yard. He knew it as well as he knew the rote of the beaches and ledges on that stretch of shore. He was meaning, at any rate, to think it over while he was out fishing where nobody could bother him. He wasn't going to be hindered by a pack of folks from doing what he liked with his own; but neither was old Ferris going to say what he had better do with his own trees.

"You put me up a bite o' somethin' hearty, mother," he made haste to say. "I sha'n't git in till along in the afternoon."

"Ain't you feelin' all right, father?" asked Lizzie, looking at him curiously.

"I be," said John packer, growing stern again for the moment. "I feel like a day out fishin'. I hope Joe won't git the start o' me. You seen his small boat go out?" He looked up at his daughter, and smiled in a friendly way, and went on with his breakfast. It was evidently one of his pleasant days he never had made such a frank acknowledgment of the lover's rights, but he had always liked Joe Banks. Lizzie's cheeks glowed; she gave her mother a happy glance of satisfaction, and looked as bright as a rose. The hard-worked little woman smiled back in sympathy. There was a piece of her best loaf cake in the round wooden luncheon box that day, and everything else that she thought her man would like and that his box would hold, but it seemed meager to her generous heart even then. The two women affectionately watched him away down the field path that led to the cove where the fish-houses were.

All the Wilton farmers near the sea took a turn now and then at fishing. They owned boats together sometimes, but John Packer had always kept a good boat of his own. Today he had no real desire to find a companion or to call for help to launch his craft, but finding that Joe Banks was busy in his fish-house, he went in to borrow the light dory and a pair of oars. Joe seemed singularly unfriendly in his manner, a little cold and strange, and went on with his work without looking up. Mr. Packer made a great effort to be pleasant; the south wind gave him even a sense of guilt.

"Don't you want to come, Joe?" he said, according to longshore etiquette; but Joe shook his head, and showed no interest whatever. It seemed then as if it would be such a good chance to talk over the tree business with Joe, and to make him understand there had been some reason in it; but John Packer could mind his own business as well as any man, and so he picked his way over the slippery stones, pushed off the dory, stepped in, and was presently well outside on his way to Fish Rock. He had forgotten to look for any bait until Joe had pushed a measure of clams along the bench; he remembered it now as he baited his cod-lines, sitting in the swaying and lifting boat, a mile or two out from shore. He had but poor luck; the cold had driven the fish into deeper water, and presently he took the oars to go farther out, and looking at the land for the first time with a consciousness of seeing it, he sighted his range, and turned the boat's head. He was still so near land that beyond the marshes, which looked narrow from the sea, he could see his own farm and his neighbors' farms on the hill that sloped gently down; the northern point of higher land that sheltered the cove and the fish-houses also kept the fury of the sea winds from these farms, which faced the east and south. The main road came along the high ridge at their upper edge, and a lane turned off down to the cove; you could see this road for three or four miles when you were as far out at sea. The whole piece of country most familiar to John Packer lay there spread out before him in the morning sunshine. The house and barn and corn-house looked like children's playthings; he made a vow that he would get out the lumber that winter for a wood-shed; he needed another building, and his wood-pile ought to be under cover. His wife had always begged him to build a shed; it was hard for a woman to manage with wet wood in stormy weather; often he was away, and they never kept a boy or man to help with farm work except in summer. "Joe Banks was terribly surly about some-thing," said Mr. Packer to himself. But Joe wanted Lizzie. When they were married he meant to put an ad-dition to the farther side of the house, and to give Joe a chance to come right there. Lizzie's mother was liable to be ailing; and needed her at hand. That eighty dollars would come in handy these hard times.

John Packer liked to be cross and autocratic, and to oppose people; but there was hidden somewhere in his heart a warm spot of affectionateness and desire for ap-proval. When he had quarreled for a certain time, he turned square about on this instinct as on a pivot. The self-love that made him wish to rule ended in making him wish to please; he could not very well bear being disliked. The bully is always a coward, but there was a good sound spot of right-mindedness, after all, in John Packer's gnarly disposition.

As the thought of the price of his trees flitted through John Packer's mind, it made him ashamed instead of pleasing him. He rowed harder for some distance, and then stopped to loosen the comforter about his neck. He looked back at the two pines where they stood black and solemn on the distant ridge against the sky. From this point of view they seemed to have taken a step nearer each other, as if each held the other fast with its branches in a desperate alliance. The bare, strong stem of one, the drooping boughs of the other, were indistinguishable, but the trees had a look as if they were in trouble. Something made John Packer feel sick and dizzy, and blurred his eyes so that he could not see them plain; the wind had weakened his eyes, and he rubbed them with his rough sleeve. A horror crept over him before he understood the reason, but in another moment his brain knew what his eyes had read. Along the ridge road came something that trailed long and black like a funeral, and he sprang to his feet in the dory, and lost his footing, then caught at the gunwale, and sat down again in despair. It was like the panic of a madman, and he cursed and swore at old Ferris for his sins, with nothing to hear him but the busy waves that glistened between him and the shore. Ferris had stolen his chance; he was coming along with his rigging as fast as he could, with his quick French wood-choppers, and their sharp saws and stubborn wedges to cant the trunks; already he was not far from the farm. Old Ferris was going to set up his yellow saw-dust-mill there—that was the plan; the great trunks were too heavy to handle or haul any distance with any trucks or sleds that were used nowadays. It would be all over before anybody could get ashore to stop them; he would risk old Ferris for that.

Packer began to row with all his might; he had left the sail ashore. The oars grew hot at the wooden tholepins, and he pulled and pulled. There would be three quarters of a mile to run up-hill to the house, and another bit to the trees themselves, after he got in. By that time the two-man saw, and the wedges, and the Frenchmen's shining axes, might have spoiled the landmark pines. "Lizzie's there—She'll hold 'em back till I come," he gasped, as he passed Fish Rock. "Oh, Lord! what a fool! I ain't goin' to have them trees murdered"; and he set his teeth hard, and rowed with all his might.

Joe Banks looked out of the little four-paned fish-house window, and saw the dory coming, and hurried to the door. "What's he puttin' in so for?" said he to himself, and looked up the coast to see if anything had happened; the house might be on fire. But all the quiet farms looked untroubled. "He's pullin' at them oars as if the devil was after him," said Joe to himself. "He couldn't have heard o' that petition they're gettin' up from none of the fish he's hauled in 'twill 'bout set him crazy, but I was bound I'd sign it with the rest. The old dory's jumpin' right out of water every stroke he pulls."

V

The next night the Packer farm-house stood in the winter landscape under the full moon, just as it had stood always, with a light in the kitchen window, and a plume of smoke above the great, square chimney. It was about half-past seven o'clock. A group of men were lurking at the back of the barn, like robbers, and speaking in low tones. Now and then the horse stamped in the barn, or a cow lowed; a dog was barking, away over on the next farm, with an anxious tone, as if something were happening that he could not understand. The sea boomed along the shore beyond the marshes; the men could hear the rote of a piece of pebble beach a mile or two to the southward; now and then there was a faint tinkle of sleigh-bells. The fields looked wide and empty; the unusual warmth of the day before had been followed by clear cold. Suddenly a straggling company of women were seen coming from the next house. The men at the barn clapped their arms, and one of them, the youngest, danced a little to keep himself warm.

"Here they all come," said somebody, and at that instant the sound of many sleigh-bells grew loud and incessant, and far-away shouts and laughter came along the wind, fainter in the hollows and loud on the hills of the uneven road. "Here they come! I guess you'd better go in, Joe; they'll want to have lights ready."

"She'll have a fire all laid for him in the fore room," said the young man; "that's all we want. She'll be expectin' you, Joe; go in now, and they'll think nothin' of it, bein' Saturday night. Just you hurry, so they'll have time to light up." And Joe went.

"Stop and have some talk with father," whispered Lizzie, affectionately, to her lover, as she came to meet him. "He's all worked up, thinking nobody'll respect him an' all that. Tell him you're glad he beat." And they opened the kitchen door.

"What's all that noise?" said John Packer, dropping his weekly newspaper, and springing out of his chair. He looked paler and thinner than he had looked the day before.

"What's all that noise, Joe?"

There was a loud sound of bells now, and of people cheering. Joe's throat had a lump in it; he knew well enough what it was, and could not find his voice to tell. Everybody in the neighborhood was coming, and they were all cheering as they passed the two old pines.

"I guess the neighbors mean to give you a little party to-night, sir," said Joe. "I see six or eight sleighs comin' along the road. They've all heard about it; some o' the boys that was here with the riggin' went down to the store last night, and they was all tellin' how you stood right up to Ferris like a king, an' drove him. You see, they're all gratified on account of having you put a stop to Ferris's tricks about them pines," he repeated. Joe did not dare to look at Lizzie or her mother, and in two minutes more the room began to fill with people, and John Packer, who usually hated company, was shaking hands hospitably with everybody that came.

Half an hour afterward, Mr. Packer and Joe Banks and Joe's friend Chauncey were down cellar together, filling some pitchers from the best barrel of cider. The guests were tramping to and fro overhead in the best room; there was a great noise of buzzing talk and laughter.

"Come, sir, give us a taste before we go up; it's master hot up there," said Chauncey, and the three men drank solemnly in turn from the smallest of the four pitchers; then Mr. Packer stooped again to replenish it.

"Whatever become o' that petition?" whispered Chauncey; but Joe Banks gave him a warning push with his elbow. "Wish ye merry Christmas!" said Chauncey, unexpectedly, to some one who called him from the stairhead. He had been king of his Christmas company up-stairs, but down here he was a little ashamed.

"Hold that light nearer," said Mr. Packer, "Come, Joe, I ain't goin' to hear no more o' that nonsense about me beatin' off old Ferris."

"Land! There's the fiddle," said Chauncey. "Le' 's hurry up"; and the three cup-bearers hastened back up the cellar stairs to the scene of festivity.

The two Christmas trees, the landmark pines, stood tall and strong on the hill looking down at the shining windows of the house. There was a sound like a summer wind in their tops; the bright moon and the stars were lighting them, and all the land and sea, that Christmas night.

A MISFIT CHRISTMAS
A MONOLOGUE: SPOKEN BY SONNY'S FATHER

BY RUTH McENERY STUART (1852-1917)

By the turn of the twentieth century, Christmas and consumerism were inextricably entwined. Stores competed for Christmas business by making the shopping experience more attractive and gift-giving more important. Most people's standard of living had improved during the Gilded Age, so they could afford to make frivolous purchases. This story is a wry account of Christmas gift-giving as seen through the eyes of an old Arkansas farmer named Deuteronomy Jones.

Well, well, well! Ef there ain't the doctor! At the steps befo' I discovered him! That's what I get for standin' on step-ladders at my time o' life. Ef you'd 'a' been a brigand you'd 'a' had me, doc—both hands up.

I was tempted o' the heathen by these big Japanese persimmons. 'Here, lay these on the banister-rail for me, doc—an' look out! Don't taste 'em, 'lessen you want yo' mouth fixed to whistle. That puckerin' trick runs in the family.

Yas, they're handsome, but gimme the little ol' woods persimmon, seedy an' wrinkled an' sugared by

199

the frost, character lines all over its face—same as a good ol' Christian.

Merry Christmas, old friend!—ef it is three days after.

This first shake is for "Merry Christmas," an' this is for thanks for yo' Christmas gif'. It did seem to be about the only one thet amounted—no, I won't say that, neither. They was all well-meant an' kind, an' I've been o' the edge of cryin' all day, thess to think—although—

But come along into my room an' see the things. Oh, yas; I reckon it was a sort of "ovation" to celebrate my seventy-fifth Christmas this-a-way an' to make it a surprise party, at that.

It seems thet Mary Elizabeth, Sonny's wife, give out along in the summer thet this was to be my seventy-fifth Christmas, an' invited accordin'ly—all the village an' country-side. She jest give it out promiscuous, tellin' everybody thet the only person thet *wasn't* to know about it was me—*on pain of not havin' it.* That was what you might call a stroke of ingeniousness. They ain't a person in the county thet would miss havin' an unusual thing like that, an' so the secret was pretty safe-t.

She never wrote no invitations. She'd thess tell every person she met to instruct the next one. So nobody's feelin's was hurted. She declares she never hinted about presents; but it must've been in her voice an' her intimations unbeknownst to herself, for not a mother's son or daughter come empty-handed. 'Sh-h-h! I notice the sewin'-machine has stopped an' she might— But I tell you here—'sh!—I say, I tell you, doc, *I can't turn around in my own room.* An' sech ridic— I tell you, *I never was so miserable in my life.*

Oh, of course, they's exceptions. There's yo' present, f'r instance. Sech a pocket-knife as that—why, it's a heredity! I've got it down in my will a'ready—that is to say, I've got it codiciled to my name-sake. What you say?

Oh, no; I wouldn't have no child named Deuteronomy, the way Sonny an' I was. He an' Mary Elizabeth, why, they offered it through excess of devotional feelin'. I see you recall the circumstance now. He's named after a certain auburn-haired doctor—an' yet, as I say, he's my namesake—named something else, for my sake. We jes call 'im doc for short.

Yas, he'll get that knife, though I hope to season it a little an' get the blades wore down some before he receives it.

It was real white in you to send sech a thing as that. A person might 'a' supposed thet you'd 'a' sent a fresh box o' porous plasters, or maybe a bottle o' lithia tab—

Why, no; of co'se I didn't fear it. How could I—an' be surprised? But ef I had been anticipatin' the party, I'd 'a' thought o' the drug-sto' show-case, an' they ain't never anything appetizin' in it to me. You cert'n'y deserve credit not even to select sech a thing as a hammock or a head-rest, although ef you had, I'd never 'a' questioned it.

Yes, I got a few head-rests, some stuffed with hops an' some with balsam, an' one poor neck-roll perfumed with something turrible—asafetida, I reckon. I've laid that out to sun. Mary Elizabeth says they're good to ward off whoopin'-cough, an' I told her I'd rather have the whoopin'-cough than it.

Oh, yas; the party was fine, an', as I said, they was a lump in my throat from the arrival of the first visitor, although it was Moreland Howe, an' you know I never hankered after Moreland. I reckon the reason my throat lumped up so at him comin' was the thought thet *even* Moreland had come to wish me joy. You see, he give my emotions a back lick—an' it's thess like 'im.

He brought me that ridic'lous thing hangin' from the swingin' lamp over my readin'-table in the hall here. What you say? "What is it?" God knows, doctor, an' he ain't told me. I suspicion it's thess a sort o' *eye-ketcher*,—to be looked at,—although I'd ruther look at almost anything I know. It's a thing thet, ef a person was anyways nervous, would either help him or hender him. He might find ease in tryin' to count the red an' purple worsted tassels, or the flies thet light on 'em; but ef he did, seem to me he would come to realize thet there was holes in the perforated paper thet couldn't be counted, an'—well, I don't like to discuss it. It's the kind o' thing *she* or *I* never liked—not thet I've ever seen its exact match.

The only use she ever had for perforated paper was to make crosses for pulpit book-marks—an' I've made 'em myself whilst she'd be darnin', thess startin' with one row o' between-holes an' cuttin' each one bigger until the desired size was reached, an' then pastin' 'em one on top o' the other, accordin' to size, so's the middle would rise up like sculpture. Then they're fastened on to the ends of ribbins to hang out in view o' the congregation. Now, there's a useful thing—an' suitable.

You know, Moreland was engaged to be married once-t, an' I suspicion thet this dangle is one of his engagement presents thet he's had laid away. I've got a consperacy in my mind thet'll rid me of it—in time. I'm goin' to tech it over keerfully with the attraction off o' fly-paper, quick as spring opens, an' when Moreland sees how they've ruined it, why, I'll drop it in the stove— *with regrets.*

He's dropped in twice-t a'ready sence it's hung there, thess to enjoy it, although he ain't crossed this threshold before but once-t in three year.

I tell you, doctor, they's nothin' thet stimulates friendship like givin'. Receivin' is cheap compared to it, as the Bible declares—in other words, of course.

Yes, but we were mighty sorry you couldn't come to the party, doctor; an' ef it had been anything but another birthday occasion thet kep' you away, we'd 'a' made a row about it. Of course the babies, bless their hearts! they must have all the attention thet they can't demand.

I tell you, things are a heap more equalized in this world than short-sighted mortals can discern.

You ain't seen the bulk o' the things yet, doctor. Wait a minute tel I have time to put on my hypocritical smile an' I'll take you in. We'll be ap' to meet Mary Elizabeth, an' I owe it to her particularly to be as deceitful an' act as cheerful as I can over it; in fact, I owe it to all them thet took part in it.

I wouldn't mind it so much ef I could shet my room door an' get into bed an' see the interior landscape thet I'm used to, but—

'Sh-h-h! I hear her slippers. She's heared you an' she's comin' out. Here's doc, daughter. An' I'm thess takin' 'im in to view my purties.

So now, I s'pose my popularity is in a manner proved, as you say, an' it's all mighty fine an' gratifyin'. But after I've lived with my constituency for a while, so to speak, I'm goin' to get you to separate 'em, Mary Elizabeth, an' let the whole house feel it. No, don't say a word! It's got to be done. Do you think I'm that selfish thet I'd appropriate all the combined popularity of daughter an' son an' gran'children!

The truth is, doc, this has got to be a turrible popular house sence Sonny has been elected school director an' little Marthy is old enough to have a choice o' hairribbins. An' Mary Elizabeth she always was popular. An' I see she's lookin' at her watch: we're keepin' 'er too long. I s'pose a watch gets looked in the face the first week of its ownership often enough to lose countenance forever except it knew it would have plenty of retirement, later on. Most ladies' watches lead lives of leisure.

Yas, I give it to her. I think every lady should have a good gold watch an' chain, ef for nothin' else on account o' the children rememberin' "ma with her watch an' chain." An' the various daguerreotypes looks well with 'em. It's a part o' gentility, a lady's watch is, whether it 's kep' wound up or not.

An' in case o' breakin' up a home, a watch looks well on the inventory. Little Marthy—her grandma's namesake—of course she's got *hers*, an' it ain't no mean timepiece, neither. It's got a live purple amethyst on one side, an' the chain goes around twice-t—an' ef the day comes when she wants to take my old picture out o' the case an' put in a younger man's, I'll be that much better pleased to know thet joy stays with us, along with time.

I wonder ef that ain't a purty fair joke, doctor, for a seventy-fiver—settin' among his troubles, too.

I'm glad she slipped away. She's sech a modest little thing—went thess as soon as I referred to her popularity. I wouldn't 'a' wanted her to stay an' look over my presents with you. It'd 'a' made me tongue-tied. Come along, doc. That's right. You lif' *that* an' I'll pull *this* back whilst I shet the door with my foot.

I tried to open that door yesterday from my bed the way I've always done, but by the time I'd got the things out o' the way they wasn't anything left to use but my teeth, an' ruther than resk my plate on that glass door-knob I got up an' h'isted a few things on to the bed—an' the rebellion thet came into my heart I'd like to forget I've doubted the doctrine of total depravity all my life, as you know, but maybe it's so, after all—in my case, at least. I reckon, like as not, all doctrines is true, more or less, in some lights, or else so many people wouldn't see their ways to belevin' 'em.

The way I've sinned over these presents has filled me with regretful remorse.

Look out! Don't step! Wait a minute! Some o' the children has wound it up. I hear it whir. Here it comes from under the bed. We must've shook the floor.

What do you think o' that, now? Sir? Why, it's said to be a seed-counter. Jim Bowers brought it. He says thet when it travels that-a-way it's prowlin' for food an' it craves peas an' beans to count.

What's that you say? "Did I give it any?" No, I didn't. Not a one. I was too nettled to give Jim that satisfaction. I know it's some dod-blasted patent thet he's been took in with, an' he thought thet bein' as I was in my second childhood, I'd be tickled over it—an' I got contrary.

I really wouldn't care so much ef the thing wasn't so all-fired big. It takes up as much floor-room as a chair, an' I'm compelled to keep it in sight for a while. Who in thunder wants seeds counted, even ef the fool thing could do it? It's more like a toe-snatcher, to me; an' I intend to have it chained to the table-leg, a safe-t distance from my bed. I never did like the idee of havin' my bare feet nabbed in the dark.

Our littlest he's mighty mischievious, an' no doubt he heared me an' you start to come in, an' he's sneaked in an' wound up— Look out there! I say he's been in here an' wound up things. That ain't nothin' but a mechanical rooster, but you don't want to step on it. See him stretch his neck an'—did you ever hear anything so ridic'lous! I s'pose I must ac' mighty childish for people to fetch me sech presents. An' yet, I ruther like that rooster. It tickles me to see the way he exerts hisself.

Hold on, doc! That's on the bureau an' it can't do you no harm. Yas, he's wound 'em all up, the little scamp, an' like as not he's watchin' us from somewheres.

Thess to think, doc, thet we was boys once-t. It's the fullest-to-the-brim of happiness of all the cups of life, boyhood is, I do believe.

Don't start! Thet's thess a donkey savin's-bank, an' it'll "yee-haw!" that-a-way now tel a nickel's dropped in its slotted ear. He's the family favoryte of all the presents, an' he's heavy with money a'ready. What's that you say? "He'll bray tel he runs down"? But he don't never run down—not within the limit of human endurance.

They say they're the best money-savers on the market. They're so ridic'lous, 'most anybody'll spend a little change to see 'em perform. The feller showed his genius in makin' the deposit go to hushin' 'em. He knew thet once-t he got started, a man would give his last cent to silence him. Did you ever hear so much sound out of sech a little— An' his last bray is as loud as his first.

Here, drop this in his ear, for gracious' sakes, so we can talk.

Oh, them? They're picture-frames constructed out o' chicken-bones.

I s'pose maybe they's jestice in this museum, but they don't seem to be mercy.

It seems thet a lady down in Ozan has been givin' lessons in makin' 'em. Yas, chicken-bones steeped in diamond dyes; an' they say they's seven kinds o' flowers an' four fruits represented. I ain't studied 'em out yet, but I can see they've used drumsticks for buds, mostly. An' the neck-j'ints, unj'inted, they're wide-open perrarer-flowers.

The heads is seed-pods, an' so is the popes'-noses; an' I have an idee thet the chrysanthe'ums an' asters is constructed mainly of ribs. Of course it'd take a number, but on a farm—

Why, yas; I s'pose it is purty—uncommon purty— considerin'; but in things of beauty I don't like to have to consider, an' the thing don't appetize me worth a cent.

Them gum-ball frames, now, an' the sycamores an' pine-cones do very well.

But when it comes to framin' my relations, I sort o' like to put my hand in my pocket an' do 'em store-jestice. An' these nature-frames they ketch dust an' harbor spiders considerable.

Between you an' me, I don't intend to give them graveyard chicken-frames house room more 'n thess so long, an' the only real use I can think to put 'em to is a raffle; so I'll donate 'em to the next county fair to be raffled for expenses. You see, they'd be suitable for the flower, fruit, an' fowl departments, an' they pleg me, thess knowin' they're here.

Mary Elizabeth she ain't give no opinion of 'em yet, an' she may consider 'em suitable to frame a couple o' stuffed birds she's got; an' ef she does, why, she's welcome. She'd likely gild hers to match the pine-cone frame round her mother. She's got it trimmed with a piece of her ma's favoryte silk dress, fastened in one corner by a little pin she used to wear. She considers suitableness in everything, Mary Elizabeth does.

These slippers I've got on was her present. She worked the initials, an' they're lined with a scrap o' one o' wife's old wool dresses, an' I like to know it.

That new readin'-lamp? Why, Sonny he give me that. The old one was good enough a-plenty, but it seems thet these new ones have special organdy burners—or no, I reckon it was the old one thet had the organdy burner, an' this one is to wear a mantle, he says. Either one reminds me of her,—either the organdy or the mantle,—an', of course, I need the best light now for my night chapter o' the gospel. The little feller—why, he made the stand it sets on, an' the mats was crocheted by the girls. Oh, I got lots of nice suitable things, an' I appreciate everything, nice or not, exceptin' that seed-counter, an' I never will be reconciled to bein' made cheap of. I hate a fool, even when it's inanimate.

Yas, that's a map o' the world. Henry Burgess brought that. Yas, it does seem a nice thing, an' I said so, too, an' I'm glad I did befo' I saw the date on it. After that, I'd 'a' been compelled either to pervaricate or to fail in politeness, an' it's always easier to fall on a piller than into a brier-patch.

I've looked for places I know on it, but it's either non-committal or I'm not observant enough. They don't seem to be no Philippine Islands on it whatsoever, but like as not they wasn't thought much of then an' they're secreted somewhere.

I always did like the look of a wall-map, —when I go into an office or court-house, —but I doubt whether I'll ever fully relish this on my own wall. A clock thet won't keep truthful time always plegs me, an' this threatens me the same way.

Oh, no; that ain't to say a toy, exac'ly—that nigger doll on the mantel. It's a pincushion; an' the heathen Chinee, why, he's a holder of shavin'-paper; an' the stuffed cat it's a foot-rest. I notice it's mouse-e't at the corners, so the connoziers ain't deceived.

I see somethin' has stole the hickory-nut head o' the toothpick lady a'ready, an' I suspect it's the flyin'-squirrel I caught sniffin' at her yesterday.

An' that pile o' ribbins? Oh, they've come off o' all the things. That was the first thing I don; rippin' them off. They'd ketch in my hands so an' gimme goose-skin the len'th o' my spine.

I've passed them over to Mary Elizabeth, an' she'll likely work 'em into crazy-patches or hair-ribbins for the girls.

That? Excuse me whistlin'. That's whisky, doctor. An' who do you reckon sent it? Who but Miss Sophia Falena Simpkins, the twin—an' they both teetotalers!

Shows their confidence in me. "How old is it?" Well, she allowed it was as old as they are, an' of co'se that stopped my inquiry, but it's old enough to be treated with respect an' not abuse. Yas, that four-in-hand neck-tie it was tied on its neck—from the other twin. Yas, it's the reverend stuff, an' that thimble-sized, hat-shaped glass over the cork seems to stand for their maidenly consciences, an' I won't never violate the hint.

That shoe-an'-slipper holder with all the nests in it was sent in by our chapter of the King's Daughters, each daughter contributin' one nest, as I understand it; an' it's ornamental on the wall, although my one contribution looks middlin' lonesome in it. Of co'se I always have on either my slippers or my boots, an' when I get into bed it's unhandy to cross the room thess to put my boots up in style.

The first night it hung there the children all come an' put in their shoes for the night, but that was awkward. They'd have to come an' go bare-feeted. Yas, the motter is suitable enough. "Rest for tired soles" is about as inoffensive as a motter could well be. An' so is this, on one o' the umbrella-holders, "Wait tel the clouds roll by," although it seems a sort o' misfit for an umbrella. "When it rains it pours" would be more to my mind. Yas, I've got three. "Little drops of water," this one seems to have on it; an' this one says—I never can read them German-tex' letters. What's that you say? "Expansion for protection only"? It's well to be highly educated like you, doctor. I wouldn't 'a' made that out in a week. But do you know it sounds sort o' deep-seated, like as ef more was meant than you see at first? I wonder ef it could refer to politics, some way. "Expansion for protection only." It cert'n'y sounds political.

Yas, they did fetch a ridic'lous lot o' pen-wipers, for a person o' my sedate habits. I never did fly to the pen much. You see, when a present is more or less obligatory, why, a pen-wiper is an easy way out. Almost any shape repeated an' tacked in the middle with some sort o' centerpiece, like an odd button, rises into prominence with the look of a present.

Of co'se I have written letters, from time to time, in days past. I was countin', only last Sunday, the letters I've written in my life, an', includin' my proposal-letter, which I wrote an' handed to her personal, on account o' the paralysis of my tongue—I say, countin' that, I've wrote seven letters all told; an' I regret to say, one of the seven was writ in anger, an' two in apology for it, so thet they's only four real creditable letters to my credit, an' one o' the four wasn't to say extry friendly, although it sounded well.

That was the one I wrote to Sally Ann, time her first husband, Teddy Brooks, died. Poor Teddy could easy 'a' been kep' livin' along a few years more, ef not permanent, ef he'd been looked after an' excused from so much motherly cradle service. Of co'se I knew Sally Ann, an' thet she was nachelly a public performer, an' would be readin' 'er letters of consolation out loud to whoever dropped in, an' I composed it accordin'. An' so she did, for she wrote me thet my note of condolence was the most eloquent of all she got—"so everybody said."

I don't suppose Sally Ann ever took a moment's comfort in seclusion in her life, no more 'n a weathervane. Poor Sally!

But talkin' about this excessive circulation of presents thet's come into fashion these last years, I don't approve of it, doctor; an' you know it ain't thet I'm stingy about doin' my part. I'll give a present, ef need be, an' I'll even command the grace to take one,—I seem to 've proved that,—but it's the principle of the thing thet troubles my mind.

Some of our best-raised girls has got flighty that-a-way after goin' to boa'din'-school, where they learn a heap more 'n Latin verbs an' finishin' behavior. Not thet I don't appreciate what they do acquire. It seems to lift 'em into a higher region of ladyhood, I know, an' it's a thing you can't locate. Wife had a year at Hilltop Academy, an' I always thought she showed it, even in the way she'd gether eggs in 'er apron, or keep still tel another person quit speakin'. But of co'se they's boa'din'-schools an' boa'din'-schools, an' them thet fosters idle hands I don't approve of; an' the fact that a parent may be able to pay for it ain't got nothin' to do with the divine responsibility as I see it. The idee of an earthly parent bein' willin' to put up big money to have his own flesh an' blood incapacited for misfortune!

Oh, yas; they give me considerable books. They've complimented my education to that extent. This "pronouncin'-Testament," for instance, I seized with delight, hopin' to get the real patriarchal pronunciations. I wanted to see if sech jokes as "Milk-easy-Dick" an' "Knee-high-miah" and "Build-dad-the-shoe-height" was legitimate frivolity, but I ain't had no luck so far. I sort o' wonder what kind of a man would aspire to write a Bible-pronouncer. You know sence Sonny's taken to writin' books, an' we've had an author's readin' here, I always seem to discern a person behind every volume.

Yas; they're usin' several of Sonny's nature-books in the schools now, an' he has mo' orders 'n he can fill, but he won't never hurry. You know he never did.

He'll study over a thing tel he's satisfied with it, before any temptation would induce him to write about it. That's why he gets sech high prices for what he does.

It don't have to be contradicted, an' no pleasure of the imagination will make him lead a dumb beast into behavior thet's too diplomatic or complicated.

He's done some jocular experimentin',—set eggs under inappropriate beasts an' sech as that,—but he ain't had no luck. All our beasts-of-a-hair seem to flock together same as birds of a feather. He 'lows thet he's often seen expressions on our dog's face thet looked as ef he might be capable of intrigue or religious exaltation, but Sonny ain't felt justifiable in ascribin' motives thess on his facial indications—not even when it's backed by the expression of his tail.

You ain't goin'? Well, I know how it is, an' I'm a friend to all the sick, so I won't keep you. Yo' visit has done me good, doctor. I always did love to hear you talk. We agree an' disagree thess enough for sugar an' spice. Oh, yas; it's been a merry Christmas; no doubt about that. An' the fun ain't fully over, either. I'll amuse myself with the presents thet's been adjudged suitable to my mind, when time hangs too heavy. I thought last night thet some time I'd empty that bottle o' iron-pills I never took—I'd empty 'em into the seed-counter when it was on some of its travels; an' ef it knew the difference an' spurned to count 'em, I'd try to have some respect for its intellect.

Good-by, doc, an' a merry Christmas!

Surely, say it again: "Merry Christmas!" That lasts here tel we can say "Happy New Year!" They say our Christmas laughter was heared clair acrost Chinque-pin Creek, an' ol' Mis' Gibbs, settin' there paralyzed in her chair, she laughed with us whilst she enjoyed the basket-dinner Mary Elizabeth sent her.

Yas, them are her cardin'-combs. She couldn't come to the surprise party, so she sent them to me. Her hands refuse to hold 'em any longer, an' she allowed no doubt thet I might while away my last moments that-away. But of co'se she didn't know me. I may be old an' childish, but even ef I was to turn baby again, I'd be a boy-baby. Yas, I know I could use 'em, but I won't. It's true I made Bible book-marks, but they was for a man to preach by, an' a housewifey woman set beside me, sewin' whilst I made 'em. That was enough to difference me. Why, ef I was to get so sedated down thet I could set up here an' do feminyne work, I'd be belittled, an' no man can stand that.

Well, good-by, ef you must. Here, ol' friend, gimme yo' hand an' lemme hold it still thess a minute. So much of our earthly hand-shakin' is thess touch an' go—an' I like to realize a friend's hand once-t in a while.

An' now I've got it, I want to keep it whilst I say somethin'. Settin' here these long hours sence this blessed Christmas day, which, after all my jocular ana-lyzin', has moved me to tears, I've had a *thought* —a thought which has give me comfort, an' I'm goin' to pass it on to you.

Settin' here, amongst my misfit presents, yesterday, mad one minute an' chokin' with laughter an' throat-lumps the next, I suddenly seemed to hear a line o' the old hymn, "My Christmas will last all the year," an' then I was thankful thet my 'Piscopal experience had fur-nished me a ready answer to that: "Good Lord, deliver us!"

An' then, with my funny-bone fairly trimblin' an' my risible eye on the fly-catcher, the sweetest thought came to me—like a white bird out of a wind-storm:

Harassed as I was with all these presents, I couldn't seem to contemplate a continuous Christmas of peace, noways, when suddenly I seemed to see the words befo' me, differently spelled. Instid of "e-n-t-s" I saw "e-n-c-e" an' right befo' my speritual vision I saw, like sky-writin', "The Christmas Presence"—thess so.

Maybe it won't strike you, but it was a great thought to me, doctor, an' "Christmas all the year" had a new sound to my ears.

Think of that, doctor—of livin' along in the azurine blue, beholdin' the face of the Little One of the manger by the near light of the Bethlehem star! Or maybe seein' the Beloved leanin' on a piller of clouds, illuminin' our listenin' faces with the gleam of his countenance whilst he'd maybe repeat the Sermon on the Mount from the book of his eternal memory. Think of what an author's readin' that would be—an' what an audience!

An' it's this Christmas Presence thet inspires all our lovin' thoughts here below, whether we discern it or not.

An' what we'll get on the other side'll be *realization*— a clair vision with all the mists of doubt dissolved.

This is the thought thet come to me yesterday, doctor, out o' the cyclone of playful good will thet got me so rattled. An' it's come to stay.

An' with it, how sweet it will be to set an' wait, with a smile to welcome the endurin' Christmas thet'll last "all the year" an' forever.

THE SNOW-BABIES'
CHRISTMAS

BY JACOB A. RIIS

This story is a fictional account of Christmas at Coney Island's Sea Breeze Hospital, which offered outdoor therapy to crippled children from the tenements. The therapy was very successful and the hospital received high praise from President Theodore Roosevelt. The Snow-Babies' Christmas tells the story of a little boy whose life view is transformed by the restorative powers of fresh air, innocent play, and the tender regard of caring adults.

All aboard for Coney Island!" The gates of the bridge train slammed, the whistle shrieked, and the cars rolled out past rows of houses that grew smaller and lower to Jim's wondering eyes, until they quite disappeared beneath the track. He felt himself launching forth above the world of men, and presently he saw, deep down below, the broad stream with ships and ferry-boats and craft going different ways, just like the tracks and traffic in a big, wide street; only so far away was it all that the pennant on the topmast of a vessel passing directly un-

215

der the train seemed as if it did not belong to his world at all. Jim followed the white foam in the wake of the sloop with fascinated stare, until a puffing tug bustled across its track and wiped it out. Then he settled back in his seat with a sigh that had been pent up within him twenty long, wondering minutes since he limped down the Subway at Twenty-third Street. It was his first journey abroad.

Jim had never been to the Brooklyn Bridge before. It is doubtful if he had ever heard of it. If he had, it was as of something so distant, so unreal, as to have been quite within the realm of fairyland, had his life experience included fairies. It had not. Jim's frail craft had been launched in Little Italy, half a dozen miles or more up-town, and there it had been moored, its rovings being limited at the outset by babyhood and the tenement, and later on by the wreck that had made of him a castaway for life. A mysterious something had attacked one of Jim's ankles, and, despite ointments and lotions prescribed by the wise women of the tenement, had eaten into the bone and stayed there. At nine the lad was a cripple with one leg shorter than the other by two or three inches, with a stepmother, a squalling baby to mind for his daily task, hard words and kicks for his wage; for Jim was an unprofitable investment, promising no returns, but, rather, constant worry and outlay. The outlook was not the most cheering in the world.

But, happily, Jim was little concerned about things to come. He lived in the day that is, fighting his way as he could with a leg and a half and a nickname,— "Gimpy" they called him for his limp,—and getting out of it what a fellow so handicapped could. After all, there were compensations. When the gang scattered before the cop, it did not occur to him to lay any of the blame to Gimpy, though the little lad with the pinched face and sharp eyes had, in fact, done scouting duty most craftily. It was partly in acknowledgment of such services, partly as a concession to his sharper wits, that Gimpy was tacitly allowed a seat in the councils of the Cave Gang, though in the far "kid" corner. He limped through their campaigns with them, learned to swim by "dropping off the dock" at the end of the street into the swirling tide, and once nearly lost his life when one of the bigger boys dared him to run through an election bonfire like his able-bodied comrades. Gimpy started to do it at once, but stumbled and fell, and was all but burned to death before the other boys could pull him out. This act of bravado earned him full membership in the gang, despite his tender years; and, indeed, it is doubtful if in all that region there was a lad of his age as tough and loveless as Gimpy. The one affection of his barren life was the baby that made it slavery by day. But, somehow, there was that in its chubby foot groping for him in its baby sleep, or in the little round head pillowed on his shoulder, that more than made up for it all.

Ill luck was surely Gimpy's portion. It was not a month after he had returned to the haunts of the gang, a battle-scarred veteran now since his encounter with the bonfire, when "the Society's" officers held up the huckster's wagon from which he was crying potatoes with his thin, shrill voice, which somehow seemed to convey the note of pain that was the prevailing strain of his life. They made Gimpy a prisoner, limp, stick, and all. The inquiry that ensued as to his years and home setting, the while Gimpy was undergoing the incredible experience of being washed and fed regularly three times a day, set in motion the train of events that was at present hurrying him toward Coney Island in midwinter, with a snow-storm draping the land in white far and near, as the train sped seaward. He gasped as he reviewed the hurrying events of the week: the visit of the doctor from Sea Breeze, who had scrutinized his ankle as if he expected to find some of the swag of the last raid hidden somewhere about it. Gimpy never took his eyes off him during the examination. No word or cry escaped him when it hurt most, but his bright, furtive eyes never left the doctor or lost one of his movements. "Just like a weasel caught in a trap," said the doctor, speaking of his charge afterward.

But when it was over, he clapped Gimpy on the shoulder and said it was all right. He was sure he could help.

"Have him at the Subway to-morrow at twelve," was his parting direction; and Gimpy had gone to bed to dream that he was being dragged down the stone stairs by three helmeted men, to be fed to a monster breathing fire and smoke at the foot of the stairs.

Now his wondering journey was disturbed by a cheery voice beside him,

"Well, bub, ever see that before?" and the doctor pointed to the gray ocean line dead ahead. Gimpy had not seen it, but he knew well enough what it was.

"It's the river," he said, "that I cross when I go to Italy."

"Right!" and his companion held out a helping hand as the train pulled up at the end of the journey. "Now let's see how we can navigate."

And, indeed, there was need of seeing about it. Right from the step of the train the snow lay deep, a pathless waste burying street and sidewalk out of sight, blocking the closed and barred gate of Dreamland, of radiant summer memory, and stalling the myriad hobby-horses of shows that slept their long winter sleep. Not a whinny came on the sharp salt breeze. The strident voice of the carpenter's saw and the rat-tat-tat of his hammer alone bore witness that there was life somewhere in the white desert. The doctor looked in dismay at Gimpy's brace and high shoe, and shook his head.

"He never can do it. Hello, there!" An express-wagon had come into view around the corner of the shed. "Here's a job for you." And before he could have said Jack Robinson, Gimpy felt himself hoisted bodily into the wagon and deposited there like any express package. From somewhere a longish something that proved to be a Christmas-tree, very much wrapped and swathed about, came to keep him company. The doctor climbed up by the driver, and they were off. Gimpy recalled with a dull sense of impending events in which for once he had no shaping hand, as he rubbed his ears where the bitter blast pinched, that to-morrow was Christmas.

A strange group was that which gathered about the supper-table at Sea Breeze that night. It would have been sufficiently odd to any one anywhere; but to Gimpy, washed, in clean, comfortable raiment, with his bad foot set in a firm bandage, and for once no longer sore with the pain that had racked his frame from babyhood, it seemed so unreal that once or twice he pinched himself covertly to see if he were really awake. They came weakly stumping with sticks and crutches and on club feet, the lame and the halt, the children of sorrow and suffering from the city slums, and stood leaning on crutch or chair for support while they sang their simple grace; but neither in their clear childish voices nor yet in the faces that were turned toward Gimpy in friendly scrutiny as the last comer, was there trace of pain. Their cheeks were ruddy and their eyes bright with the health of outdoors, and when they sang about the "Frog in the Pond," in response to a spontaneous demand, laughter bubbled over around the table. Gimpy, sizing his fellow boarders up according to the standards of the gang, with the mental conclusion that he "could lick the bunch," felt a warm little hand worming its way into his, and, looking into a pair of trustful baby eyes, choked with a sudden reminiscent pang, but smiled back at his friend and felt suddenly at home. Little Ellen, with the pervading affections, had added him to her family of brothers. What honors were in store for him in that relation Gimpy never guessed. Ellen left no one out. When summer came again she enlarged the family further by adopting the President of the United States as her papa, when he came visiting to Sea Breeze; and by rights Gimpy should have achieved a pull such as would have turned the boss of his ward green with envy.

It appeared speedily that something unusual was on foot. There was a subdued excitement among the children which his experience diagnosed at first flush as the symptoms of a raid. But the fact that in all the waste of snow on the way over he had seen nothing rising to the apparent dignity of candy-shop or grocery-store made him dismiss the notion as untenable. Presently unfamiliar doings developed. The children who could write scribbled notes on odd sheets of paper, which the nurses burned in the fireplace with solemn incantations. Something in the locked dining-room was an object of pointed interest. Things were going on there, and expeditions to penetrate the mystery were organized at brief intervals, and as often headed off by watchful nurses.

When, finally, the children were gotten up-stairs and undressed, from the head-post of each of thirty-six beds there swung a little stocking, limp and yawning with mute appeal. Gimpy had "caught on" by this time: it was a wishing-bee, and old Santa Claus was supposed to fill the stockings with what each had most desired. The consultation over, baby George had let him into the game. Baby George did not know enough to do his own wishing, and the thirty-five took it in hand while he was being put to bed.

"Let's wish for some little dresses for him," said big Mariano, who was the baby's champion and court of last resort; "that's what he needs." And it was done. Gimpy smiled a little disdainfully at the credulity of the "kids." The Santa Claus fake was out of date a long while in his tenement. But he voted for baby George's dresses, all the same, and even went to the length of recording his own wish for a good baseball bat. Gimpy was coming on.

Going to bed in that queer place fairly "stumped" Gimpy. "Peelin" had been the simplest of processes in Little Italy. Here they pulled a fellow's clothes off only to put on another lot, heavier every way, with sweater and hood and flannel socks and mittens to boot, as if the boy were bound for a tussle with the storm outside rather than for his own warm bed. And so, in fact, he was. For no sooner had he been tucked under the blankets, warm and snug, than the nurses threw open all the windows, every one, and let the gale from without surge in and through as it listed; and so they left them. Gimpy shivered as be felt the frosty breath of the ocean nipping his nose, and crept under the blanket for shelter. But presently he looked up and saw the other boys snoozing happily like so many little Eskimos equipped for the North Pole, and decided to keep them company. For a while he lay thinking of the strange things that had happened that day, since his descent into the Subway. If the gang could see him now. But it seemed far away, with all his past life—farther than the river with the ships deep down below. Out there upon the dark waters, in the storm, were they sailing now, and all the lights of the city swallowed up in gloom? Presently he heard through it all the train roaring far off in the Subway and many hurrying feet on the stairs. The iron gates clanked—and he fell asleep with the song of the sea for his lullaby. Mother Nature had gathered her child to her bosom, and the slum had lost in the battle for a life.

The clock had not struck two when from the biggest boy's bed in the corner there came in a clear, strong alto the strains of "Ring, ring, happy bells!" and from every room childish voices chimed in. The nurses hurried to stop the chorus with the message that it was yet five hours to daylight. They were up, trimming the tree in the dining-room; at the last moment the crushing announcement had been made that the candy had been forgotten, and a midnight expedition had set out for the city through the storm to procure it. A semblance of order was restored, but catnaps ruled after that, till, at daybreak, a gleeful shout from Ellen's bed proclaimed that Santa Claus had been there, in very truth, and had left a dolly in her stocking. It was the signal for such an uproar as had not been heard on that beach since Port Arthur fell for the last time upon its defenders three months before. From thirty-six stockings came forth a veritable army of tops, balls, wooden animals of unknown pedigree, oranges, music-boxes, and cunning little pocket-books, each with a shining silver quarter in, love-tokens of one in the great city whose heart must have been light with happy dreams in that hour. Gimpy drew forth from his stocking a very able-bodied baseball bat and considered it with a stunned look. Santa Claus was a fake, but the bat—there was no denying that, and he *had* wished for one the very last thing before he fell asleep!

Daylight struggled still with a heavy snow-squall when the signal was given for the carol "Christmas time has come again," and the march down for breakfast. That march! On the third step the carol was forgotten and the band broke into one long cheer that was kept up till the door of the dining-room was reached. At the first glimpse within, baby George's wail rose loud and grievous: "My chair, my chair!" But it died in a shriek of joy as he saw what it was that had taken its place. There stood the Christmas-tree, one mass of shining candles, and silver and gold, and angels with wings, and wondrous things of colored paper all over it from top to bottom. Was there ever such a Christmas-tree before? Gimpy's eyes sparkled at the sight, skeptic though he was at nine; and in the depth of his soul he came over, then and there, to Santa Claus, to abide forever— only he did not know it yet.

To make the children eat any breakfast, with three gay sleds waiting to take the girls out in the snow, was no easy matter; but it was done at last, and they swarmed forth for a holiday in the open. All days are spent in the open at Sea Breeze—even the school is a tent, and very cold weather only shortens the brief school hour; but this day was to be given over to play altogether. Winter it was "for fair," but never was coasting enjoyed on New England hills as these sledding journeys on the sands where the surf beat in with crash of thunder. The sea itself had joined in making Christmas for its little friends. The day before, a regiment of crabs had come ashore and surrendered to the cook at Sea Breeze.

Christmas morn found the children's "floor"—they called the stretch of clean, hard sand between high-water mark and the surf-line by that name—filled with gorgeous shells and pebbles, and strange fishes left there by the tide overnight. The fair-weather friends who turn their backs upon old ocean with the first rude blasts of autumn little know what wonderful surprises it keeps for those who stand by it in good and in evil report.

When the very biggest turkey that ever strutted in barnyard was discovered steaming in the middle of the dinner-table and the report went around in whispers that ice-cream had been seen carried in in pails, and when, in response to a pull at the bell, Matron Thomsen ushered in a squad of smiling mamas and papas to help eat the dinner, even Gimpy gave in to the general joy, and avowed that Christmas was "bully." Perhaps his acceptance of the fact was made easier by a hasty survey of the group of papas and mamas, which assured him that his own were not among them. A fleeting glimpse of "the baby," deserted and disconsolate, brought the old pucker to his brow for a passing moment; but just then big Fred set off a snapper at his very ear, and thrusting a pea-green fool's-cap upon his head, pushed him into the roistering procession that bobbled round and round the table, cheering fit to burst. And the babies that had been brought down from their cribs, strapped, because their backs were crooked, in the frames that look so cruel and are so kind, lifted up their feeble voices as they watched the show with shining eyes. Little baby Helen, who could only smile and wave "by-by" with one fat hand, piped in with her tiny voice, "Here I is!" It was all she knew, and she gave that with a right good will, which is as much as one can ask of anybody, even of a snow-baby.

If there were still lacking a last link to rivet Gimpy's loyalty to his new home for good and all, he himself supplied it when the band gathered under the leafless trees—for Sea Breeze has a grove in summer, the only one on the island—and whiled away the afternoon making a "park" in the snow, with sea-shells for curbing and boundary stones. When it was all but completed, Gimpy, with an inspiration that then and there installed him leader, gave it the finishing touch by drawing a policeman on the corner with a club, and a sign, "Keep off the grass." Together they gave it the air of reality and the true local color that made them feel, one and all, that now indeed they were at home.

Toward evening a snow-storm blew in from the sea, but instead of scurrying for shelter, the little Eskimos joined the doctor in hauling wood for a big bonfire on the beach. There, while the surf beat upon the shore hardly a dozen steps away, and the storm whirled the snow-clouds in weird drifts over sea and land, they drew near the fire, and heard the doctor tell stories that seemed to come right out of the darkness and grow real while they listened. Dr. Wallace is a Southerner and lived his childhood with Br'er Rabbit and Mr. Fox, and they saw them plainly gamboling in the fire-light as the story went on. For the doctor knows boys and loves them, that is how.

No one would have guessed that they were cripples, every one of that rugged band that sat down around the Christmas supper-table, rosy-cheeked and jolly— cripples condemned, but for Sea Breeze, to lives of misery and pain, most of them to an early death and suffering to others. For their enemy was that foe of mankind, the White Plague that for thousands of years has taken tithe and toll of the ignorance and greed and selfishness of man, which sometimes we call with one name—the slum. Gimpy never would have dreamed that the tenement held no worse threat for the baby he yearned for than himself, with his crippled foot, when he was there. These things you could not have told even the fathers and mothers; or if you had, no one there but the doctor and the nurses would have believed you. They knew only too well. But two things you could make out, with no trouble at all, by the lamplight: one, that they were one and all on the homeward stretch to health and vigor—Gimpy himself was a different lad from the one who had crept shivering to bed the night before; and this other, that they were the sleepiest crew of young-sters ever got together. Before they had finished the first verse of "America" as their good night, standing up like little men, half of them were down and asleep with their heads pillowed upon their arms. And so Miss Brass, the head nurse, gathered them in and off to bed.

"And now, boys," she said as they were being tucked in, "your prayers." And of those who were awake each said his own: Willie his "Now I lay me," Mariano his "Ave," but little Bent from the East-side tenement wailed that he didn't have any. Bent was a newcomer like Gimpy.

"Then," said six-year old Morris, resolutely,—he also was a Jew,—"I learn him mine vat my fader tol' me." And getting into Bent's crib, he crept under the blanket with his little comrade. Gimpy saw them reverently pull their worsted caps down over their heads, and presently their tiny voices whispered together, in the jargon of the East Side, their petition to the Father of all, who looked lovingly down through the storm upon his children of many folds.

The last prayer was said, and all was still. Through the peaceful breathing of the boys all about him, Gimpy, alone wakeful, heard the deep bass of the troubled sea. The storm had blown over. Through the open windows shone the eternal stars, as on that night in the Judean hills when shepherds herded their flocks and

"The angels of the Lord came down."

He did not know. He was not thinking of angels; none had ever come to his slum.

But a great peace came over him and filled his child-soul. It may be that the nurse saw it shining in his eyes and thought it fever. It may be that she, too, was thinking in that holy hour. She bent over him and laid a soothing hand upon his brow.

"You must sleep now," she said.

Something that was not of the tenement, something vital, with which his old life had no concern, welled up in Gimpy at the touch. He caught her hand and held it.

"I will if you will sit here," he said. He could not help it.

"Why, Jimmy?" She stroked back his shock of stubborn hair. Something glistened on her eyelashes as she looked at the forlorn little face on the pillow. How should Gimpy know that he was that moment leading another struggling soul by the hand toward the light that never dies?

"Cause"—he gulped hard, but finished manfully—"'cause I love you."

Gimpy had learned the lesson of Christmas,

"And glory shone around."

AUTHOR BIOGRAPHIES

Alexander Wilson Drake, born 1843, American painter, wood engraver, Art Director *Scribner's Monthly* and *The Century*, died 1916, further reading: The Literary Gothic http://www.litgothic.com/index_html.html

Mary Hallock Foote, born 1847, American illustrator and author, died 1938, further reading: Johnson, Lee Ann, *American Women Writers: A Critical Reference Guide from Colonial Times to the Present* (Detroit: St James Press, 2000).

Sarah Orne Jewett, born 1849, American author, died 1909, further reading: Stein, Marc, *LGBT: Encyclopedia of Lesbian, Gay, Bisexual, and Transgender History in America* (New York: Gale Group, 2004).

Charles Battell Loomis, born 1861, American author and humorist, died 1911, further reading: Garraty, John A. and Carnes, Mark C., eds., *American National Biography* (New York: Oxford University Press, 1999).

Thomas Nelson Page, born 1853, American author and lawyer, died 1922, further reading: Ferris, William, ed., *The South: The Greenwood Encyclopedia of American Cultures* (Westport, CT: Greenwood Press, 2004).

Albert Bigelow Paine, born 1861, American editor, author, secretary and biographer of Mark Twain, died 1937, further reading: Camfield, Gregg, ed., *The Oxford Companion to Mark Twain* (New York: Oxford University Press, 2003).

Jacob A Riis, born 1849, American/Danish journalist, photo-journalist, author, died 1914, further reading: Shumsky, Neil Larry, ed., *Encyclopedia of Urban America: the Cities and Suburbs* (Santa Barbara, CA: ABC-CLIO, 1998).

Vida Dutton Scudder, born 1861, American professor of English, author, died 1954, further reading: Five College Archives & Manuscript Collections http://asteria.fivecolleges.edu/findaids/sophiasmith/mnsss111_bioghist.html

Florence Watters Snedeker, died 1893.

Frank R Stockton, born 1834, American author, journalist, died 1902, further reading: Griffin, Martin I. J. *Frank Stockton: A Critical Biography* (Philadelphia: University of Pennsylvania Press, 1939).

Ruth McEnery Stuart, born 1852, American author, died 1917, further reading: Perry, Carolyn and Weaks, Mary Louise, eds., *The History of Southern Women's Literature* (Baton Rouge: LSU Press, 2002).

Waltz, Elizabeth Cherry, born 1866, American author, died 1903, further reading: Townsend, John Wilson, *Kentucky in American Letters 1784-1912* (Cedar Rapids: Torch Press, 1913).

BIBLIOGRAPHY

"A Christmas Dilemma (A True Story)." *Century Illustrated Magazine* Dec. 1903: 316-319.

Drake, Alexander Wilson. "The Curious Vehicle." *Century Illustrated Magazine* Dec. 1893: 217-223.

Foote, Mary Hallock. "The Rapture of Hetty." *Century Illustrated Magazine* Dec. 1891: 198-201.

Jewett, Sarah Orne. "A Neighbor's Landmark." *Century Illustrated Magazine* Dec. 1894: 235-242.

Loomis, Charles Battell. "While the Automobile Ran Down." *Century Illustrated Magazine* Dec. 1900: 187-193.

Page, Thomas Nelson. "My Cousin Fanny." *Century Illustrated Magazine* Dec. 1892: 178-187.

Paine, Albert Bigelow. "A Christmas Rescue." *Century Illustrated Magazine* Dec. 1903: 213-215.

Riis, Jacob A. "Merry Christmas in the Tenements." *Century Illustrated Magazine* Dec. 1897: 163-182.

Riis, Jacob A. "The Kid Hangs Up His Stocking." *Century Illustrated Magazine* Dec. 1899: 174-177.

Riis, Jacob A. "The Snow-Babies' Christmas." *Century Illustrated Magazine* Dec. 1905: 226-232.

Scudder, Vida Dutton. "Wulfy: a Waif." *Century Illustrated Magazine* Dec. 1891: 276-280.

Snedeker, Florence Watters. "Their Christmas Meeting." *Century Illustrated Magazine* Dec. 1892: 304-309.

Stockton, Frank R. "The Christmas Shadrach." *Century Illustrated Magazine* Dec. 1891: 176-185.

Stuart, Ruth McEnery. "A Misfit Christmas." *Century Illustrated Magazine* Dec. 1904: 226-232.

Waltz, Elizabeth Cherry. "How 'Sandy Claws' Treated Pop Baker." *Century Illustrated Magazine* Dec. 1903: 230-235.

ABOUT THE EDITOR

Barbara Quarton is reference coordinator in the John M. Pfau Library at California State University, San Bernardino. She is a member of California Academic & Research Libraries and the California Library Association. She lives in Claremont, California.

THE HENLEY COLLEGE LIBRARY

Printed in Great Britain
by Amazon.co.uk, Ltd.,
Marston Gate.